DONALD F. AVERILL

Missing Notes, Hidden Talents, and Other Stories

REVISED EDITION

ISBN 978-1-970529-01-2 (softcover)
ISBN 978-1-970529-02-9 (ebook)

This book is a work of fiction. Names, characters, places, and incidents are the product of the author's imagination or are used fictitiously. Any resemblance to actual locales, events, or persons, living or dead, is purely coincidental.

Printed in the United States of America.

INK START MEDIA
265 Eastchester Dr Ste 133 #102
High Point NC 27262

Missing Notes

New Environment

Crystal was in Carnegie Hall randomly hitting the white keys on a grand piano. Only five, she couldn't reach the pedals with her short legs and bare feet. She smiled proudly at the audience and pressed down on more keys but ignored the black ones. The piano and sousaphone duet was supposed to represent a mouse and an elephant. Her mother was playing the same note, over and over on the gleaming brass sousaphone.

Crystal suddenly woke up and realized the sounds of the sousaphone were from her alarm clock. Her left ear was buried in a fluffy pillow, and a soft, light-blue sheet covered her right ear. Eyes closed, she reached toward the noise, and pressed buttons until she found the off switch, silencing the irritating sounds. She slowly opened her eyes and spent a few moments adjusting to her first morning in the basement apartment. Crystal was not an early riser but today was different. She had a morning appointment on campus.

Last night, Sunday night, she had set the digital alarm clock for 6:00 a.m. and placed it on the triangular white nightstand beside her keys and some pocket change. She had touched the base of the reading light to turn it off and had relaxed into the pillow. The clock preparation and surroundings reminded her of staying in a modestly priced motel except this place was much nicer. She wasn't worried in the least about bed bugs or soiled sheets. Everything was clean and the fresh pillowcase smelled so good!

Crystal had been instructed to come a week before classes began to get acquainted with the campus at Whiting College, New Hampshire, and meet her professors and fellow graduate students.

It was her first semester as a graduate student in the Music Department and she couldn't be late for her initial meeting. Scheduled to meet Dr. Zhukov at 8:00 a.m., Crystal was to find out what her Fall Semester duties were going to be. Her assistantship would be enough to support her for the academic year if she adhered to a strict budget. She wouldn't be getting rich as a teaching assistant, but grad students weren't supposed to make big bucks. They were there to prepare for more grandiose things; Crystal understood that.

She hadn't eaten much on Sunday but didn't want her stomach to be growling during her meeting with Professor Zhukov. In her underwear, she slipped into a soft, yellow bathrobe and had breakfast. The Corn Flakes were crunchy and needed some sugar which she didn't have. She splashed some milk on the flakes, quickly ate the crispy cereal, and sipped a small glass of orange juice.

Crystal asked herself, *Why am I so nervous?* The answer was simple; it was fear of the unknown that unsettled her. A hot shower would help remove some of the tension from both mind and body. She left her dirty bowl on the counter next to the sink and took a quick shower. Dressed in a black skirt, white blouse, and black high heels, she started toward the campus. She didn't have far to go, only three blocks, so she told herself to calm down and walk slowly. She tried to absorb some of the essence of the small college town on that chilly morning, wishing she had worn a sweater.

Two days ago as she rode the bus, Crystal had seen a sign posted outside of town stating the population was 3,502. But a brochure stated over seven thousand inhabitants were present if college students were counted. The town owed its existence to the college. Crystal was renting a basement apartment for $135 a month from a family of four, the Brennan's. Mike Brennan was about thirty years old, taught high school math, and was the assistant football coach. His wife, Sherry, a cute brunette, had a small Internet business, selling vitamin supplements. Brennans had a three year old daughter, Lexis, and a five-month-old boy, Lee.

There were about a dozen concrete steps leading to the imposing front entrance of Harwick Hall, the Music Building. Crystal had been attracted to the Music Department at the college because of its solid reputation. Over the years, a large number of graduates had been accepted into prestigious music programs. Crystal had her sights set on The Brighton Conservatory of Music in Boston after completing her master's degree. The elite Brighton was rated as one of the top three schools in North America.

The door to Harwick Hall was heavy. Crystal had to lean into it and push to force it to swing open. Crystal entered the building and saw OFFICE written in gold letters on the translucent glass in the door to the right across the white marble floor. The lobby seemed more likely to belong to an office building in Washington, DC than a small college music building. Several award plaques were mounted on the walls, which added to the lobby's air of department's importance. She entered the office and saw a mature, gray-haired woman at a desk on the left. The lady looked away from her monitor at Crystal.

"May I help you?"

"Yes. I'm Crystal Salsman. I have an appointment with Professor Zhukov."

"Oh, yes. I remember your name from our departmental meeting the other day. It's nice to meet you. I hope you like it here. We'll have eight graduate students this year. You are the second of the four new students to report in. I'm Mrs. Farnsworth, the department secretary. You can call me Betty."

Crystal glanced at the nameplate on the lady's desk. It said Mrs. B. Farnsworth.

"It's nice to meet you, Betty. Where will I find Dr. Zhukov? I'm supposed to meet with him at 8:00 a.m."

The secretary looked up at the large wall clock and said, "You're two minutes late dear, but not to worry, Professor Zhukov looks kind of mean, but he is really a nice man. Room 131—down the hall on the left." She gave Crystal a motherly smile.

"Thank you." Crystal spoke cheerfully and smiled. She thought she'd better be on the good side of the woman who was probably in charge of the department, second to the chairman, Dr. Johansson.

Crystal's heels echoed in the polished, well-lit hallway. She watched the room numbers for 131 to appear. *There it is. It says Dr. Zhukov on the door.* She knocked and heard a deep baritone voice say, "Come in."

Crystal opened the door and stuck her head in the room. She saw a large man over six feet tall in a gray-blue suit standing at a desk reading from a piece of paper. It was Dr. Zhukov. She had seen his picture in the graduate studies catalog.

"Yes?" he asked as he looked up over his reading glasses.

"I'm Crystal Salsman, your new graduate student."

"Come in, come in. Take a seat. You're five minutes late," he said quietly, but with a disapproving look on his face. "You're fired!"

Crystal blinked her eyes, frowned, and nearly stumbled into the nearest chair.

"Just kidding!" the professor grinned.

"Boy, you had me there for a second. My first symphony flashed before my eyes."

"That was a good one, Crystal. You have a good sense of humor. I always imagine what the new students look like from reading their applications. You are just about what I expected, maybe a little taller." Zhukov had evaluated Crystal's appearance. She wasn't beautiful, but nice looking and very well groomed.

"Your references described you fairly accurately. I'll put you right to work. We have to convert a storage room into an office for graduate students, but we have to clean out and remove some old file cabinets. That will be your project for this afternoon. However, it will be a dirty job. The room is dusty, so I want you to come back at 1:00 p.m. dressed in jeans and a sweatshirt, or at least some grubby clothes. Did Betty give you a lunch voucher?"

"No sir. What is that?"

"It's a little card for a free lunch at the Burger and Tunes Café over on Washington and Clarinet. It's the way they try to get your business for the upcoming year," he smiled.

"Oh, I see. You'd think it would be on Washington and Cherry," Crystal smiled.

The professor thought for a moment and said, "Very clever. You have a quick mind. We're going to have a fun time this year," he smiled. "Well, pick up a voucher from Betty, and I'll see you back here at one o'clock. Okay?"

"Okay. Thank you Professor. Bye."

"Bye Crystal. See you later."

Crystal left Zhukov's office, was careful not to slam the door and returned to the departmental office. With voucher in hand, she walked down Washington Street to Clarinet Avenue. It was about three blocks away from where she had rented the basement apartment. She looked at her watch. It was only nine o'clock. Crystal stopped at a clothing shop and spent about half an hour looking around before continuing to the Burger and Tunes Café. She entered the sandwich shop and took a seat in a large booth near the door. A young boy, about fourteen or fifteen years old, wearing a red T-shirt and a white apron over his jeans, approached.

"May I help you?" he asked.

"Yes please. I'd like a cup of coffee, black."

"Anything else?"

"No thank you."

Crystal looked around the sandwich shop. The walls were decorated with various sandwiches adorned with little flags. The little designs resembled eighth notes.

The boy reappeared with a mug of coffee and a small oatmeal-raisin muffin.

"The muffin is on the house until classes start next week. Creamer, sugar and artificial sweetener are over there." He pointed to a small oblong tray on a semicircular table against the wall.

"Thank you," Crystal replied with a smile.

"You're welcome. Thank you for coming to the B & T Café. The music begins at eleven o'clock."

Crystal watched the young man wave to someone passing by, straighten out some menus by the cash register, and disappear through an arched doorway behind the counter.

As Crystal sipped her steaming hot coffee and took the first bite from the muffin, she reflected on her impressions of Professor Zhukov.

He was at least five inches taller than she was and had a humorous side to him. Crystal's heels made her at least five-ten so Zhukov must be about six-three. His eyebrows were bushy and looked like they were trying to escape from behind his plastic-framed reading glasses. She imagined his eyebrows to be two hurdlers, racing over high hurdles. The right hurdler was slightly ahead of the left one. Zhukov's facial features seemed almost chiseled from stone, and his high cheek bones reminded Crystal of a Native American chief she had seen in a western movie. His hands, although large, were strangely delicate, his fingers long and slender. Crystal concluded he was a pianist. She thought he would look very regal sitting at a piano playing classical music. She smiled. Zhukov was probably a jazz pianist. Her impressions of people were only about half right.

She wondered what his wife looked like and if they had any children. Crystal smiled as she imagined his kids out smoking, drinking, and taking drugs, just the opposite of their parents. *No, the children were probably very smart and had earned scholarships to top rated universities.*

She took the second and final bite of the miniature muffin. The owners hadn't splurged on the mini-muffins, but it was a nice touch. As she familiarized herself with the café, several young people sat down in the adjoining booth. They looked like high school kids, but she could hear them talking about starting their first semester in college next week. Crystal was happy to be finished with her undergraduate work but suddenly realized she was a kind of freshman herself, starting her first year of graduate school.

CHAPTER 2

Tory

Pretty good coffee, Crystal thought as she slid out of the booth, and if the dinky muffin was an example of the real thing, she would have to buy a regular one someday. She started to walk out of the café and a voice from behind her said, "Miss, you forgot to pay for the coffee."

Crystal turned toward the voice and looked at the young waiter. "Oh, I'm so sorry. How much do I owe you?"

"Seventy-five cents please."

"I'm really sorry about that. I'm adjusting to everything today; I'm a new student. Here's a dollar, keep the change," Crystal smiled. Feeling rather foolish, she hoped the tip would make up for her negligence.

"Thank you."

"You're welcome. I'll be back again. I hope you don't have to remind me about paying next time," she smiled.

"I probably won't. I'm still in high school and only work on Saturday during the school year. I'll warn my mother about you though," he laughed.

Crystal turned back toward the door and pulled on the handle. The door swung open and she stepped out onto the sidewalk colliding with another pedestrian. Whoever she had walked into was very large and solid, nearly immoveable.

"Oh! Excuse me. I didn't look where I was going," Crystal apologized as she struggled to maintain her balance. She had slammed into a young man. He was crouching to retrieve the book he had dropped.

"It was my fault. I had my head in my book and wasn't watching where I was going. I shouldn't be walking and reading at the same time," he explained and smiled. "I guess I'm not good at multitasking."

The young man adjusted the cover of his book and stood up in front of Crystal. He was tall, at least as tall as Dr. Zhukov. She noticed the title of the book, *Computer Algorithms for Signal Processing*.

"So you work with computers?" she asked.

"Yeah. I'm a new grad student. This is a text for one of my classes," he said shyly.

"I'm also a new grad student—in music." She extended her hand and said, "I'm Crystal."

Tory's enormous hand engulfed Crystal's, but he held her hand gently.

"Glad to meet you, Crystal. I'm Tory. Say, would you like to have lunch with me here at noon? I don't know anybody yet. I arrived on campus late last night and stayed at the Student Union Building."

Crystal was going to go back to her apartment, change clothes, finish unpacking, and wait until noon to get her free lunch, so she said, "Sure. I'll see you here at twelve o'clock, and it won't cost you a penny. I have a voucher for a free meal."

Tory smiled and said, "That sounds great, a cheap date! Ah—I didn't mean that the way it sounded." He gave a nervous laugh.

"Don't worry. I wasn't offended. I'll see you at noon. I'll be wearing different clothes, something I won't ruin if I get dirty, not that I'm a sloppy eater," she giggled. "This afternoon I'll be working in a dusty storage room. Bye Tory."

"Bye Crystal. See you at noon."

High heels and all the walking were not doing Crystal's feet any favors, so she headed to her apartment. It was 10:37. She changed to a red sweatshirt, slipped into jeans, and some black flats. She sat down and started a grocery list, enough food to keep her going for a week. Surprised by a knock at the door, she saw Sherry Brennan with her two kids. Sherry and Crystal talked for about fifteen minutes before the kids got anxious to go on their morning stroll. Sherry excused herself and Crystal returned to her list. She decided to finish unpacking later.

After completing the grocery list, Crystal combed her hair, brushed her teeth and started toward the café. As she sauntered along, she thought about her chance meeting with Tory. Crystal wondered if she would have met Tory if she hadn't forgotten to pay for the coffee. She would have left the café sooner and wouldn't have bumped into him. He seemed to be a nice guy. He wasn't Hollywood handsome, but nice looking. She wondered if he had broken his nose playing football; it wasn't quite straight. Crystal noticed his dark blue eyes and his height, over six feet. He must be pretty smart. She didn't have a clue what the title of that book meant, unless it involved the analysis of sound waves. She had something to ask him.

When Crystal was about half a block from the café, she could see Tory looking in the window of the shop. She quickened her pace, watching Tory turn and lean against the red brick wall reading a book. She was almost breathless, so she slowed down and took several deep breaths before she reached out, poked the book, and said, "Hi Tory!"

Tory glanced up from the book, looking over the top of his glasses. He looked a little puzzled at first but then dropped his hand holding the book and looked through the lenses.

"Oh! Hi Crystal. You look so different. I barely recognized you."

"Is that good or bad?" Crystal inquired.

"Well, I mean you look ordinary. I'm sorry. That didn't come out right. I meant you look like a regular student now—not all dressed up."

"I'm just joking with you, Tory. I know what you mean," Crystal laughed.

"I like your laugh. I was afraid when you laughed you might sound like a hyena or a donkey. I dated a girl once that laughed like a donkey. We only had one date. I was embarrassed to be with her in public. You know what I mean? Let's find a seat."

Tory opened the door for Crystal and they entered the café. They sat at a small window table. The café was already crowded. The table was dirty and the two waitresses were busy. As Tory grinned at Crystal, a waitress arrived and said, "Our special today is a chili burger and fries. Would you like the special?" Before either of them could answer, the waitress wiped the table and said, "Sorry about that, we are really busy today."

Crystal thought about the special. She was going to be working all afternoon cleaning a room, probably moving furniture, including file cabinets. The extra calories would probably be all right this time and gas wouldn't be a problem as long as she worked by herself. She laughed to herself hoping to not let one slip out if she wasn't alone.

"Okay, I'll have the special and iced tea please."

The waitress looked at Tory questioningly.

"Ah—the vegetarian salad and black coffee for me please."

"Thank you. I'll be right back with your drinks."

Crystal looked at Tory with a bit of a frown.

Tory responded, "I'm on a diet. I've lost fifty-one pounds in the past two months, but I need to lose thirty more. I was a lineman on the football team at Idaho. I weighed 294 and now that extra weight serves no purpose."

"Good for you, Tory. I was heavy in high school and lost the extra baggage when I was in the marching band at Nebraska. Say, how tall are you?"

"Six-four in bare feet, about six-six in heels," he chuckled.

"I'm glad you aren't serious, you'd have a hard time finding a date," Crystal grinned.

The waitress returned with the iced tea and coffee.

Tory took a sip of coffee and placed the cup back on the saucer. "Wow! That is really hot!" he exclaimed. Crystal took a sip of tea. Tory waited for her response. "You fooled me, Crystal. I thought you were going to say, "Wow! That is really cold!"

"Why did you think that?" she asked grinning.

"It was that mischievous look in your eyes," he said smiling.

Crystal had taken another sip of tea. She started laughing and coughing at the same time. She picked up a napkin and wiped her mouth.

"You're pretty sharp, Tory. I was going to say that, but I decided not to. I didn't want you to think I was a smart ass. It looks like we think along the same lines."

The waitress arrived with the specials, and Crystal asked for some ketchup.

"I don't know the rest of your name, Tory. What are your middle and last names?"

"Actually, Tory is my middle name. My first name is Ernest and my last is Clayton," he answered as Crystal inverted the bottle of ketchup and shook it. He was going to warn her but decided to keep his mouth shut. A little dribble of ketchup came out of the bottle, so she shook it again, and a little bit more came out. She put the bottle down on the table and looked at Tory.

"You thought I was going to take a bath in ketchup, didn't you?"

"Yeah. I almost warned you, but you seemed to know what you were doing, so I didn't say anything."

"So, your initials are *ETC*," Crystal smiled.

"Don't say it. I've heard all the jokes. But I don't like Ernie, so I use Tory."

"Well, I like Tory."

"Thank you. So, is your middle name Linn?" he asked.

Crystal gave him a puzzled look.

"You know, crystalline."

"Oh! That's very clever. Strange, I never thought of that. I don't have a middle name, but Linn would be a good one."

Crystal looked at her watch and said, "I've got to get to work. I enjoyed your company. When you have some time, stop by the Music Department and I'll show you around. Maybe we can take a break and you can tell me what you're computing," she grinned, "Some computer music?"

"Sounds good. Give me your voucher and I'll take care of the bill. Thanks for meeting me for lunch. It's been fun."

Crystal slid back her chair and stood up. Tory stood and pointed at her shirt. There was a spot of ketchup the size of a dime about waist high.

"That ketchup bottle did get you. You've got something for a snack," Tory laughed.

Crystal picked up a napkin and wiped her shirt.

"Oh well, it's just a work shirt. Thanks Tory. See you later." She smiled, turned, and walked out of the little restaurant headed for the music building.

CHAPTER 3

Missing Tones

When Crystal reached Harwick Hall, she heard a single ringing tone reverberating from above her head. The loud sound seemed to have come from the tower atop the Music Building. As she ascended the stairs, she said aloud, *"It must be one o'clock."* She went to Dr. Zhukov's office and knocked. No answer.

She turned around and leaned against the wall to wait for the professor. The natural stone wall was cold, so she stepped away from it, scanned the hallway for students or faculty, but saw no one. She heard a door open and a woman walked down the hall toward the departmental office. Crystal lifted the bottom of her shirt, looked at the reddish stain, and decided to visit the lady's room to remove the spot.

In a couple of minutes, her shirt sporting a large wet area, she returned to the door and knocked again—still no answer. Then, she noticed a small pink Post-it note taped to the door near the knob. It said, "I'm in Room 219. Come on up Crystal–Zhukov." At the end of the hall, a black-lettered wall sign displayed Rooms 201-245, followed by an up arrow. She walked to a translucent glass door and pushed on the brass plate. A motor swung the door open and she started up the stairs.

There were pictures of university musical groups on the walls. She didn't recognize any of the names or faces. However, after she entered the hallway on the second floor, Crystal noticed pictures and names of some well-known musicians. The second floor hallway was labeled the Hall of Honor.

Down the right corridor a door was ajar. As Crystal approached, she could hear someone moving furniture, table legs were vibrating against the floor like a fingernail scratching a blackboard, only much louder, and of a lower pitch. She leaned into the room and stuck her head around the half-opened door. Professor Zhukov was dragging a large table across the marble floor. He had removed his suit coat and rolled up his sleeves. He paused for a moment to take in a few deep breaths and saw Crystal enter the room.

"I need some help, Crystal. This heavy table is in the way of the file cabinets we need to clean out. If you will grab that end and push, we'll get this beast over against the wall."

They slid the table against a wall below a blackboard. Zhukov was right, the room was very dusty. Tracks made by the table legs could be clearly seen on the dusty floor. Crystal surveyed the medium sized room. There were three, four-drawer, wooden file cabinets against the outside wall between two large windows. Some rolled-up banners, covered with plastic wrap, were piled on top of the cabinets.

Dr. Zhukov pointed at the cabinets and said, "Those are the objectives for today. We need to go through them and discard most of the contents. We'll be very selective about anything we keep. I'll help you get started and you can continue while I'm gone. I have to attend a faculty meeting at two o'clock."

The first plywood cabinet was pretty beat up. When Zhukov pulled open the top drawer, the rollers came off the tracks. Crystal and the professor stepped back to avoid being struck as the drawer and its contents fell to the floor.

"I guess we know why these old cabinets have to be disposed of, don't we?"

Crystal smiled and answered, "Yes. That was kind of exciting!"

Small notebooks, old, faded papers from mimeographs, several chalkboard erasers, and a pencil sharpener for mounting on a wall formed a scattered pile at their feet. As the cloud of dust settled, Zhukov said, "I'll bring a broom and some dust rags with me after my meeting. Ask Mrs. Farnsworth where to dump the wastebaskets. There's a dumpster behind the building, but I'm not sure if we put materials for recycling in it. You'd better ask her. In fact, if you need to know anything, ask Mrs. Farnsworth. She's our encyclopedia." Zhukov knelt by the pile and scanned the debris. "Except for the erasers and pencil sharpener, there's nothing here we need to keep."

"Professor Zhukov, you have a meeting in ten minutes." Mrs. Farnsworth was standing at the door holding a desk schedule in one hand and a ballpoint pen in the other.

Zhukov stood and brushed off his trousers. "Thank you Betty. Could you please tell Crystal where to put recyclables and where to dump the trash?"

Crystal was kneeling next to the debris. She sneezed twice with only a short pause between sudden outbursts.

"Bless you!" came from Mrs. Farnsworth. "Come by the office and I'll give you a small box of tissues."

Crystal wiped her nose with the back of her hand and said, "Thank you. Right now, I think I'd better get some toilet paper so I can blow my nose. The dust is going to be a problem. My old allergies are acting up," she smiled.

The two women left the room and walked down the hall together. Betty told Crystal more than she needed to know about trash and recyclables. Crystal went in the lady's room, then the office, and returned to Room 219 with a box of tissues. Ten minutes had passed and she was ready for drawer number two. Crystal cautiously opened the drawer, expecting a disaster but the drawer didn't fall to the floor. All she found in the drawer was old sheet music that had been marked with colored ink. She put it all in the recyclables and went to the next drawer.

The third drawer was more interesting than the other two, although the papers had the same musty smell. It was full of old final exams for Introduction to Music 101 taught by a Dr. Kinneer, who was a former faculty member. Exams covering a period of twelve years were in that drawer. All the old tests were tossed in the recycle basket.

Crystal stopped for a few minutes, pulled a couple of tissues from the box, blew her nose and looked out a window. She saw Professor Zhukov approaching the building walking with a short chubby woman and gesturing toward the music building. The woman was probably another professor. Crystal got back to work. Dr. Zhukov would be here in a few minutes and Crystal wanted him to see she had made significant progress while he was gone.

The fourth, and last, drawer of the first file cabinet was a bit of a surprise. It was full of audiotapes of small ensembles. Crystal didn't want to throw them away until she checked with the professor. She set them aside, scooped up odds and ends of paper that were beneath the bottom drawer and tossed them in the recyclables. Zhukov entered the room with a broom, metal dustpan, and some rags.

"I'm back!" he announced as if relieved. "That was a terrible meeting. The administration is going to cut some of our funding, and they didn't consult us. Even if the cuts have to take place, they could have warned us ahead of time. Sometimes I think those inn charge are inconsiderate boneheads. Sorry Crystal, it doesn't concern you."

"That's okay. I'm used to my mom getting angry with my dad, only she used more colorful language," Crystal laughed. "What about these tapes. Should we keep them?"

Zhukov looked at the tapes and said, "Throw them out. I listened to them once and there's nothing of any value on them. I should have ditched them long ago."

"Okay. I've finished the first file cabinet. It's not in very good shape."

"I know what to do with it. I've got a hammer in my car trunk. I'll get it."

Zhukov left the room and Crystal started looking through the drawers of the second cabinet. She found more of the same except it was a little newer. Someone had organized the material in the cabinet. Crystal processed the second cabinet in less than ten minutes.

Zhukov returned holding a large claw hammer as if he were ready for a street fight. He said, "I just got off the phone with the maintenance people. They say they can't fix the clock tower on top of the building. Boy, this day is not going well!"

The professor tipped the first empty cabinet on its side and pulled it away from Crystal. She watched as he raised the hammer repeatedly and pounded the old cabinet into a heap of splintered wood. He stood back, grinned, and glanced at Crystal.

"Now I feel better!" he laughed. Crystal joined him in laughter.

"This one is empty too, Professor," Crystal informed him smiling.

Three notes sounded from the steeple above them. Crystal glanced at her watch. It was three o'clock. She hadn't heard any sound at two o'clock so she mentioned it to the professor.

"Dr. Zhukov, did you say there's something wrong with the clock in the tower?"

"There sure is. It only works on odd numbers up to seven, and we don't have anyone to fix it."

"I think I know someone who can fix it. Would it be all right for me to ask him to take a look?"

"That would be a God's send, Crystal. The department will pay for the parts as long as they don't cost more than a hundred dollars. The university was supposed to fix it, but they told us to unplug it. Fixing it would have to wait."

"How do we get up there?"

"Come by my office and I'll show you. I've got a key to the access door. I'm acting Chairman until Dr. Johansson returns from Iceland next week. Maybe we can surprise him when he comes back from vacation. It would be nice to get that thing fixed. That clock has been a problem for the last six months."

"Okay, I'll talk to my friend Tory about it in the next couple of days. I'll bet he can fix it."

CHAPTER 4

Interesting Find

While Professor Zhukov attacked the second file cabinet, Crystal opened drawers and sifted through old papers. However, the bottom drawer of cabinet three held something quite different than what she had encountered in the other two old storage containers. Tied together with heavy twine were a dozen small student notebooks. Crystal, curious to see what the student journals contained, sat down cross-legged on the cold marble floor, untied the knotted twine, and opened the first book.

The introductory page was labeled: Music Composition 435: *Sonata for Somnambulation*, Semester Project by William Cox, Spring Semester 1965, Prof. Maxine Rheinhold. Crystal looked at the music and began to laugh. It was written for a sousaphone and cello. She hummed a bit of the music; it sounded like a funeral hymn. Professor Zhukov stopped swinging his hammer, smiled, and said, "Is that for the cabinets I just destroyed?"

"Appropriate music, don't you think, Professor?" Crystal grinned.

Zhukov laughed. "Sounds like someone knew a passing grade wasn't in the cards. What have you found?"

"These are notebooks from Music Composition taught by Professor Maxine Rheinhold in 1965," she replied.

"Ah yes. Max retired about fifteen years ago. She lives just north of the campus on Lincoln avenue. She attends all of our student performances and loves to discuss music with the students. The department benefits by having her around, although some students find her a bit different. I'm surprised those old notebooks are still here, they should have been discarded long ago."

Crystal continued glancing through the books until she arrived at a symphony entitled *Galactic Family*. She turned through the pages, noting it was for brass only, no strings, woodwinds or percussion. The composer was Chris Sandman.

As she slowly scanned the pages, the notes began to form sounds in her mind, some ponderous, and some lyrical. She began to imagine how cellos, violins and other instruments would contribute to the symphony. On the last page, there was a notation:

Professor Rheinhold: I'm sorry I turned this in unfinished. Can you give me an incomplete? I've nearly finished—. But when Crystal looked for the next page to continue reading, it was gone. The remainder of the passage from the student was missing. It had been torn out.

"Professor, would it be all right for me to take this notebook home and review the music more thoroughly?"

"I don't see why not. Help yourself. The notebook would be recycled anyway."

That was what Crystal had hoped for. Now she could study the symphony to see if her first impression was accurate. It could be an important find. If it were as good as her first opinion, it led her to believe the student and the university could gain immensely from it, both financially and in reputation.

She set the book aside and continued searching through the old cabinets.

After her fourth trip to empty the wastebaskets and the third trip to the paper-recycling bin, she asked Dr. Zhukov, "Professor, what will I be doing this semester for my assistantship?"

"Several things, Crystal. You will proctor exams, especially evening ones; you will grade most of my exams; and you will assist

Professor Winslow with the student orchestra. Mrs. Farnsworth will give you an assignment sheet with all the information on it. It is pretty detailed and you will have to check your mailbox daily because changes can occur. Everyone has a mailbox in the main office. There is compulsory attendance for all graduate student meetings and seminars. We intend to keep you very busy in addition to your classes. However, you'll have help with some of the tasks."

"Thank you, I think," Crystal smiled, "I just hope I don't have to get up early every day of the week. After two cups of coffee and a bowl of instant oatmeal, I'm ready to go—but cautiously. A half-hour later I'm going full speed. However, if I have to get going early, I can do it."

"I used to be that way until I had children of school age. They were the force that got me going in the morning," remarked Zhukov.

"How old are your kids?"

"Ben is twenty-one and Caroline is nineteen. Ben's studying finance at Boston University and Caroline is at the University of Washington studying microbiology."

"They're not musicians?"

"Nope, but they love music." Professor Zhukov put the hammer on the intact cabinet. "Well, Crystal, that will be all for today. Tomorrow we'll clean up, find some furniture, and get the room ready for occupancy. Let's get out of here and I'll lock up. See you tomorrow at eight o'clock. Thanks for all the work you did today."

"You're welcome. It was fun watching you destroy those cabinets."

Crystal picked up the notebook and started down the hall.

Zhukov shut and locked the door. "Have a good evening, Crystal. Bye."

Crystal turned around and, while walking backward a few steps, said, "Bye Professor. See you tomorrow."

As Crystal descended to the first floor, she began thinking about Sandman's music. Tonight she would look over the unfinished symphony and give it a complete evaluation. She tightened her fingers on the book as she left the music building. She didn't want to lose possession of the exciting music she had discovered in that old cabinet drawer. She hoped her initial evaluation of the music was right.

She arrived at her apartment at 4:27 p.m. She hadn't planned for meals yet, except for breakfast for a few days. Fortunately, the voucher had taken care of her lunch but what would she do for dinner? She made a cup of coffee and sat down at the little dining room table. She opened the notebook and began scanning the staves. Questioning some of what she saw caused her to get a pencil. She needed to make some notations that were erasable. Sandman's music was in black ink.

Instead of returning to the notebook, she picked up the list of groceries and stuck it in her pocket. She would be getting hungry before long. It was five o'clock. Crystal could faintly hear the tones from the tower on the music building. Her watch indicated 5:02. One of the timepieces was off a little, perhaps both of them.

Crystal grabbed her purse, went out the door and locked it. In five minutes she was pushing a large grocery cart through the supermarket aisles. She heard loud squeaking wheels of another grocery cart approaching as she neared the end of an aisle. Crystal stopped and waited—she didn't want another collision today. The squeaking stopped. She continued to wait, not wanting to push her cart forward and run into another shopper. The annoying squeak resumed and got louder.

The front of a cart appeared around the cans of fruit and jars of applesauce. The noisy cart was being pushed by a very large man. It was Tory! Crystal got the giggles and couldn't talk. Crystal saw Tory frown and look at her as if she were crazy.

"Hi Crystal! Did you just come from the dentist, a little too much nitrous oxide?"

That comment made it worse. She couldn't stop laughing. She turned away from Tory, took a deep breath, and held it. That was a trick courtesy of her mother.

Crystal finally regained her composure, took a breath, and said, "I'm sorry Tory. The situation tickled my funny bone. I expected a little old lady to be pushing the cart, but it was a giant young man.

And to top it off, I knew who it was. For some reason the whole thing just seemed too silly! Oh! I've got a proposition for you."

"Crystal, we hardly know each other!" Tory grinned.

"Not that kind of proposition, you nut. If you aren't busy tomorrow morning, could you come over to Harwick Hall? I'd like you to look at the mechanism that produces the hour tones in the clock tower and see if you can fix it."

"Okay. I'll come over about nine o'clock. Where will you be?"

"I'll be working in room two one nine with Dr. Zhukov. We're getting the room ready for teaching assistants to use as an office. By the way, your cart needs a lube job," she grinned.

Tory smiled and said, "I like the squeaky ones, people keep out of my way. See you tomorrow. I might be a few minutes late."

"Bye Tory."

Crystal had almost forgotten why she had been moving down that aisle. She thought for a second and went to the fresh fruit and lettuce sections and filled up the bottom of the cart. She went through the express lane and headed home, happy to have seen Tory. Now she wouldn't have to track him down; he would come to the Music Department looking for her. When she unpacked her groceries, Crystal realized she had forgotten to buy sugar, even though it had been on her list.

CHAPTER 5

The Clock Tower

Following dinner, Crystal examined the written music critically. She had made some notations earlier, but as she continued to investigate, almost all her questions were answered. She spent nearly three hours pouring over the notebook before realizing it was time for bed. As she brushed her teeth, it occurred to her that perhaps Tory could program a computer to play the music written in the notebook. Before turning off her light, she wrote a reminder note to ask Tory if he could do it. She set her alarm for 7:00 a.m.

Groping for the alarm clock as usual, she stopped the beeping. She could hear some footsteps upstairs and a truck passing by on the street. Crystal tossed back the covers and sat on the edge of the bed for a minute. After a quick shower, she fixed her curly blond hair and had breakfast. While she was eating, an idea popped into her head. She had to find Chris Sandman and the rest of the music, if it still existed. What if he had passed away and the music had been lost? Crystal hated to think of that possibility. Mr. Sandman would be near retirement age now, assuming he was about 20 when he wrote the music. Maybe Dr. Zhukov could help find him. The professor might have access to student records to obtain an address or something else to trace the former student.

At eight o'clock, Crystal arrived at the professor's office door. The door was open about four inches. She tapped lightly on the glass.

"Come in Crystal."

She pressed on the door and it swung open. Dr. Zhukov was thumbing through a stack of mail he had picked up in the office when he entered the building. Instead of a suit, he wore jeans, a yellow shirt and athletic shoes. He looked strangely out of place dressed in work clothes rather than a tailored dark blue suit.

"Hi Professor! Good morning!"

"I thought that was you, Crystal. Good morning. Are you ready to work?"

"Yes sir. My friend Tory is coming over at nine to look at the tower clock. I told him we would be in room 219."

"That's great. Maybe he can get that mechanism working properly again. The guys from Physical Plant are bringing over some desks and new cabinets for 219. I guess we'd better get up there. I unlocked the door when I came in this morning."

Crystal and the professor took the stairs to the second floor. There were three husky men leaning against the wall conversing.

"Good morning, gentlemen," Zhukov greeted the three men.

They nodded, walked into the room, and stood beside the wood pile checking out Crystal. The new cabinets and desks had already been moved into the room. Crystal opened one of the file cabinets and saw that it was clean and empty. Zhukov checked the desks to make sure they functioned properly.

One of the young men said, "We have a small table and eight chairs to bring in from the truck, and what about this pile of wood? Should we get rid of it?"

Zhukov answered, "Yes, please take the wood and that old file cabinet. It's empty. After the table and chairs are brought in, that should do. We'll move things around to set up the room. Thank you for your help."

The tallest of the three men said, "You're welcome. We'll bring the rest of the furniture right up. Let the Physical Plant secretary know if you need anything else."

Crystal and the professor went to the blackboard and drew an overhead view of the room. They tried various combinations of desks and cabinets and finally came up with a plan that looked to be the best. Just as Crystal checked her watch, Tory appeared at the door. Her watch read 9:00:24.

"Hi Tory! You're 24 seconds late," she laughed.

Crystal saw Tory look at his watch and smile. He didn't say a word. Apparently he wasn't in the mood or couldn't come up with a wisecrack response. Maybe he was just adjusting to his new surroundings; he didn't know the professor.

Crystal introduced the two men, and Zhukov showed the graduates the tower access door at the end of the hallway. He unlocked the door, reached in, and flipped a switch to turn on a light at eye level and another light in the tower. They would have to climb a ladder about twelve feet high to get to the clock circuit.

"I'll let you two go up there since you have student insurance. My ladder climbing days are way behind me. I believe there is another light at the top. You can direct it to see what you are dealing with. Yell if you need me for anything."

Tory had already climbed the first six feet of the ladder before the professor had turned to go back to room 219. Crystal started the ascent and felt a little claustrophobic. The shaft was rectangular about three feet square. She watched Tory disappear into the tower.

Tory's face appeared at the top of the shaft as he said, "Don't climb any higher, Crystal, there's a hunchback up here with an ax."

"You big dummy! That's not even scary! If you had said there were bats and mice, I might have gone back down."

Tory laughed, "Now I know what you're afraid of. Come on up, it's kind of cozy, but a bit dusty."

Crystal reached the top of the ladder and looked around. She didn't think there was enough room for both of them up there. Wiring was attached to a gray metal box about the size of two shoeboxes, and four large speakers were mounted in front of louvers, covered by window screen, on the inside of the tower. Tory found the light Dr. Zhukov mentioned and turned it on. He removed the top of the metal box and looked inside.

"Holy cow! This thing is ancient. It's made from discrete parts, no integrated circuits here." There was a switch in the box which he moved to the off position before touching anything else. "I've got to remove this old circuit and replace it with a new integrated circuit board. I think it will cost forty or fifty bucks, maybe a little more.. Let's see—transformer, bridge diode, voltage regulator, capacitors and resistors, and a four-digit counter for a start. Once I get that built I'll figure out the sound generator. But I might be able to use what's already here."

"Jeez, Tory, you lost me after the transformer," Crystal confided.

"Crystal, do you have a screwdriver?"

"Not on me." She smiled. "Regular or Philips?" she asked.

Tory was surprised. He had no idea Crystal knew what a Philips screwdriver was.

"I could use one of each, but not too big. I have to get my hand and the screwdriver into the box."

"Okay, I'll get them from the professor."

She descended the ladder and returned in a few minutes. She stuck her head above the tower floor and held up the screwdrivers. Tory took them from her outstretched hand.

"Thanks, Crystal! You do good work!"

"Yes, I know," she grinned. "I'm a wonder with tools. Say, could you write a computer program to play music?"

"I'm sure I could, but it might take me a year to figure out how to do it. I would have to learn something about music, construct some circuits, take my classes, and do my TA duties. It would be easier to have a band, or an orchestra, perform the music."

"Okay. Thanks. It was just a thought."

In a couple of minutes Tory had removed the circuit board and they returned to room 219. He told the professor what he was going to do, and Zhukov asked Tory if he needed money to purchase the parts. Tory said no. He would retain the receipts and turn them in when he got the clock working again.

Zhukov said, "Fair enough, but if you need any money, let me know."

"Okay, Professor. I'm going to work on this now. I'll see you this afternoon to make a progress report. Oh, by the way, the clock is turned off, so you won't have any clock tones today, maybe for a couple of days. Bye Crystal. Bye Professor."

Tory left the building headed for Radio Shack. Crystal and Zhukov got back to work arranging the furniture in the teaching assistant's office. While Crystal and Tory were in the tower, the table and chairs were delivered. The pile of boards, now firewood, and the last old cabinet had been hauled away.

CHAPTER 6

Conversation with Max

Dr. Zhukov and Crystal spent the rest of the morning configuring and reconfiguring the furniture. The original plan had to be altered; they had neglected the table and chairs. It was nearly noon, so they quit for lunch. As they were leaving room 219, Crystal asked the professor, "Could you please get me a list of the students that took Music 435 during the spring semester of 1965? I'd like to see who took that class from Dr. Rheinhold."

"That's easy. Come down to my office and I'll print a class list. I can get it from the main computer at the Registrar's Office."

"Oh, that would be awesome!" Crystal grinned.

Five minutes later, Crystal had the list and was strolling home. As she walked, she scanned the class list. There were twelve names, but Chris Sandman was not one of them—nor was William Cox. That didn't make any sense. She had Sandman's notebook with the date and course number written on it, and William Cox had written that strange sonata.

After lunch, Crystal began the return trip to Harwick Hall. As she walked slowly, the warming effect of the sunlight on her skin and having just eaten seemed to induce a dream-like state. However, on the verge of being lost in the soothing influence, her mind was still mulling over the fact that Chris Sandman's name was not on the class list. She should have checked more of the notebooks for names, but it was too late now, the notebooks had been taken to be recycled. She passed into a shaded area beneath some trees and began to shiver, even though the temperature was in the high seventies. Crystal had never experienced anything this confusing. Perhaps Dr. Zhukov would know something about the missing name.

When she reached room 219, Zhukov was standing with his left hand under his jaw looking at the placement of the desks and chairs. Crystal entered the room and said, "You know, Professor, we need to put some rugs under the desks and chairs. I'll bet the marble floor gets awfully cold during the winter."

"Hi Crystal. What a good idea! We need to get a rug from Physical Plant. I'll bet there are some remnants from the Administration Building. The administrators get new rugs installed every year and we get the hand-me-downs."

"Professor, do you know why the name of a student that was in a class does not appear on the class list?"

"Are you talking about Dr. Rheinhold's Music 435 class?"

"Yes. Chris Sandman, the name on the notebook, isn't on the list you gave me, and neither is that sonata's composer, William Cox."

"Well, I remember Max had the students use a pseudonym for their class projects so she could grade them more fairly. If she didn't know for sure who wrote the music, she would not be biased when she gave them grades. At least that was the intent, but I think she would recognize the writing."

"Oh! No wonder the name Chris Sandman isn't on the class list. Do you think Dr. Rheinhold would remember who Chris Sandman really was . . . or is?"

"You bet! She has a memory like an elephant's. She probably remembers the name of every student who ever took that class. She loved to teach four thirty five."

"Do you think if I paid her a visit, she would tell me who used the name Chris Sandman?"

"I'm sure she would love to talk to you and tell you who used that name."

"That's great! I'll see if I can get Tory to walk over to her house with me this evening."

"Tell her hello for me, would you? She lives at three one one West Lincoln Avenue. Oh yes, she has a yippy little dog named Staff. It's a Chihuahua. We are mutual enemies," he smiled.

Mrs. Farnsworth entered the room followed by a petite young woman with short black hair. Her stature made her appear quite young, but her horn-rimmed glasses gave her a scholarly appearance.

"Hi Betty. Who's following you?"

"Dr. Zhukov, I'd like you to meet Barbara Collins, another new graduate student. Barbara came to us from Ohio. She'll be working with Dr. Welker this semester."

Zhukov introduced Barbara to Crystal and commented, "You ladies will be the first to occupy the room. You can choose your desks and move the furniture anywhere you want, as long as it stays in the room," he grinned. "How would you like to come with me to Physical Plant and pick out a rug? There might not be much choice of color."

Zhukov led the way, talking about the money crunch and the impact on the Music Department. Crystal and Barbara walked rapidly, trying to keep up with the professor. They got acquainted as they walked the equivalent of four blocks to a Physical Plant warehouse. Zhukov pulled out his cell phone and called ahead. When they arrived at a large, light-green, metal building bordering the northern edge of the campus, the right half of a giant double door slid to the side.

A large man, slightly taller than Crystal, wearing a plaid shirt and black work pants, greeted them. Jack Morgan was about fifty years old and probably had a sore back. His belly was trying to escape from his shirt, straining the buttons. He wasn't fat; he was obese. Jack did everything he could to keep the faculty and administration comfortable in the campus buildings. Everyone liked his jovial manner.

"Hello Ivan. I understand you're looking for a large rug. We've got several stored here."

"That's right, about fifteen by twenty. These young women need to keep their feet warm during the winter," he smiled as they shook hands.

"Who are these pretty young ladies?" Jack inquired exhibiting a big grin.

Zhukov introduced the young women. "Crystal and Barbara are two of our new graduate students."

Mr. Morgan said, "Well, ladies, we have beige, dark-green, and blue carpets that would fit that room. I'll show you."

Jack led them to rolls of carpet mounted along one wall of the warehouse.

Crystal liked the beige carpet and Barbara preferred the blue one. They flipped a coin and Barbara won.

"Okay. I'll have a team over there in about an hour and we'll get you fixed up. The installation will take ninety minutes to two hours, depending on how much furniture you have for us to move. We'll put down a thick pad underneath the carpet."

When the trio stepped out of the warehouse, Zhukov pointed to a house across the

street from an adjacent campus storage building and said, "That's Max Rheinhold's house, Crystal."

"Thank you. Now I know where she lives."

Barbara looked at Crystal with a little frown and said, "Who's Max Rheinfold?"

"*Rheinhold*, Barb. She was a professor in the department and retired in 1996."

During the walk back to Harwick Hall, Crystal explained the notebook, the compelling music the student had written, and the missing student name in the class list.

"So you think Dr. Rheinhold would remember who Chris Sandman was?"

"According to Zhukov, she remembers all the students that took Composition from her. Would you like to go with me and find out the real name of that student? We could walk out there after dinner. Please come with me," Crystal asked excitedly. Crystal waited for

Barbara's answer. After a few seconds, Crystal said, "Come over to my place and look at the music, then decide if you want to come with me."

"Okay. If I think the music has promise, I'll go with you. We'll talk to the old bag. I'm curious to meet someone with a memory like that. Where do you live? I'll come by and we'll try to have an interesting evening. It should be better than reading a book."

"You think she's an old bag? Where's your respect?" Crystal spoke seriously and then grinned.

"Jeez, Crystal, she must be at least eighty. She's got to be an old raisin!"

Crystal began to laugh and said, "Barb, you are too funny. We're going to be great friends! I live in the basement apartment at three one one Hawthorne. Come by at six o'clock. I'll be waiting."

Barbara thought for a moment, and said, "Hey! I live only a block from you! I'll see you at six tonight, for sure."

When they got back to room 219, Dr. Zhukov told the girls to take the rest of the afternoon off. The rug installation would prevent them from using the room. He would see them tomorrow morning at eight.. The girls left the building together and began walking home.

"Crystal!"

The loud voice yelling at Crystal came from behind them. Crystal turned around and saw Tory approaching at a run.

"Who is *that*?" Barbara asked as she raised her eyebrows.

"That's Tory, a computer whiz. He's a grad student in Computer Science. The clock tone from the tower on the Music Building was broken, and I asked him if he could fix it. I just met him two days ago. He's a former football player from Idaho."

Tory was breathing hard and said, "I'm glad I caught up to you. It's going to take me a couple more days to get that thing fixed."

Crystal replied, "That's okay. Tory, this is Barbara Collins. She's a grad student in music too. Barbara, meet Tory Clayton."

They talked for a few minutes and Tory excused himself. Radio Shack closed at 5:00, and he needed some more parts.

Barbara, wearing a light-blue denim jacket, arrived at Crystal's promptly at 6:00 p.m. Crystal handed the notebook to Barbara, and they sat on the sofa and reviewed the music.

Crystal watched as Barbara pushed her glasses back and said, "Very interesting—but it needs some strings, don't you think?"

"That's what I think is in the second notebook. Are you coming with me?"

"Sure. Let's go see what the old lady has to say."

It was still warm outside, so they decided to leave their jackets in the apartment and walked north across campus. They skirted the Physical Plant buildings and found Lincoln Avenue after walking several blocks. They could tell where they were by watching the Physical Plant buildings. Sure enough, 311 Lincoln was directly across the street from the second storage building.

The little house was set back from the street at least ten yards. The girls opened the white picket-fence gate and started toward the porch on a brick pathway. Barking could be heard from the house as they stepped on the wooden porch. The railing needed a coat of paint and some of the balusters were cracked and coming loose. Before they had a chance to knock, an elderly woman appeared at the screen door.

"Staff! Be quiet!" she spoke harshly with a gravelly voice to her dog. Staff walked slowly into another room. "May I help you young ladies?"

"Dr. Rheinhold?" Crystal inquired.

"That's correct. Dr. Maxine Rheinhold, retired. At your service," she smiled.

"We're new graduate students from the Music Department. We wondered if we could ask you some questions."

"Well, sure. Come right in. I just finished dinner and was cleaning up the kitchen. If you don't mind, we can talk while I wipe off the counters."

Crystal and Barbara followed Max and Staff into the kitchen. Professor Rheinhold picked up a washcloth from the sink.

"What can I do for you?" she asked as she busied herself cleaning the tile counter tops. She turned her back to the girls to wipe around the kitchen sink.

"Do you remember the actual name of a student of yours from your composition class? His pseudonym was Chris Sandman. It was in 1965; spring semester."

There was a long pause as Max stopped cleaning and stood riveted in place. She laid down the dishrag and turned around to face the girls.

"May I ask why you want the name?"

Crystal explained her interest in the intriguing music Chris Sandman had written in her notebook. Crystal also wondered about the unfinished note in the back of the book, and if the student finished the composition. If Chris Sandman had finished the music, where was the second notebook?

Dr. Rheinhold took in Crystal's words and appeared to be thinking. Her eye movement and the lack of any facial expression said a lot. The music students watched the former professor with anticipation, expecting her to tell them the student's name. Professor Rheinhold wouldn't make eye contact with the young women.

"You know, that's one name I've forgotten. I'm sorry I can't help you, but good luck with your investigation. If you will excuse me, I have some things to do before I retire for the evening."

Crystal said, "Well, thank you for your time. We'll figure it out somehow. Have a good evening Dr. Rheinhold."

"Good evening, ladies."

Barbara looked at her watch. It was 7:18. Staff, tail wagging, followed Barbara and Crystal to the door.

CHAPTER 7

Phone Calls

As the young women headed back across campus, Barbara spoke first. "You know, Crystal, I think that old biddy was lying. Did you notice how she reacted when you said Chris Sandman?"

"I sure did. I think you're right. She was lying, but I wonder why?"

Barb stopped and turned toward Crystal with her eyebrows raised.

"This is great! I've always liked a mystery. What do you think our next step is?" Barbara asked excitedly.

"We have the actual names of the students, so why not see if any of them are in the phone book? We can call them and see what they remember. We can also do a computer search and see what addresses and phone numbers come up. Maybe Tory can help us."

They walked quietly for a minute or two. Barbara broke the silence. "I'll make up a list of questions we can ask if we get a former student on the phone. With three of us making calls, it shouldn't take long. But, I don't have a phone, do you?"

Crystal answered, "I don't have one either. I wonder if Tory has one, or if we get a microphone, we could use one of the computers. We might have to make some long distance calls. Tory might know of a cheap long distance deal on a computer. Let's borrow the phone book in the department office tomorrow to see if any of the people on the class list are living in this area. Wouldn't it be cool if one of them lives here in Whiting?"

It was 8:05 a.m. when Crystal arrived at Dr. Zhukov's office the next morning. She found two notes taped to the door, one from the professor and the other from Barbara. Zhukov's note said he would be an hour late today. Barbara had left a handwritten note also, saying she had the phone book in room 219.

Crystal climbed the steps thinking about getting access to a telephone. She had the list of students in her pocket. Crystal entered room 219 and saw a young man sitting at one of the desks.

He stood and introduced himself, "I'm Brad Cooper, second year grad student. I work with Professor Armitage. I guess we're going to be office mates."

The girls introduced themselves and told Brad about the mystery. He said he knew about Professor Rheinhold but had never met her. Several professors had commented that Max possessed a phenomenal memory. She could listen to a piece of music and later write it down without missing a note.

Barb looked at Crystal, smiled, and said, "Maybe she has Alzheimer's."

"I don't think so. I think she just lied," Crystal responded a little indignantly.

"You guys said you needed a phone." As Brad pulled a cell phone out of his pocket, he said, "You can use my phone if you like."

"Awesome, Brad. So you'll help us figure this out?" asked Barbara.

"Sure. I don't have anything else to do until next Monday."

"That's great! Look at the list of names. There are seven women and five men. Let's see if we can talk with one of the men. Maybe we'll be lucky and get the person that used Chris Sandman as their pseudonym," suggested Crystal.

"Okay. I'll make the first call," Barbara volunteered.

They searched through the phone book and found one name that coincided with a name on the class list. Barbara dialed the phone, stared into space and listened. When the phone was answered, she asked for the name on the list, smiled at Brad and Crystal, and gave a thumbs up with her left hand. She talked nearly five minutes and hung up after thanking the person for the information.

"Well? Come on Barb, tell us what you heard!" Crystal asked excitedly.

"As you know, I called Paul Wofford. He was in the class and so was his wife. Her maiden name was Jocelyn Toy. They don't know who used the name Chris Sandman, but in their opinion, the student in the class with the most ability was Sharon Tilfield. She was really smart and kind of a flower child. They said she had a hippie boyfriend that looked like a creep and smoked weed. Mrs. Wofford said Dr. Rheinhold didn't approve of Sharon's boyfriend. Rheinhold told Sharon she was wasting her talent running around with an idiot."

Crystal thought for a moment and then said, "Do you guys think Chris Sandman stands for chrysanthemum? If Sharon was a flower child—."

Brad said, "Hey, Crystal, you could be right. That's a good idea. But Rheinhold was a smart cookie. She would have figured that out. Well, maybe not, she was probably so involved with music she might not have put those things together. Whoever makes the next call, make sure to press the speakerphone button so we can hear all of the conversation."

Crystal and Barbara looked at the phone to find the speakerphone button.

"So, now we need to find Sharon Tilfield. I think we should Google that name and see what comes up," suggested Crystal.

The planning to trace Sharon Tilfield stopped with the appearance of Dr. Zhukov.

He entered the room and spoke to Brad after saying hello to the two women, "How was your summer, Brad? I see you have met two of our new students."

Brad told Dr. Zhukov about his summer activities and said, "How was your summer?"

"Well, it has been good except for today." Zhukov exhibited a look of concern and lacked the usual smile he exhibited in the morning. "I got a call this morning, a little after eight o'clock. Dr. Rheinhold died last night. That's why I wasn't here at eight." He looked at the two young women.

"Are you kidding me? Barbara and I just talked to her last evening."

Barbara said, "She appeared fine when we saw her. What happened?"

"When Jack Morgan came to work early this morning, he went out to the storage building. Barking from Dr. Rheinhold's house attracted his attention, so he went across the street to investigate. After knocking on the door and getting no answer, he looked in the windows and saw Dr. Rheinhold sleeping in her bed. Her dog came to the window and barked, but she didn't get up or say anything to the dog, which made Jack suspicious. Jack went around to the front door and opened it with his master key, entered, and found Max dead. He called nine one one and the ambulance *EMT* confirmed the death. She was transported to the hospital; the coroner checked the body and took some blood samples for analysis. They'll know more this afternoon."

"Boy, I'll bet Mr. Morgan was scared," commented Crystal.

"What did you ladies say to Max?" asked Zhukov.

Barbara answered, "We just asked her if she could remember who used the name Chris Sandman on his compositions. She told us she didn't remember so we left. We were only there for about ten minutes. On the way back home, Crystal and I talked about what she had said. We felt she had lied to us."

"Why did you think she lied?"

Crystal answered, "It was the look on her face and her lack of eye motion. She appeared to be troubled with our question about the name Chris Sandman. Do you think she committed suicide? Maybe our questions upset her."

CHAPTER 8

Midnight Search

The remainder of the day at Harwick Hall was spent preparing materials for lower division music courses. The three graduate students talked about a variety of things, including their families and undergraduate backgrounds. Tory stopped by to tell Crystal the electronic module for the clock tower was almost ready. He wanted to install it next week but had to wait for a special clock to arrive. Tory was on his way to a meeting of the graduate teaching assistants for the Computer Sciences Department, so he couldn't stay to shoot the breeze.

At 4:15, Dr. Zhukov came by to tell the students they could leave for the day. He would see them tomorrow at 8:00 a.m. for a meeting of the eight Music Department teaching assistants. In the afternoon, attendance by all assistants at a university faculty meeting was mandatory. They would be welcomed and introduced to the faculty and administration at the meeting.

The girls said goodbye to Brad and started walking home.

"Well, doesn't that sound like fun," Barbara said sarcastically. "I just love for everyone to see how short I am. They'll think I came from a group of pygmies!"

"Yeah, a musical pygmy group, or maybe a Gypsy family! You can wear heels and you'll be almost normal height," Crystal smiled.

"Jeez, thanks a lot! I know who I can call on when I need uplifting," she joked.

Nothing was said while they walked for about a half block. Barbara spoke first. "Do you think that old bitty had Chris Sandman's other notebook?"

"Hey! You could be right Barb. We could go over to her house tonight and check it out. No, on second thought, if we got caught they'd probably throw us out of the university."

"I think we should risk it. If the music is there, it might get thrown out when they clean that raisin's house. The music in that first notebook looked very interesting. Think of what humanity would lose!"

"Hey! Don't get overdramatic," Crystal smiled. "But I would like to find that other notebook—if it still exists."

"All we need is a couple of those LED flashlights. We can dress in black clothes," Barbara said excitedly as she grabbed Crystal's arm. "I've always wanted to sneak around at night in black clothes! You know, black ops!"

Crystal looked into Barbara's face and said, "You're really serious?"

"You can bet your sweet whole notes on it!" laughed Barbara. "Let's go by the Dollar Store and get a couple of those little flashlights."

Detouring from their regular path home, they walked a couple of blocks out of their way and bought two small flashlights and some extra batteries. They stopped at Barbara's to test the flashlights in a closet to make sure they could operate them in the dark.

Crystal grinned and said, "Okay, except for the dark clothes, we're ready to rumble. I'll come and get you at 11:30 tonight. I hope there isn't much of a moon."

Following the late TV news, the young women, dressed in black, walked across the nearly deserted campus to the Physical Plant lot. Barbara looked at her watch. It was close to midnight when they arrived at the storage building across from Professor Rheinhold's house. They had scurried from the shadows of one building to another to avoid being noticed in the glaring spotlights illuminating the parking areas around the buildings.

Barbara whispered, "I noticed the fence wasn't tight against the wall of the building when we were here before. I think we can squeeze through." Barbara watched Crystal step through the opening and squat down against the big building next to a shrub. Barbara, being vertically challenged, had to hop through the tight space.

When Barbara joined Crystal, she whispered, "I was afraid I was going to rip my crotch out on that wire fence. I almost didn't make it."

Fortunately, the streetlights were nearly half a block away, and few of the house lights along the street were on. Barbara dashed across the street and crouched beside the gate into Max Rheinhold's yard. Crystal ran across the street after looking for cars and joined her buddy. They knelt beside the gate and smiled at each other.

Barbara murmured, "I don't know when I've had so much fun. But I feel like I've had too much caffeine."

"I know what you mean. My heart is pounding. Can you hear it?"

They unlatched the wooden gate, crawled through on all fours and closed the gate.

Barbara whispered, "Let's go around to the back of the house and check for an open window."

They crept to the side of the house where it was darker. The back of the house was really dark. There were large shade trees blocking out the streetlights, and only a small amount of light came from the thin crescent moon. Barbara tripped on the garden hose and fell to her knees.

"Shit!" she muttered.

"Are you all right?" Crystal quizzed.

"Yeah, I'm okay. I just got my knees wet."

"That's not so bad. I thought you fell in some dog poop. You'd smell great!"

Crystal leaned over a boxwood bush and tried to lift the kitchen window. It was either locked or painted shut and wouldn't budge. She tried the backdoor. It was locked. Barbara had gone to the bedroom window and pushed up on the top of the sash with a stick. The window moved up about an inch.

"Hey! This window isn't locked," she whispered. "Give me a boost. I'll go in and unlock the back door."

Crystal interlocked her hands and Barbara stepped into the assist and pushed the window wide open. Crystal watched Barbara vanish into the darkness and observed the window close. Barbara's flashlight went on momentarily, and Crystal moved to the back door. The lock clicked, the door creaked and swung open like out of a horror movie. She hesitated at the open door, looking into the black void.

"Get in here!" Barbara hissed. "This place is creeping me out."

Crystal relaxed and grinned. She joined Barbara in the house, aimed her flashlight at the floor and turned it on. They moved into the bedroom slowly to prevent collisions with unseen furniture. Crystal noticed that the bedding had been stripped from the queen-sized bed. There was a white mattress cover stretched over the casing of coiled springs. It looked as if no one had lived there in some time.

Barbara said, "Let's start in the closet. The old bat might have stashed her important stuff in there."

Crystal moved toward the closet, avoiding a chest of drawers and slowly opened the door. There were a few dresses and two coats on hangers, and some shoes on the floor. The shelf above the cloth-ing was packed about a foot high with stacks of manila folders full of papers on top of some boxes. She stood on her tiptoes and grabbed a handful of folders and gave them to Barb. Just as Crystal reached for another bunch of folders, the girls heard the sounds of a key being inserted into a lock—someone was coming in the front door.

Crystal whispered, "Quick, Barb, get under the bed. I'll stay in the closet."

Barbara dropped to her knees, rolled to the floor and slid under the bed. Crystal pulled the closet door closed but didn't want to latch it for fear of making a noise. The closet door swung open about an inch. Heavy footsteps on the hardwood floor in the hallway sounded like hammers as someone approached the bedroom. The light from a large flashlight scanned the room. Crystal had never been so scared. She held her breath and tried to make herself as small as possible against the closet wall, hiding behind the dresses.

"All right, whoever you are, come out from under the bed or I'll shoot," boomed a male voice.

"Don't shoot! I don't have a gun or anything."

Barbara slid out from under the bed as far as possible from the voice and stood up in the space between the bed and the wall. The beam from the man's flashlight panned from the edge of the bed and traversed her black clothing from her waist to her face.

"I know you! What are you doing here at this hour of the night? Did you have something to do with Professor Rheinhold's death?"

Crystal had silently stepped out from the closet, took a deep breath, and shoved her flashlight into the big man's back. She tried to lower her voice and growled, "Drop the gun, buster, or I'll blow your head off! Raise 'em!"

The surprised man said, "I don't have a gun, just my flashlight. Don't shoot."

"Give me that flashlight!" Crystal hissed.

The man lifted the flashlight above his head and bent his arm back so Crystal could take the tube full of batteries from him. Barbara started laughing almost hysterically. She pressed the button on her little flashlight and illuminated the face of the man. It was Mr. Morgan from the Physical Plant. Barbara continued to laugh and Crystal began to laugh when she recognized the large man with the potbelly.

Crystal shined the light on her face and then on Mr. Morgan's.

"Hi Mr. Morgan!" was all Crystal could get out of her mouth as she laughed.

"What in the hell are you two girls doing here? It's after midnight! Jeez, young lady, you scared the bejesus out of me! May I have my flashlight?"

Barbara squeezed out a few words between laughs. "Sorry Crystal, but when you said drop the gun, buster, or I'll blow your head off, I couldn't help but laugh. Where did you come up with that? You've been watching too many police TV shows. That was so funny!"

Crystal gave Jack his flashlight, looked at Barbara, and said, "I think we'd better tell Mr. Morgan why we're here. Mr. Morgan, can we turn on the lights?"

CHAPTER 9

Christmas Cards

"Sorry, ladies, the electricity is turned off."

Crystal and Barbara told Jack about the music in the notebooks and the suspected dishonesty of Dr. Rheinhold. Jack thought for a moment and said, "So, what does this notebook look like?"

"You're going to help us look for it? That's awesome. Oh, thank you! The cover looks like granite, in black and white, with a black binding about this big." Crystal indicated the size of the notebook with her hands.

Jack asked, "Do you think she would have hidden it?"

"Probably. I'll bet that old raisin was nasty when she was younger," answered Barbara.

"Why don't you gals look in the closet in the hallway, and I'll start going through the chest of drawers here in the bedroom."

Barbara started to laugh and whispered to Crystal, "I'll bet he wants to look though her underwear."

Crystal elbowed Barbara and said, "That's gross, Barb. Where did you get that idea?"

"Well, Jack's going through her drawers," Barbara snickered.

The young women moved down the hallway and opened the closet door. Barbara stepped back releasing the doorknob.

"Oh, God! That little dog must have peed in here, more than once! Hold your nose!"

"Barb, hold the flashlights, and I'll look through the stuff in there. We can't hold our nose and the flashlight at the same time. I'll sacrifice my nose. I'll try to hold my breath."

Crystal searched through several boxes on the floor and a couple of smaller boxes on the closet shelf. She set a box marked Christmas cards down on the other boxes, looked in it briefly, and put the lid back on.

Jack joined the girls in the hallway and said, "No luck in the bedroom. I even looked under the mattress, behind the pictures, and behind the headboard."

Barbara asked, "Mr. Morgan, why did you come here tonight?"

"One of our workers lives a couple of houses down the street. He was outside smoking a cigarette and noticed you coming across the road. He figured you were here to carry out some sort of prank so called me. Since I was doing a security check of the Physical Plant Buildings, I walked over here. This house belongs to the university."

Crystal said, "Nuts! There's no notebook here. Where else can we look?"

Jack panned the living room with his flashlight and said, "Let's check out the furniture in there and then we'll go in the kitchen."

Barbara gave Crystal her flashlight, followed Jack into the living room, and started looking under the chair and sofa cushions. Crystal started putting things back in the closet. She lifted the Christmas card box over her head, gave it a shove with her right hand, and turned away. But the push wasn't strong enough; the box teetered and crashed to the floor.

"Damn!" she uttered.

"Drop your watch, Crystal?" Barbara kidded.

Crystal didn't answer. She placed her flashlight on the floor, bent down and started scooping up scattered cards and envelopes. As the stationery was stacked and placed in the box, she bumped her flashlight and it rolled against a book.

"Where did that come from?" she uttered.

Then she knew what had happened, the notebook had been under the Christmas cards at the bottom of the box. Crystal picked up her flashlight and illuminated the back of the book. She flipped the book over and there it was: Chris Sandman, Music 435-Book 2. It was the missing notebook!

She yelled at the others in the living room, "I found it! I found it!" Barbara rushed to where Crystal was, followed by Mr. Morgan. "Look Barb! Look what's written on the front cover."

Crystal turned the notebook so Barbara could read the writing.

"Okay ladies, it looks like you found what you were looking for. Let's get out of here. It's almost one o'clock in the morning. We'll walk over to my pickup and I'll drive you home."

Mr. Morgan dropped both young women off at Crystal's apartment. After they climbed out of the truck, thanked Jack for the help, and the ride, Crystal looked at Barbara and held her right index finger to her lips. Barbara nodded her head, indicating she understood they were to be quiet. Crystal inserted her key into the lock and turned it cautiously. There was a slight click; Crystal opened the door very slowly and flipped on the light. She gave the prized notebook to Barbara and relocked the door.

They tiptoed to the overstuffed, beige sofa, sat down and opened the notebook.

The first page was not attached—it was the page torn from the other notebook. The girls saw what looked to be a hurriedly written note to Dr. Rheinhold.

the rest of my project. I'll turn it in on Monday. Something happened and I didn't have enough time to finish the symphony. I need the weekend to complete it. Thank you Dr. Rheinhold.

Crystal recognized the note to be the continuation from the last remaining page in the other notebook.

She whispered to Barbara, "Why would Professor Rheinhold still have this notebook and the ripped out page from the other notebook? Wouldn't she have put this book with the rest of the Music 435 notebooks? I don't get it."

"Hmm. I think I need to sleep so I can think up a dastardly plan that old hen would have hatched. I'd better go home; it's almost two a.m."

"Why don't you stay here? You'll just fit on the couch even if you stretch your legs," suggested Crystal as she smiled. "Besides, you don't want to be walking out there at this time of night; it's pitch black outside. You could trip and fall into a pothole and we'd never find you," Crystal chuckled.

"Now, *that was* funny. Okay, you twisted my arm. Got a blanket and an extra pillow?"

"Sure. We've only got four hours, so we're going to have to sleep twice as hard to get in eight hours," Crystal grinned.

"Oh, that's right! We have to dress up for that stupid meeting at eight a.m."

"No! We don't have to dress up in the morning, just in the afternoon," corrected Crystal.

"Okay! Let's go dressed in black. We'll just wear these clothes," Barbara smiled.

"Yeah, they'll think we are mourning the death of that old liar," Crystal laughed.

Barbara grinned, "Now you're talkin'. I could've said that!"

"Shush," Crystal whispered.

CHAPTER 10

Police Investigation

Crystal's alarm scared both young women. They felt like no time had passed at all; they had just turned out the lights. However, the big red LEDs on the clock showed 6:00. Crystal jumped up and was already in the kitchen making coffee when Barbara stretched and sat up. Crystal noticed Barbara's frown as her petite friend looked around trying to figure out where she was. Four hours sleep had certainly not sharpened Barbara's senses.

"Barbara. You should probably go home and get ready for the departmental meeting at eight, unless you want to smell bad until noon."

Crystal's voice triggered the mental processes for Barbara to recall the early morning's episode, which flashed through her memory. She had always been slow to wake up. However, a cup of coffee always catalyzed the process of completing all the crucial cranial connections and she was ready to tackle the new day.

Crystal handed Barbara a mug of hot coffee and said, "Here, drink this. You'll be awake in no time. It's high test!"

Barbara took a few sips, looked at her watch, suddenly stood up and said, "Jeez! I've got to get ready for that meeting at eight o'clock."

Barb put the coffee mug on the end table, pulled on her pants, shoes, and sweatshirt and hurried to the door. Crystal heard the noise of the lock opening and walked toward the living room. Barbara stopped halfway out the door and said, "Come by and get me in about an hour, okay?"

"Okay!" Crystal smiled and thought Barbara's idiosyncrasies made her fun to be around. *There will never be a dull moment with Barbara; she's such a character and becoming a good friend. I hope a friend for life.*

Barb and Crystal arrived at Harwick Hall a few minutes before eight o'clock. They were on their way upstairs to their office when Betty called to them.

"Ladies, Police Lieutenant Porter would like a word with you."

Crystal grabbed Barbara's arm and they froze in place like stone statues. Barb looked at Crystal and whispered, "Did Mr. Morgan call the police?"

"I don't think so. He was helping us look for the notebook," Crystal replied.

"I guess we'd better talk with the police; if we run, we'll be fugitives," Barb laughed.

The girls, with facial looks of concern, walked toward Betty.

"Lieutenant Porter is waiting in the Department Chair's office. Follow me."

Betty led the girls past her desk to a door that opened into a nice wood-paneled room that smelled fresh, as if someone had just dusted, vacuumed and polished. The custodial staff probably cleaned the room during the night. As the three women entered the room, a uniformed police officer stood up from a padded chair next to the Chairman's desk. He looked to be about fifty years old and was little taller than Crystal, and much heavier.

"Are these two girls Crystal and Barbara?" he asked Mrs. Farnsworth.

"Yes Lieutenant," Betty replied and smiled.

Betty introduced the graduate students to the officer and then said, "I'll leave you here to talk."

"It's nice to meet you. Please sit down."

He motioned to a polished, high-back, wooden bench against the wall. The elongated seat reminded Crystal of a church pew.

"Did you see Professor Rheinhold two days ago at her home?"

Crystal and Barbara looked at each other and answered in unison, "Yes sir."

"Well, she left you a note. We found it folded up in her sweater pocket."

The lieutenant pulled a folded piece of paper from his shirt pocket. As he began to unfold the paper, the young women looked at each other in surprise.

"I don't want to alarm you, but Dr. Rheinhold might have committed suicide. The coroner found some sleeping pills in her stomach. Four or five pills would have been fatal, but he only found two, and they were almost completely dissolved. We're not sure why she died. The coroner is going to carry out some further tests. Ms. Rheinhold might have had a heart condition."

The girls glanced at each other with raised eyebrows, a little shocked by the words they had just heard.

Crystal spoke first, "I don't understand. Why would she do such a thing? Was she ill? I sure hope the questions we asked didn't result in her taking her life."

"I don't believe she was ill," replied the lieutenant. "Maybe the note will mean something to you. I don't know what she is referencing. Read this and tell me what it means."

The Lieutenant handed the paper to Crystal. Barbara moved closer to her and they read the handwriting from Professor Rheinhold.

"I made a big mistake many years ago and it has finally caught up to me. When you ladies came to see me, I perpetuated the lie. I do remember Chris Sandman; she is Sharon Tilfield. Her pothead boyfriend's name was Nick Weems. Her ability to compose music was extraordinary, and I was terribly jealous. I couldn't let her show me up, so I made sure her music was never finished. I was a tough grader, and when she missed the deadline for her project, I gave her an F. I couldn't throw her second composition book away, so I hid it. I think she might have been pregnant and dropped out of school, never to return to Whiting. I have her notebook for you. Maybe you can publish or perform her work and show her talent to the world. I'm sorry for what I did. I didn't mean to ruin her life. I don't want to think about this anymore, so I am going to sleep."

Barbara and Crystal looked at each other. Barbara noticed Crystal's tears. Crystal laid the paper down on the bench beside her and wiped her eyes.

Barbara sniffed and said, "We'll tell you the story Lieutenant. I guess she just couldn't face the music." Barbara grinned and looked at Crystal.

Crystal jabbed her with an elbow and said, "Always a joke!"

"Sorry, I couldn't help myself."

Crystal began with her discovery of the notebook in the storage cabinet and ended with finding the second notebook in Max Reinhold's closet. At the conclusion of the story, the Lieutenant said, "Wow. What a thing to live with for nearly fifty years. She punished herself for a long time. I'll get the notebook for you ladies. I need to go out to the Professor's house anyway."

Crystal volunteered, "Thank you, Lieutenant, but we already have it. Mr. Morgan from the Physical Plant helped us find it last night. The notebook was boxed with some Christmas cards in a closet. We searched for about thirty minutes before we discovered where it was."

Barbara touched Crystal's wrist and said, "Look at the time."

Crystal glanced at the big wall clock behind the Chairman's desk and said, "Oh, sh—shucks, we're twenty minutes late for that meeting. Dr. Zhukov will kill us!"

The women looked at the Lieutenant, smiled, and said in unison, "Just kidding!"

Porter smiled and said, "That's okay, I know what you mean. I'll speak to Professor Zhukov for you and tell him you cleared up the mysterious note Dr. Rheinhold left."

"Thank you Lieutenant. Is it all right if we go now?" inquired Crystal.

"Sure. If I have any other questions, I know where you are. I'll leave my number with Mrs. Farnsworth in case you think of anything else. Thank you for your time."

The two girls moved quickly from the chairman's office to the second floor stairway. They ran up the steps, down the hall and entered their office slightly out of breath. Zhukov was standing at the blackboard writing, and six students were sitting in chairs. They all looked at Crystal and Barbara. The girls recognized Brad; they hadn't met the other five graduates.

Crystal said, "I'm sorry we're late, Professor, but we had to talk to the police. Lieutenant Porter said he would speak to you about it."

Professor Zhukov introduced Crystal and Barbara to the other students. After the introductions, the professor continued with his instructions for about ten minutes and took the eight students on a tour of the music building. Since Barbara, Brad, and Crystal were already familiar with the building, they lagged behind the others. As the group returned to Mrs. Farnsworth's office, Tory came in the front door, smiled, and waved to Crystal. He was carrying a box and pointed toward the ceiling with his free hand. Crystal frowned and then realized what he meant. Tory was ready to install the new electronic circuit in the tower. Crystal realized what he was waiting for must have arrived.

CHAPTER 11

Return to the Tower

Professor Zhukov had just asked the students to check Mrs. Farnsworth's records to make sure their social security numbers, addresses, and phone numbers were correct. Crystal stepped up to the secretary's desk, quickly checked her data, returned the paper to Betty, and said, "Everything's correct."

"Thank you, Crystal. Be sure you are at the faculty meeting at one o'clock. It's in the Student Union Building, the White Mountain Room. That's the large room on the first floor just to the left of the reception desk. They'll serve lunch."

"Thanks Betty, I'll be there," she smiled.

She turned to leave the office but stopped momentarily to tell Barbara she was going to see Tory out in the hallway. She assumed Tory was ready to install the new circuit for the clock tones. Barbara should meet them at the tower access door as soon as she verified her data. Barbara nodded and waved to Crystal.

Crystal saw Tory leaning against the wall. He was standing over the box. Tory smiled as Crystal walked toward him.

"Hi Tory! Have you got the circuit ready to install?"

"Yep. I got the parts sooner than expected, so I worked on the system last night until I got it finished. I finally went to bed about 2:00 a.m. I just hope I considered everything and it works as planned."

"I believe in you, Tory. Let's check it out."

"We've got about two hours until our meeting. Maybe we can get it going by then. At least we can give it the old college try!" he smiled as he bent down and picked up the new box.

As they walked toward the stairs, Barbara ran up behind them.

"I get to be the hunchback!" she whispered.

Crystal smiled and said, "Sorry Barb—wrong gender!"

"You're not old enough, and no hunchback, either! But you don't need a mask," Tory added with a big grin.

"Careful now! You're no Don Juan," chimed Crystal.

"Maybe Dumb One!" added Barb as she grinned.

Crystal added, "Don't listen to him Barb. You're very cute."

Tory led the way up the stairs and Barbara followed closely behind. She looked back at Crystal and pointed at Tory's butt and gave a thumbs up. Crystal broke out laughing. Tory stopped abruptly and Barbara ran into him. Tory looked around and noticed the embarrassed looks on the girl's faces.

"Okay, you two go ahead of me and let me see what I think," he raised his eyebrows and smiled.

They hesitated and Crystal said, "That's all right, Tory, we just have a little more sway in our tushies."

"I know that. I just want to observe and make the evaluation for myself!" he smiled. "Oh forget it! Let's go, we're wasting time."

Tory took the last few steps, went into the hallway, and stopped at the entrance to the tower. Crystal opened the door and turned on the light. Tory started the awkward climb up the tower ladder, carrying the box in his right hand and holding the ladder with his left. When he reached the top, he plugged in the extra light and began to unpack the materials from the box. In less than a half minute, Tory leaned over the opening to the floor below and said, "Crystal, I need a second set of hands to hold some things. Could you please come up here?"

Crystal responded, "Barbara's coming up. The space up there is too small for two big people. Barb is about half my size. Well—maybe two-thirds."

Barbara looked a little surprised at Crystal's comment but started climbing the rungs a little hesitantly; not knowing what was in store for her. She slowly ascended the ladder attached to the wall of the tower access shaft. Each step made her hang on with a stronger grip; Barbara was afraid of heights. The small tower access shaft gave her some comfort; the shaft walls were close to her on all four sides. She relaxed a little realizing it was almost impossible to fall. When she reached the top and stuck her head above the tower floor opening, Tory reached over, grabbed her arm and pulled Barbara into the tower.

Tory noticed her face looked a little pale and said, "Are you okay?"

"I'm all right, thank you. Don't worry; I won't barf on you."

"I hope you don't," Troy laughed. "You don't like climbing ladders?"

"Yeah. Anytime I get above my height, I think I'm going to fall."

"Well, relax and hold these two wires for me. I have to solder them together."

Barbara pinched the two wires between her fingers and held them where Tory pointed. As the fumes from the melting solder drifted up, Barbara turned her head away and said, "Oh God, I think I'm going to vomit!"

"Close your eyes, Barb!"

She closed her eyes. Tory leaned over and kissed her on the lips.

When she felt his lips touch hers, she kissed him back. She opened her eyes and said, "Why did you do that?"

"I just wanted to make up for the crack I made about you not needing a mask. Do you feel nauseous now?"

Barbara thought for a couple of seconds and said, "No," and then smiled.

"How did you know to do that, Tory?"

"It was the only thing I could think of that would take your mind off barfing. That was the best idea I've had in a long time," he smiled.

"Don't tell Crystal! I want her as a friend."

"C'mon Barbara, it's not like we're getting married! Nice kiss though."

"Here, hold these wires, but first, take a breath of fresh air from the louvers and hold your breath so you don't smell the solder fumes."

It only took a few more minutes and the circuit was ready to test. Tory set the clock to 12:59 and flipped the test switch to ON. Nearly a minute later, Tory said, "Cover your ears, Barb!" They both plugged their ears and a loud gong sounded from the four large speakers in the tower. It was almost noon, so Tory inserted the batteries into the standard clock, reset the time, and flipped the master switch to RUN.

"Okay, Barb, let's get out of here, or get ready to plug your ears for twelve loud gongs. We only have about two minutes to get down the ladder before noon."

Barbara scooted over to the shaft opening and started down the ladder. Tory followed her, closing the tower shaft door behind him. He had decided to leave his tools in the nearly empty box until later, after the clock had completed a full cycle. When he reached the floor at the bottom of the shaft, he heard the sequence of twelve gongs begin. Tory set his wristwatch to midday. He stood with the girls, counting the sounds from the tower.

Crystal and Barbara looked at each other, then at Tory, and said, "Awesome!"

Tory bowed and said, "Thank you ladies! I might have to make some adjustments so I left my box and tools up there. I also have a doorbell to install."

"Doorbell?" quizzed Crystal.

"Yep! When the battery on the standard clock needs to be replaced, a signal will ring a doorbell every hour to indicate the battery voltage is low. I just don't know where to put the doorbell. What do you guys think?"

"Barbara said, "Mrs. Farnsworth's office! Or, maybe it should be in the Chairman's office. What do you think Crystal?"

"The only other person that might respond would be Dr. Zhukov. He would send a graduate student, probably me, up there to replace the battery. We'd better ask him what he thinks."

Barbara smiled and offered, "Well, let's go to the B & T Café. We can have some coffee and a mini-muffin before we have to go to the meeting. We have nearly an hour to kill. We're getting something to eat at this afternoon's meeting, aren't we?"

"I think we're to have sandwiches and something to drink; probably Gatorade," grinned Crystal.

Tory smiled and said, "Gatorade—that reminds me of my football days."

They locked the tower access door and left the building. As they walked toward the café, they noticed many young faces. Classes would be starting Monday, and there was a large freshman class.

Just as they crossed the street leaving the campus, a police car pulled up to the curb beside them. The window rolled down and Lt. Porter said, "I need to talk to you ladies."

Barbara and Crystal moved toward the car, but the door started swinging open and they quickly stepped back. The lieutenant stepped out of the car and closed the door. He turned to the girls and said, "I'm glad I saw you. I wanted to inform you that you are suspects in the murder of Dr. Rheinhold."

The two young women looked at each other in disbelief. Tory stepped over to the women and the lieutenant put his hand up to Tory's chest.

Tory said, "What the hell are you talking about! That's ridiculous!"

"Step back! Who are you?"

"I'm Tory Clayton. Barbara and Crystal are my friends."

The Lieutenant had reached toward his handgun since he was six inches shorter and fifty pounds lighter than Tory.

Crystal saw the policeman's reaction and said, "It's all right Tory. There's been some mistake."

"I'm afraid not, Crystal. Dr. Reinhold was poisoned with cyanide. She was murdered, and you girls were the last people with her."

"Obviously not, Lieutenant. We didn't kill that old lady," refuted Barbara.

"I'm not going to arrest you, but I want you to stay in town if further questioning is required. If you have to leave town, tell me where you're going and give me contact information."

Crystal replied, "All right, Lieutenant. Good luck with the case. I hope you find out who did it."

While they walked to the café, the women told Tory about their talk with Dr. Reinhold and how they found the missing notebook. They had Tory's rapt attention. Crystal and Barbara had been wondering who might have poisoned Professor Reinhold.

"So who do you think might have done it?" Tory inquired. "Are you girls members of Charlie's Angels, out to solve a crime?"

Without hesitation, Barbara said, "The butler!" She giggled and said, "That was a good one! And I don't qualify as an angel, I'm too short."

Crystal smiled and said, "That was funny, Barb, but I don't think there is a height requirement for angels. The killer must have been someone like Sharon Tilfield or Nick Weems. Anyway, we need to see if we can contact Sharon to find out more about her composition. We should leave the murder investigation to the police, don't you think?"

Tory said, "Good idea. I wonder if Dr. Reinhold had any siblings. Maybe they didn't get along . . . a family dispute."

Barbara quipped, "Yes! Perhaps there were more raisins in the family, or maybe an old goat."

The café was nearly packed with students when the three graduate students arrived. They ordered coffee, took their drinks and mini-muffins outside, and began walking back toward the campus. They talked about the murder and fall semester classes. The rest of the music grad students joined them near the music building.

Tory looked at his watch and said, "Jeez! I have to go! The computer department grad students are all supposed to sit together. It was nice meeting all of you. See you and Barbara later, Crystal."

"Bye Tory." Crystal looked at the others and said, "We'd better get over to the Student Union Building so we can enjoy a catered lunch." She grinned and said, "I hope you all like sushi."

CHAPTER 12

Faculty Luncheon

The Student Union Building was bustling with activity when the music grads entered the large white-brick building. The lobby contained several strategically-placed stanchions with arrows pointing to the oversized double doors of the White Mountain Room. The students followed the other people entering the building.

Crystal and Barbara found their seats at a table adjacent to the Music Department Faculty. Crystal sat down and opened a packet that had been placed on each chair. The instructions said to pick up their luncheon plate from a nearby serving table. Barbara had already located the serving table, so Crystal just followed her pixie friend. She saw Tory waving to her from two tables away, but he was moving in the opposite direction.

There was a line at the serving table, so Crystal began looking through the packet at the rest of the papers. There was a list of former faculty members that had passed away since the previous academic year. Of the four names, the only one she recognized was Dr. Maxine Rheinhold. The short obituary said a younger brother, Robert Rheinhold, survived the professor.

"Lettuce or potato?" a voice broke Crystal's thoughts. A young lady, probably an undergraduate, asked the same question to each person as they approached the serving table.

"Lettuce, please," answered Crystal. Barbara stood beside Crystal and poked her in the ribs. Crystal turned and Barbara pointed to the obituary.

"Did you see this?" Barbara asked. "There's a younger brother! Do you think he did it?"

Crystal shrugged her shoulders and looked at her plate. It was almost full. She had been lost in thought about Robert Rheinhold and hadn't observed what she was being served. She added some dressing to her lettuce and started back to her seat. When she approached her chair, she looked where Tory had been. He was holding up his information packet and pointing at the obituary page. Crystal didn't want to raise her voice to be heard by Tory, so she nodded, waved and took her seat.

Barbara sat down beside Crystal and said, "I wonder what Robert looks like. Do you think he's a raisin sprinkled with powdered sugar and also a killer?"

"Jeez, Barb! Could be he's much younger and doesn't have gray hair. He could be a nice guy that has just lost his sister," commented Crystal. "He may be the only remaining member of the family. You could be right though; he might have poisoned her. I wonder what she left him in her will."

A distinguished looking, middle-aged man in a gray suit, began speaking into a microphone, "Welcome to the fall semester at Whiting. I trust you all had an enjoyable summer break. I would like to start the proceedings with a sad note. A former faculty member, Dr. Maxine Rheinhold, recently passed on this summer. She was a pillar of strength in the Department of Music for many years. She was to be presented the Distinguished Faculty Award for her contributions to the university for fifty years. Her passing saddens us. Her younger brother, Robert Rheinhold, will accept the award."

A fairly tall man, in a brown suit, walked from the side of the stage, and approached the man at the microphone. They shook hands and Mr. Rheinhold stepped up to the microphone.

"Thank you, President Ames. Maxine would have been very proud to receive this acknowledgement of her many years of service to the university. She loved being here and taking part in the molding of many talented students. About ten years ago, I asked Max why she wanted to remain here. She could have returned to our family home and taken part in the music activities in the city. She told me she wanted to make up for some mistakes she had made by continuing to contribute to the education of young musicians. She would have cherished this award. Thank you very much." Mr. Rheinhold received an energetic round of applause.

Mr. Rheinhold moved gracefully and talked with confidence, apparently no novice at communicating to large groups, although the amassed faculty were not a really large assemblage. Crystal felt compelled to tell him that she had talked with Max the afternoon before her death. She watched as Mr. Rheinhold left the stage and shook hands with several people as he moved to a table where the Music Department faculty was sitting. Crystal kept an eye on him as the proceedings continued.

All the graduate teaching assistants were introduced by the chairs of the departments. President Ames continued with other topics, but Crystal wasn't paying much attention. She was thinking about how to approach Mr. Rheinhold.

Barbara leaned over to Crystal and said, "Do you think we should talk with Mr. Rheinhold?"

"I was just about to ask you the same question. As soon as this is over, let's visit with him. I'm sure talking with him won't be as boring as this stuff."

The audience sat through another five minutes of remarks that a memo could have covered and the luncheon ended. The noise level in the room abruptly increased as people began moving toward the large double doors at both ends of the room. Crystal and Barbara moved in the direction of Mr. Rheinhold. They could see him speaking with several people as he neared the exit.

Barbara began to move faster and passed several wide-bodies as she tried to catch up with Bob Rheinhold. Crystal tried to keep up, but the crowding at the doorway prevented her from seeing where Barb had vanished. Crystal reflected, *if only Barb were four or five inches taller*. But Crystal knew Barbara would catch up to Mr. Rheinhold.

Sure enough, just outside the glass doors to the building, Mr. Rheinhold and Barbara were engaged in conversation. A young man, probably a student, was with them. He was dressed in navy blue slacks and a white dress shirt with the sleeves rolled up. Crystal thought he looked familiar. Then she recalled—*He was one of the servers at the luncheon*. His short blond hair and young appearance made him look like a high school student, but he was probably a freshman. Barbara was undoubtedly encouraging him to be in one of her classes. When Crystal caught up to them, they were standing next to a concrete bench on the large patio outside the building.

Barbara introduced Crystal to the two men and motioned to the large bench, "Let's sit down."

Reinhold said, "You young ladies saw my sister the day she died."

"How did you know?" quizzed Barbara.

"Lieutenant Porter gave me the names of two suspects."

"That's a laugh," Barbara responded. "We'll tell you what happened, Mr. Rheinhold."

Barbara glanced at Crystal, who nodded to proceed, and Barbara related the high points of their brief meeting with Maxine and how they had discovered Chris Sandman to be Sharon Tilfield. During Barbara's explanation, she noticed Russ was trying to interrupt her. She finally looked at him and said, "Russ, did you want to say something?"

"Yes. Sharon Tilfield is my grandmother's maiden name."

"You're kidding!" Barbara exclaimed.

"Nope. Tilfield is my middle name."

"Wow! Crystal and I have to talk to you about her."

Rheinhold commented, "Well, I can't see that you girls had any-thing to do with what happened to Max. The Lieutenant told me that the local police thought the note she left had been altered. The last line originally said she was going to bed, not to sleep. The change in that word made it appear she was committing suicide. I can't imagine her doing that. The police are going to do a handwriting analysis of Maxine's note. Lieutenant Porter sent some examples of her hand-writing to an expert in Boston. The police think she didn't write the note. Also, she normally carried about a hundred dollars in her purse, but the money was gone."

Barbara replied, "This is really getting to be a mystery!" She looked at Robert and said, "Your sister was poisoned and robbed! I wonder what the police are doing, in addition to handwriting analysis, to find the person responsible. Crystal and I were thinking Sharon Tilfield might have had something to do with it. That's why we want to talk to you about your grandmother, Russ. We also need to talk to your grandmother about the music she wrote for Professor Rheinhold's class."

Russ stood up and said defiantly, "You're crazy if you think my grandmother had anything to do with Professor Rheinhold's death. She just isn't that type of person. She wouldn't kill anyone in a mil-lion years, and besides, she liked the professor."

CHAPTER 13

Steaks

Crystal replied, "But Russ, your grandmother had a motive, Barbara and I don't. We were thinking your grandmother might have been mad at Professor Rheinhold for giving her a bad grade and never recognizing how good her music was."

"Well, I don't believe my grandmother thought her music was anything more than a class project. Last night Gram and I talked about Dr. Rheinhold. She told me about handing in the second notebook after the deadline. Gram expected a low grade, but she still liked the professor."

Crystal asked, "Where does your grandmother live? We'd like to talk with her."

"She lives in Chester. It's about 35 miles west of here," Russ replied.

"Could you give us her phone number?" requested Crystal.

"Sure. If you want to see her, come over to my trailer and talk to her."

"What? You mean she's here in Whiting?"

"Sure, she drove me here from Chester four days ago. She's been visiting with some old friends of hers for the last few days, but she's planning on going home tomorrow. I'll give you my address. Gram will be there after seven o'clock tonight."

Crystal handed Russ a pen, and he wrote his address on the back of a sheet of paper torn from the luncheon packet. Crystal folded the piece of paper and stuck it in her skirt pocket.

Russ stood up and said, "Oh! Gram calls me Rusty. You know, Russ T. Neill. It's her little joke. She's always asking if I had my tetanus shot. In spite of what you think, it was nice meeting you. I'll tell Gram you're coming over this evening. I'm sure she will enjoy talking to you, especially Mr. Rheinhold. Your idea about her killing Dr. Rheinhold will make her laugh."

Robert said, "It was nice meeting you, Russ. We'll see you this evening, and I, for one, don't believe your grandmother had anything to do with Max's death. I'm sure she's a very nice lady."

Russ turned away and walked toward the student union building. Barbara and Crystal didn't know what to say. The chance meeting of Sharon Tilfield's grandson had taken them by surprise. They were anticipating a difficult search for Professor Rheinhold's former student.

Robert sensed the tension in the silence of the two young women and wanted to know more about what they were thinking. "Well, ladies, how would you like to have dinner with me? I hate to eat alone. I was thinking of having dinner at Harley's Steak House on Winsome. I'll get my car and meet you at the campus entrance next to the Music Building at five o'clock." Robert looked at his watch. "That will give me plenty of time to check on Staff over at the veterinarian's, talk to Lieutenant Porter, and get some things from my motel room."

Crystal and Barbara looked at each other uneasily, and Barbara answered, "That would be very nice, Mr. Rheinhold, but we're on tight budgets and can't afford to eat at a restaurant."

"Don't even think about it. It's my treat. I'd like to hear more of your thoughts about Sharon Tilfield and my sister. Besides, I can write it off on my expense account," he smiled.

Barbara raised her eyebrows, glanced at Crystal, smiled, and replied, "Well, all right, Mr. Rheinhold, it's a date! We'll see you at five o'clock. What kind of car do you drive?"

"A gold Aztek. You can't miss it. It has a ski rack and a black storage pod on top."

Barbara and Crystal returned to Harwick Hall, checked to see who the fourth member of their office was, and then went to the bookstore to buy some office supplies. Having no more duties at Harwick Hall, Crystal and Barbara went to Crystal's apartment for another review of the music Russ's grandmother had written years ago. They decided to take the notebooks with them so they could discuss the music when they met with Sharon Tilfield.

While the girls were freshening up at Crystal's apartment, they talked about Bob Rheinhold. They wondered what he did for a living, and how close he had been with his sister. It was 4:50 p.m. when they left the apartment and headed toward the campus.

Barbara said, "I've never had a sugar daddy before, have you?"

"Jeez, Barb, are you serious? Rheinhold is at least 65 years old, and eating dinner with him is not a lavish gift. He's just lonely, wants to hear more about Sharon Tilfield and his sister, and we're getting a free meal. That's got to be a bargain for us."

As they approached the stone pillars flanking the southern entrance to the Whiting campus, they saw a gold-colored SUV, just as Rheinhold had described. He had been parked near the campus entrance for about five minutes, watching for the young women. When they reached the car, Rheinhold got out and stepped to the passenger side.

"Hello ladies, your chariot awaits," he smiled and motioned to the car with his hand. He opened both front and back doors of the car. The girls noted Bob had changed from his suit coat to a more casual sports coat. Barbara climbed in the front seat and Crystal hopped in the back. Barbara turned to Crystal, gave her a funny look, and whispered, "Is this guy for real?"

The drive to the steak house took less than five minutes. During that brief time, the young ladies found that Bob Rheinhold raised money for several large charity organizations. Many of his contacts had been cultivated during the time he had spent working for the State Department at the United Nations. The girls were thoroughly impressed.

The party of three was seated at a nice table. Crystal and Barbara picked up their menus and scanned them apprehensively. The price for one steak dinner was enough to pay for a college student's food for an entire week. They doubted if they would ever come to the restaurant again, short of having a real sugar daddy. Neither young lady imagined being in that situation.

Robert noticed the silence and watched the girls closely. He realized they were out of their element, so he offered some help. "If you would like, I'll order for you, and we'll have some wine. I believe you are both of age. Isn't that correct?"

Both answered affirmatively and Rheinhold placed the order. While they waited, Robert asked some questions.

"What made you begin the search for the lost notebook, Crystal?"

Crystal explained the note at the end of the first notebook and the unfinished music. Barbara filled in the portion about their belief that the music was extraordinary and should be performed, published, and recorded.

"And then you went to see my sister?"

"Yes sir," answered Crystal.

"When we heard your sister tell us she didn't remember who Chris Sandman was, we both felt she wasn't telling the truth." Barbara added, "But we weren't sure."

"That doesn't surprise me. Max never was a very good liar. I, however, can tell some whoppers without blinking an eye. I had to learn how to lie when I worked for the State Department. In my opinion, nearly everyone working in the Department lies most of the time," he smiled. "It's a wonder anything is ever done legitimately. Oh! I think I'd better tell you now that if I am lying to you, I will give you a wink. I don't want to lead you young ladies astray."

Barbara replied, "Well, that sure makes me feel better." Barbara looked at Crystal and winked.

"Me too." smiled Crystal. Crystal had to keep from laughing at Barbara.

As they ate, the conversation broadened to several different topics, and before long, it was a quarter to seven. Robert looked at his watch and said, "Let's take a little ride to see Sharon Tilfield, shall we?"

CHAPTER 14

Unknown Meeting

The gold Aztek moved through the Whiting streets and slowly entered Pine Butte Trailer Park. There was no evidence of a butte. Robert braked inside the gravel road entrance and glanced at the slip of paper Crystal had given him.

"Help me ladies. We're looking for number 16."

Barbara and Crystal lowered their windows and began looking at the numbers painted on Frisbees nailed to stakes driven in the ground.

"What a classy place to live." quipped Barbara.

Crystal added, "Some of these trailers look pretty nice but some are real dumps, aren't they?"

"I think this is typical student living for those on limited budgets," commented Robert. "There's number 12 on the right."

Rheinhold guided the car slowly past several more trailers but they didn't see 16. The numbering stopped at 15. They came to a T in the road and Robert stopped.

"Right or left, ladies?"

Barbara said, "Left," and Crystal said, "Right." They all laughed.

Rheinhold said, "Shall we flip a coin?"

"No, let's go right," answered Barbara.

Right was a good choice; the next trailer was number 16. It was the largest and newest mobile home they had seen and was parked on a large lot. There was a good-sized concrete pad surrounded by a white picket fence a person of normal height could step over. Two young men and an older woman were sitting near the trailer door.

Rheinhold and the two girls got out of the SUV and walked slowly toward the picket fence. Russ stood and waved to them as they approached.

"Just step over the fence," he laughed. "Barbara, you might have to jump."

Barbara replied, "Funny, Russ."

The older woman stood and said, "Rusty! Mind your manners! Enough with the jokes!"

The elderly lady's chiding of Russ betrayed her identity. The lady had to be Sharon Tilfield, or more properly, Mrs. William Jenkins, or Sharon Jenkins. Her hair was pulled back, the roots dark brown with an occasional strand of gray. Crystal's quick estimate of Sharon's age was mid-sixties, but she looked ten years younger.

Crystal introduced everyone and asked the other young man his name.

"I'm Sean Wiggins, Russ's trailer mate. Nice to meet you," he answered with a broad smile. Sean had medium-length, brown hair, an athletic build, and was about six feet tall. Sean's resemblance to Russ was remarkable; they might be mistaken for brothers.

Sharon looked at Crystal, smiled, and said, "Rusty told me you ladies think I killed Dr. Rheinhold."

"That's not really what we said. Lieutenant Porter told us we were suspects, but we don't have a motive. We thought you might, though. You could have been mad at Dr. Rheinhold for giving you a failing grade in her class."

"Oh, I see, but why would I have waited so long to act?"

Crystal replied, "That's a good question."

Barbara surreptitiously elbowed Crystal and whispered, "I saw him at the coffee shop a couple of days ago."

Crystal noticed the interest the others had in the whispering and said, "Barb just told me she saw Sean at the coffee shop a couple of days ago."

Sharon replied, "Oh yes! I took Sean and Rusty to the Student Union to get a sandwich when I went to visit with Dr. Rheinhold the first time."

Crystal was shocked. "You met with Dr. Rheinhold?"

"Well, not while the boys were at the coffee shop. She wasn't home then. I went to see her again Tuesday after dinner. I talked with some old friends in the afternoon and lost track of time. I went to see her after we ate."

Barbara said, "Crystal and I went to see Dr. Rheinhold that evening. When were you at Rheinhold's, Mrs. Jenkins?"

"Let's see—it must have been about 8:40 to 8:45 p.m. She was getting ready for bed and I was only there for a little while. I thanked her for being such a good teacher and that I was sorry I hadn't done better in her class. I also told her I had appreciated what she said about Nick Weems. He was a real jerk. She apologized for flunking me, but I knew I had turned in my notebook too late. It was my fault."

"What time did you leave the professor?" quizzed Crystal.

"It must have been around nine o'clock. Do you remember when I got back, Rusty?"

"Uh, let's see. Sean and I were watching the sports channel. The NFL program came on at 10:00. You were home before then. I guess around nine-thirty."

"The professor didn't mention having the notebook?" asked Barbara.

"She had my notebook?" Sharon queried.

"Yes, she had your second notebook from your 1965 class with her," Barbara replied.

Sharon frowned and scanned the faces of her guests. "I thought those notebooks were destroyed long ago. I remember there were two books. I think the brass and percussion were in the first one and the strings in the second, but I'm not sure."

"Let me tell you the whole story, at least the part Barbara and I have uncovered."

Crystal related how she found the first notebook and how they found out what Chris Sandman's name was after traveling down a blind alley at Professor Rheinhold's.

Sharon said, "Gosh, I don't remember the Wofford name. Of course, at that time, I didn't pay much attention to anything. Wait a minute. There were two students sitting behind me, always holding hands. Perhaps they are the Woffords. However, I do remember trying to avoid drugs my stupid boy friend kept shoving at me. I did try—." She looked at the two freshmen and cut her comment off. She saw no reason to offer any encouragement to them to experiment with marijuana. "When I talked with Professor Rheinhold, she remembered my name and my pseudonym, but she didn't say anything about the notebooks."

Barbara snapped her fingers and said, "I knew it! She lied to us."

Crystal continued, "After we heard the Professor was dead, Barbara and I decided to look for the second notebook. We entered Professor Rheinhold's house through a back window. Jack Morgan, from the university, helped us look for the notebook. I found it in a hall closet in a box of Christmas cards."

Mrs. Jenkins said, "Well, when I left the Professor's house, she was fine. She seemed to be in a rush to get me out of the house so she could go to bed. I said good night, got in the car and drove away. Mr. Rheinhold, what did you and Max talk about?"

"What do you mean?" Rheinhold replied. He was surprised by Sharon's question.

"I looked in my rearview mirror as I pulled away from the Professor's and I saw your car stop in front of your sister's house." Sharon pointed at the gold Aztek. "That's your car, isn't it? I saw that car in my mirror as I was driving away."

Barbara frowned at Robert and said, "You didn't tell us you had talked to your sister that night!"

There was a hush as they all focused their attention on Robert.

"Okay, I admit it. I stopped to talk with Max right after I saw a car leaving her house. That must have been you, Mrs. Jenkins." Robert continued, "I had called Max earlier in the day. I wanted to talk about her investments and contributions to charities. I had met with President Ames that morning and he informed me about the award Max was to be given. I was supposed to make sure she went to the luncheon. I was to take her to the luncheon where she would be surprised with the award."

Crystal quizzed, "You helped with her investments?"

"That's right. My job on Wall Street gave me some opportunities to help my sister with her finances. I started and managed a portfolio for her."

When Robert said Wall Street, he winked at Crystal.

Barbara injected, "But I thought you worked for——."

Crystal caught Barbara's eyes and winked, cutting her off in mid sentence.

"Well, when I arrived, Max was a little upset. She told me the story about Sharon Tilfield and how, when a professor, she had made no exceptions when assigning grades. Max said the music Sharon had composed was very good and she had brought the notebook home to study it. She didn't know if the first notebook still existed, but she kept the second one so the music wouldn't be lost, and to remind her how inflexible she had been when younger."

Crystal said, "I found the first notebook when I was cleaning out some old file cabinets. We have both notebooks in the car. Barbara and I have been studying them. We want to make the music available to the student orchestra and present it at the Christmas concert."

Sharon was intrigued and said, "You girls have my old notebooks? God, I put writing music out of my mind long ago. I can't remember what I wrote back then. After college, I shifted my interests to art and became a graphic designer. That's how I met my husband."

"How did that happen?" Crystal inquired.

"I had written some announcements for Senator Wilkins when his daughter got married. President Ford had seen one of them and the senator gave him my address. One day a young man from the Secret Service arrived with a contract for me to do all the designs for invitations to various social functions for the President. He was very handsome—not the President; I mean the agent," Sharon smiled. "I married him."

Sharon looked at Bob Rheinhold and said, "Mr. Rheinhold, I don't believe you finished your explanation of what you and Max talked about."

CHAPTER 15

Murderer?

Rheinhold leaned back in his chair, put his right palm under his chin and looked down as if deeply thinking about what to say. "Max and I talked about her finances until after ten o'clock. She said she was going to bed, and if I wanted, I could sleep on the couch. She went into the bedroom and I watched the late news. I wasn't tired and at eleven o'clock, I turned the TV off. That's when Max opened her bedroom door—said she couldn't go to sleep. She asked if I would get her two sleeping pills and a glass of water, which I did."

Robert looked at Crystal and Barbara and continued, "I went in the kitchen and put the capsules on a saucer. I tossed the empty bottle in the trash and took a glass of water and the capsules to Max. She thanked me and closed the bedroom door. I turned out the lights and went to sleep on the couch. At six o'clock, I woke up and made some coffee, expecting Max to get up, but she didn't seem to be rousing. I couldn't hear any sounds coming from her bedroom, so I knocked on her door, but she didn't answer. Then I heard Staff scratching at the bedroom door, so I opened it. Max was still asleep. Well, that's what I thought. I called to her, but she didn't move, so I moved to the bed and touched her arm and forehead. She was cold and had no pulse. She had expired in her sleep."

Mrs. Jenkins inquired, "Did you call 911?"

"No, it was too late for that. It wasn't an emergency. That's when I got scared."

"What would you be afraid of?" asked Mrs. Jenkins.

"I'm the chief heir of her estate. She had a large sum of money in an account I managed for her as well as an insurance policy I wrote for her."

"Wait a minute! You said you worked for the State Department!" exclaimed Crystal.

Sharon added, "No, he said he worked on Wall Street."

Robert stood up and dropped his hands to his sides and looked at the ground. "I'm sorry I lied to you. I'm an insurance salesman. That's the truth. I just said those things to seem more important. I always looked up to Max because she had a PhD and taught at an influential school. I admired her ability to remember almost every-thing she saw and did. I was disappointed that she never used her talent to create wonderful music. But I have found out things about her in the past few days that made me realize things changed over the years. When she was younger, she was very stingy. She wouldn't help me go to a university to get an education, so I went to a community college and learned all about insurance. In fact, she was so stingy that if she had a hundred candied apples, she wouldn't even give one to a hypoglycemic diabetic."

Russ looked at Sean, leaned toward him and whispered, "What did he say?"

Sean whispered back, "Hell, I don't know. I'm only a freshman."

Robert continued, "Well after thinking I might be in real trou-ble, I sat down at the kitchen table and wrote a note to make it look like Max was overwhelmed with the situation and decided to end it all. My handwriting is almost the same as Max's. When I was learn-ing to write, Max had me copy her writing. She had very nice hand-writing. I copied it over and over, until I couldn't tell the difference between her writing and mine.

Max told me I got an A in penmanship. I was proud of that. After I wrote the note, I folded it and stuck it in Max's sweater pocket. Then, I straightened up the living room and left. I went back to my motel room. I guess Staff started barking, Mr. Morgan investigated and found Max's body."

"Did the police contact you?" asked Crystal.

"Nope. They didn't even know I was in town. President Ames called me to tell me Max had died during the night and the police would contact me after their investigation."

Crystal inquired, "So, what did the police tell you?"

"I haven't talked with them yet," replied Robert. "I was going to, but I chickened out."

"Speak of the Devil! Look who just drove up," Sharon announced.

"Grandma! Put away your marijuana!"

"Hush Rusty! That's not funny!"

Barbara was laughing and poked Crystal. "He's hilarious!"

A patrol car rolled to a stop next to the Aztek and Lieutenant Porter climbed from the cruiser. He walked slowly toward the group and said, "Hello. Barbara, you and Crystal are no longer suspects."

Crystal introduced the Lieutenant to the two boys, Sharon Jenkins, and Robert.

"It's nice to meet you. Mr. Rheinhold, you are under arrest for murdering your sister. Please come with me. I have to place you in handcuffs."

Porter read Robert his rights, placed the older man in cuffs, and began to usher him toward the police car.

Robert said, "Just a moment Lieutenant. Crystal, could you please drive my car to the motel and check me out? You can keep the car at your house until I'm set free. Lieutenant, please take the motel and car keys out of my right front pocket and give them to Crystal."

Crystal replied, "Okay. Barbara and I will take good care of your things. We'll come see you tomorrow."

"Thank you, ladies."

Porter retrieved the keys and handed them to Crystal. Robert was placed in the back seat of the patrol car, and the lieutenant walked back to talk to the girls.

"Don't worry about your friend. We're still analyzing data and he might be out of jail in a couple of days. We're following up on some information, but we'll have to hold Mr. Rheinhold for now. We need to question him thoroughly. We think he wrote the note we found, and his prints were on the pill bottle in the trash. He has tampered with evidence of a crime, so we must incarcerate him for at least the weekend. You can visit him after ten o'clock tomorrow morning."

Barbara smiled and said, "Remember Lieutenant, Robert isn't the butler! He couldn't have done it."

Lieutenant Porter looked at Barbara, frowned, shook his head, and walked to his car. He climbed into the cruiser, backed up to the road and drove away.

Crystal grinned at Barbara and said, "God, Barbara. Will you ever quit?"

CHAPTER 16

Confession

"I don't think he did it," Sharon stated emphatically. "In spite of what Robert said about Max being stingy, I think he loved his sister. He would never have poisoned her."

"Gram, I've heard you say you would like to kill Grandpa. How would you do it? It would be easy for you to put poison in his food."

"Rusty! What I say and what I do are two entirely different things. When I've said I would like to kill your grandpa, it was just a statement of frustration. You must know that!"

Russ smiled, "I sure pushed your button, didn't I? I just wanted to see what you would say."

"You'd better watch it buddy. I'll take my trailer and go home. Where would you be then?" Sharon inquired, "What do you young ladies think?"

There was a pause as everyone sat down in the yard chairs. Barbara spoke first, "Could it have been some sort of mistake? What do you think, Crystal?"

"Well, Robert lied about working for the State Department at the United Nations, and again about working on Wall Street. I wonder what other lies he's told us. I'm a little suspicious of him, to tell the truth. And remember, Robert is the heir to most of Dr. Rheinhold's estate. I'll bet Max left several hundred thousand dollars."

"I think the police investigation will expose the murderer," stated Sharon.

"Good thinking Grandma. That's what I think."

Crystal looked at her watch and glanced at Barbara. Barbara looked bored and was looking around trying to find something to focus on.

Barbara asked, "Where's your dog, Russ?"

"Don't have one—yet. I'd like to get a medium sized one. Maybe I'll get a puppy and name him or her Max," he smiled. "I like that name. Maybe it'll like music," he laughed. "The dog might even sing along."

Barbara grinned and commented, "Maybe you can teach the puppy to howl when you sing, although your singing might not be considered music. That's to repay you for that short joke."

Crystal stood up and turned toward Mrs. Jenkins. "It was nice meeting you and talking with all of you. When Barbara and I get your music ready for the student orchestra, we'll give you a call. Maybe you can come to a rehearsal and listen to your creation."

"I'd like that, Crystal. Thank you for your interest in my old class project, and for saving the notebook from being recycled. It was nice to meet such devoted and considerate young ladies."

Barbara had begun to drift toward the Aztek and seemed anxious to get back to the campus area. As Crystal joined her, they both turned and waved to Sharon and the boys. Crystal looked at the keys in her hand and pressed the unlock button. The car lights blinked and the locks clicked.

Barbara said, "Let's get out of here! I have something I have to tell you."

The evening sunlight was dimming and Crystal was glad they chose to leave the trailer park before darkness arrived. She didn't like driving an unfamiliar car at night, but she could still locate the controls before it got completely dark. She didn't like driving with the dome light on. She checked the headlight control, gearshift, brakes, and started the engine. After adjusting the rearview mirror and backing onto the street, she put the car in drive and exited the trailer park.

"So what is it you need to tell me? Something you figured out about the murder?"

"No, nothing like that. Remember when I was in the tower with Tory?"

"Yeah?"

"Well, I'm afraid of heights, and when I got up there, I felt like I was going to barf, but I held it back. Then, I smelled the fumes from the melting solder, and I *really was* going to barf!"

"But you didn't. What stopped you?"

"Tory kissed me!"

"Really?"

"Yeah! I was worried about our friendship, so I didn't say anything, but Tory said the kiss was only medicinal. He said it was the only thing he could think of to keep me from vomiting all over the tower floor. That would make him barf."

"I guess it worked. Look, Tory and I haven't even been on a real date. We had lunch together on Monday. I had a voucher and he even commented it was a cheap date. I don't think either of us interpreted it as courtship. We just wanted someone to talk to since we were both new on campus. However, if you get serious with him, I'll have to buy some cyanide. So you'd better be careful if you eat anything at my place." Crystal scrunched up her face, bared her teeth, and gave Barbara a mean look. They both started laughing.

"Jeez, I wish I had my recorder. If the police find me dead from cyanide poisoning, they will know who did it," Barbara grinned.

"Actually, I wouldn't kill you. I'd just make you suffer. I would make you listen to a kid learning how to play a clarinet."

"That would be mean! If Tory asks me out, I'll tell him I have a boyfriend."

"I don't think either of us has to worry much about going out. After classes start, we probably won't have time to go on dates," concluded Crystal.

Crystal drove to Barbara's apartment and dropped her off. A minute later, when Crystal got home, she saw Tory sitting on the concrete steps leading to her apartment. Crystal parked at the curb and walked slowly toward Brennan's house.

Crystal's face was all smiles. "Hi Tory. How did you find out where I lived?"

Tory grinned. "Hi Crystal. I went over to the Music Department to ask you to help me get my tools from the clock tower, and they gave me your address. They knew we were friends. What's with the car?"

"That's Rheinhold's *SUV*. He asked me to take care of it for a few days. He's in jail."

"I thought he looked and sounded too smooth! So they got him for killing his sister?"

"We don't think he did it, maybe someone else. I'll tell you what we've been doing. Come in and we can talk."

They sat down at the kitchen table. After relating the evening's events to Tory, Crystal said, "Barbara told me what happened in the tower the other day."

"Did she tell you that it was only a medicinal kiss?" Tory inquired seriously.

"No. She said you told her you were entranced with her beauty and you couldn't help yourself."

"Hey! That's not true! That little skunk lied!"

"Don't get excited. I'm just kidding. She told me what happened. You prevented her from barfing. She said the kiss was medicinal, but I've never heard of such a thing. Let's forget it. Besides, we've only had lunch together. It's not like we're going steady."

"Whew! I'm glad you know the truth."

"Why don't you meet me in my office tomorrow morning? I'll let you into the tower so you can get your tools. Oh! You need to complete the doorbell wiring, don't you?"

"Yep! That's why I came over tonight, plus I wanted to see you again," Tory answered displaying a sheepish grin.

"Would you like some coffee? I can reheat some."

"Uh—I'd better not, thanks. It will keep me awake, and I need my beauty sleep," Tory grinned as he stood up.

"Okay Tory. I'll see you in the morning about nine o'clock."

"It's a date! Thanks for filling me in about Sharon Tilfield and Mr. Rheinhold. I'm still wondering if Rheinhold had something to do with the professor's death. People have been killed for a lot less money than she had. Good night."

"Good night Tory, see you tomorrow."

CHAPTER 17

Back in the Tower

Loud knocking awakened Crystal. She glanced at her clock. It was almost 7:20 a.m. She threw back the covers, went to the door, and looked through the curtain. It was Barb.

"Hey Crystal! Let me in!"

Crystal unlocked the door and Barbara rushed in.

"Did you hear the radio? Robert Rheinhold is getting out of jail!"

"Hey, slow down. What are you talking about?"

"Well, I got up at six, turned on the radio, and while I was propping my eyes open, I heard that Robert Rheinhold was being released from jail. The death of Professor Maxine Rheinhold was ruled accidental!"

"Gosh! I wonder what happened."

"I don't know, but if we go down to the jail to return Robert's car, maybe we can find out all the gruesome details!"

"Hmm. You just woke me up. I forgot to set the switch on my alarm last night. Guess what, Tory came over. Hey, do you want some coffee?"

"No wonder you slept in! Did you guys do anything? Tell me all about it! This is exciting!"

"Hold it, Miss Pixie, nothing happened. I told him what you said about the kiss in the tower, but I first said that you told me he was overcome by your beauty, and he couldn't resist kissing you."

"You said that? You're kidding!"

"I'm not kidding, but then I told him the truth."

"Jeez, Crystal, you're gonna get me in trouble!"

"No, it's all straightened out. I'm to meet with him today at nine o'clock so he can get his tools from the tower and finish installing the doorbell alarm that indicates a low battery on the clock."

"Well, you'd better get dressed. Take a shower and I'll get your breakfast ready. I need some more coffee. I'll make a big pot for us."

"Okay. It should take less than ten minutes."

As Crystal disappeared into the bathroom, she yelled to Barbara, "Turn on the radio and the TV! Maybe you'll hear some more about Rheinhold."

Barbara made the coffee and popped two pieces of bread in the toaster. She listened and watched for more information about the accidental death of the professor, but nothing more was said.

"Nine minutes thirty-seven seconds!" Barbara announced as Crystal rejoined her in the kitchen.

"You actually timed me?"

"Nope! I made that up. But that was a quick shower, and you're presentable too! Oh, I buttered the toast with some of that fake, spray-on butter."

After having toast, oatmeal, orange juice, and a mug of coffee, the girls set off toward Harwick Hall. It was 8:21 a.m. The sun was out and the girls didn't wear jackets, just light sweaters. There wasn't much activity on campus yet. Student registration was complete, and a few students were wandering around checking out locations of classes in preparation for Monday.

Normally they would have checked their mailboxes in the departmental office, but the door was locked, so they went upstairs. No last-minute notes from their professors were found.

"We've got thirty-five minutes to kill, Crystal. Got any ideas?"

"Why not go back to my place and clean up Rheinhold's car? I noticed some scraps of paper and a napkin on the floor behind the front seat."

Barbara grinned and replied, "Why not? We'll be good Girl Scouts."

"I never made it through Brownies," Crystal laughed.

Rheinhold's car was fairly clean, and it only took the young women a few minutes to pick up the small bits of trash that were on the floor and shake out the floor mats. Crystal kept an eye on her watch. When the time was 8:50, they locked the car and walked back to the Music Building.

Tory was waiting for them at the front door. He grinned and greeted them. "Hello ladies!"

The girls smiled and said, "Hi!" in unison.

Tory opened the heavy front door, and they walked to the tower access door on the second floor. Crystal unlocked the door and pushed it open. Tory stepped into the small space and started up the ladder.

"Crystal, please flip that light on for me. I forgot to turn it on."

Barbara reached into the little space and flipped the switch. In a minute or so, Tory yelled down the access shaft, "Barbara, could you help me?"

Barbara looked at Crystal, frowned, and shook her head.

"No way! I went through that once before. Once was enough!"

Crystal acquiesced. "All right, I'll come up." Crystal started up the ladder.

When she was halfway up the ladder, Tory said, "Is anyone coming up?"

Tory looked down the shaft and could see curly blond hair approaching. He grinned, just what he wanted. Crystal stuck her head above the trap door, smiled and said, "Barb doesn't want to come up here again. She doesn't want to risk getting another medicinal kiss."

"I had hoped you would come up, Crystal. I have something to show you."

Crystal sat on the floor with her legs dangling through the opening and looked up at Tory.

"What is it?"

"You'll have to come over here."

Tory pointed at the circuit box.

Crystal got to her feet and squeezed close to Tory. He detected a slight scent of perfume and felt like kissing her but held back the impulse. He showed Crystal the battery that would have to be replaced occasionally, when a radio signal was sent to a doorbell located in Mrs. Farnsworth's office.

"We'll have to tell the secretary what the buzzer means so she can send someone up to change the battery. The buzzer will sound every hour until the battery is changed. This battery should last about a year," Tory stated.

He placed the cover on the metal box and snapped it into place.

"Now, there is one last thing."

"What's that?"

"This."

Tory leaned over and kissed Crystal. She kissed him back and grinned.

Tory smiled and said, "That was not medicinal! And thank you for helping me."

"But I didn't do anything."

"Yes you did. You kissed me back. The score is tied! Let's get out of here."

They descended the ladder carrying Tory's tools and flipped off the light. Crystal locked the door, and they went down the hall to the TA's office. Barbara was waiting for them.

"Did you get everything accomplished?" Barbara quizzed.

Tory quickly replied, "Oh yeah," and grinned.

Barbara glanced at Crystal. Crystal smiled and gave a thumbs up.

Crystal looked at the wall clock and said, "Let's go to jail!"

Tory had to take his tools back to his dorm room, so he said he would see the girls later. Barbara and Crystal got in Rheinhold's car and drove off campus toward town.

CHAPTER 18

Nothing to Do

The ladies had only driven a block when Barbara inquired, "Where's the Police Station?"

Crystal started laughing and said, "I don't know. We'd better pull over and ask somebody."

An elderly lady, walking her dog, was approaching the Aztek. Barbara lowered her window and asked, "Could you please tell me how to get to the Police Station?"

"Sure. Go three more blocks, turn right, and drive four blocks. It's the light-blue building on the left. You can't miss it; you'll see the police cars."

"Thank you." Barbara replied in a cheery voice.

Crystal followed the lady's directions and parked diagonally beside a patrol car. When the young ladies entered the building, they saw Robert sitting in a large, comfortable looking, leather-covered chair. He was drinking coffee and reading the New York Times.

Robert stood, put down his cup, folded the paper, and said, "Good morning ladies. How nice of you to come by."

"Nuts! I though we were going to look through some bars and see you sitting on a cot in a cell," Barbara replied with a grin.

"Barbara! That's not funny. He had to stay in jail overnight!" retorted Crystal.

Robert commented, "No big deal ladies. My stay in—this establishment was quite comfortable. I was in a private guest room you know." He smiled and tossed the newspaper on a small table next to a magazine rack.

"Did you meet any hardened criminals or see any fights?" Barbara quizzed.

"Nope. I was the only visitor. Currently there are several vacancies."

Barbara said, "Tell us what happened, Mr. Rheinhold."

"The County Sheriff and the Lieutenant sat down with me, and I told them my story. Then they went through the evidence box with me. We found a business card from Pests Down Under, owned by Joe Wilagur. There was a handwritten note, in black ink, on the back of the card, saying Potassium Cyanide—POISON—Do Not Eat! The business card was in a plastic evidence bag from the first shelf of the medicine cabinet. The card was found with the remnants of a rubber band behind a plastic container of foot powder. The sheriff called Mr. Wilagur and asked him about the potassium cyanide. He remembered giving Max four capsules. He put them in an empty sleeping pill bottle. He and Max used two capsules to set a rodent trap in the back yard. That left two remaining capsules in the bottle. Max told Mr. Wilagur to put the poison up high in the medicine cabinet where she couldn't reach it. Remember, Max was only about five feet two.

When Max asked me to get her some sleeping pills, I saw the bottle on the top shelf. Since I'm six-three, I took the two pills from the bottle within easy reach, and gave them to Max. I didn't see there was another bottle of capsules on the bottom shelf. Apparently, the rubber band had dried out, broken, and fell off the higher bottle. The card warning of the poison had dropped down behind the foot powder.

The police thought, if I had been trying to poison Max, I would have wiped my prints from the empty sleeping pill bottle. They decided not to arrest me for the note I wrote pretending that Max had committed suicide."

"Oh yes, the police found five twenty-dollar bills in her night-stand. She wasn't robbed."

"Wow! That's really too bad about the professor, but her death was an accident," stated Crystal. "You didn't have any idea those pills weren't sleeping pills."

Barbara smiled, "So, it wasn't the butler! It was a good mystery though!"

"Well ladies, let's get out of this free hotel. Where's my car? I'll take you back home or wherever you want. How about lunch?"

Barbara quizzed, "Your treat?"

"Yep! My treat."

As they drove toward the Burger and Tunes Café, Barbara reached into her pocket and pulled out a piece of yellow paper.

"Crystal, I forgot to tell you about the barbeque at Professor Welker's house on Saturday. When I was waiting for you and Tory to come down from the tower, I found this note on my desk. All the members of the Music Department, their families, the support staff, teaching assistants, and their dates are invited. I was thinking we should recruit some of the other teaching assistants to help us with Mrs. Jenkins's music. What do you think?"

"That sounds like fun. Good idea about recruiting. We'll need some help with the strings. I think I'll ask Tory to go to the barbeque. You'll need to find a date, Barb." Crystal laughed, "Maybe not, there will be some kids about your size that you can play with."

"That's mean, Crystal. After I helped you find the notebook, you came up with a short joke! I thought you were my friend," Barbara pouted.

Crystal looked at Barbara, not knowing whether her diminutive friend was serious or not. Crystal smiled when she thought of the quip she had made.

When Barbara saw Crystal smile, she broke out laughing. "I actually thought that was pretty funny. I just acted mad to keep from laughing. I know who I'm going to ask to come to the barbeque."

"Who?"

"Mr. Rheinhold! How about it Mr. Rheinhold? Would you like to be my date to the barbeque on Saturday?"

"I would be delighted, Barbara. I don't have to be home until Monday. My taxi service is available, too. You ladies, Tory, and I can go together."

Barbara looked at Rheinhold and said, "That's a great idea Mr. Rheinhold." Then Barbara glanced at Crystal. "Crystal, think about this. After the barbeque, we won't have anything to do until Monday."

Crystal replied, "We'll think of something."

The Canoe

Morning Walk

Samuel Kelly's morning walk usually began around eight-thirty and was completed in a half-hour or so. When he didn't stop to give a biscuit to a dog or scratch a cat, his shortest time was twenty-two minutes. Sam's Timex read 8:17, so he was starting a little early today. Breakfast had been quick; just enough fuel for the morning's activities. He slipped into his heavy coat, which had a hood, and opened the front door.

Sam stepped outside, locked the door, and started north along Eagle Creek Lane, the street next to the green belt where the big pines offered the nearby homes some shelter from the East wind, which so often blew through the Columbia River Gorge. The gorge wind sometimes blew for several days, indicating a low pressure area off the Pacific Northwest coast was moving inland. The sky was a uniform gray and the wind had stopped.

It had rained lightly before dawn, and there had been sporadic sprinkles since he arose at 6:00 a.m. He had gotten up at that time for most of his sixty-nine years. The grass and pavement were wet, and the air smelled clean, with a barely detectable scent of pine and smoke from chimneys. He crossed Kilgore Street and hopped over a small puddle onto the concrete curb, then stepped over the wet grass onto the sidewalk. Sam was slightly over six feet tall, weighed one-seventy, and was in pretty good shape. His graying brown hair was very thin on top. Sam wasn't handsome but he was better than average looking.

Sam decided to take his time and enjoy the sights and sounds of the green belt. He began to walk more slowly than usual and tried to identify birds from their songs. Sam had never been a bird watcher, but he could easily identify seagulls, hawks, robins, and blue jays. He had never owned a pair of binoculars. Approximately a half-mile from his front door, roughly one-third through his walk, Sam began the uphill portion of his exercise, which usually left him breathing hard when he reached the top of the grade.

It began to sprinkle, and he could see his pant legs beginning to get wet. The drops striking his hood made barely audible thumps. He thought of turning back but decided to continue, hoping there wouldn't be a real downpour. If the rain started to drench him, he could always wait it out under a big tree, but Sam had little concern for the weather; he could walk in the rain if he wanted and lightning was rare. Sam had thought about getting one of those fold-up umbrellas, but he hated carrying things around, they were too easy to lose.

A few minutes went by and it did begin to rain harder. Sam chose a spot under a tree to wait out the heavy precipitation. He relaxed against a big pine and noticed a canoe inverted on a couple of weathered sawhorses across the street between a garage and two trees that provided shelter for the small inverted boat. It amused Sam that he had never seen the canoe when he had walked up the other side of the street. Then he was reminded why.

A young lady came out of the house next to where Sam stood, ran to a car, and drove off. She was probably on her way to classes or work. The community college wasn't far away. She looked pretty fine, was about fifty years younger than Sam, but he still appreciated a nice looking young woman. The car was loud, maybe a boyfriend's. That noise was a big part of strutting to attract potential mates. Sam smiled. He remembered seeing films of male birds displaying highly colored feathers to attract females of the species. These days, boys used loud cars and loud music to attract girls. Sam questioned the logic.

It was quiet on the street then, except for the sound of the rain-drops pummeling the sidewalks, asphalt, and rooftops. An occasional car drove by, tires kicking up small rooster tails from the wet pavement. Sam was fairly dry and enjoying the serenade. His thoughts drifted back to Lake Breeze, Michigan, a few years after the end of the second world war.

"Grandpa . . . are we goin' fishin' sometime?" five-year old Sam asked.

"Sure Samuel. How about today? Let's get some worms and the fishing poles. You carry the poles and worms, and I'll tote the canoe," replied Grandpa Bud. Grandpa had bushy white eyebrows, fairly long white hair, a hint of a potbelly, and was very strong. He was average height, about five-nine.

Sam got the war surplus shovel from the garage, and the two fishermen went to the garden and dug up a dozen juicy worms. Each fat, writhing worm was about six inches long, so the anglers wouldn't run out of bait before they caught several lake trout.

Sam liked the feeling of the worms wiggling in his hands. Grandpa had an empty can to which he added a handful of moist dirt and the worms.

Sam was a little above average size for his age, and a little skinny. His ears were bigger than average, just like his dad's, but he was a nice-looking boy with short brown hair. Sam carried the bait and two bamboo fishing poles.

When Grandpa was walking with the canoe resting on his head, Sam imagined it was one of those giant Texas cowboy hats. When they arrived at the lake, a distance of a quarter mile, Sam watched his grandpa lower the canoe from above his head and slide it halfway into the water. A few kids were playing in the water while their parents watched, but no one was fishing. Sam wondered if the people knew fish were in Lake Bliss. He was eager to get out on the water, so jumped into the boat.

Sam heard Bud call out, "Hey! You forgot something."

Grandpa handed Sam the poles and the bait can, pushed the canoe farther into the water, and said, "Ready?" Grandpa smiled at Sam, who was big eyed with expectations.

"Yes, Grandpa!" Sam answered with a big grin.

Grandpa Bud pushed the canoe farther out in the water and hopped in. They began floating slowly away from the shoreline. Sam picked up an oar and started paddling. Grandpa knelt in the boat and paddled from the other side. One of Grandpa's strokes was equivalent to two of Sam's and the canoe slipped quietly across the still water. When they were about a hundred yards offshore, the oars were placed in the bottom of the boat and the fishing poles were made ready for hauling in the "big ones," as Grandpa often said. The hooks were baited and the two fishermen waited for a strike. Sam looked across the water to a small lump of land some distance away.

"Is that an island, Grandpa?" Sam inquired as he pointed with his left hand.

"Sure is! That's Hum—Handy Island. Not much is there Samuel, just some sand, rocks and a few small scraggly trees. Someday you'll probably go there and see for yourself," Grandpa chuckled.

Sam felt his line go taut and could feel the pulling on his pole.

"Grandpa! I've got one!"

"Need help, Samuel?"

"No Sir! I think I can pull it in," Sam answered with guarded confidence.

Sam struggled, but Grandpa let him wrestle with the fishing pole. Sam finally got the line reeled in and hoisted the fish from the water. Grandpa removed the hook and tossed the eight-inch squirming trout on the bottom of the canoe. Sam looked at the fish and said, "It's trying to get its breath! I want to put it back in the water so it won't die."

Grandpa realized Sam had never seen a living thing bigger than a bug die in front of him, so he said, "Okay Samuel. Pick it up, hold your hand under its belly, and lower it into the water."

Sam followed Grandpa Bud's instructions. After a few seconds, the fish flapped its tail and swam away from Sam's hand. Sam looked at Grandpa and said seriously, "I think maybe I'll keep the next one, Grandpa."

From then on, all the fish Sam caught were kept for eating, but he still remembered that first one. That was the only time Sam and Grandpa went fishing. Grandpa Bud had a heart attack and passed away just before Halloween.

The rain ceased and Sam continued on his walk, returning home after forty-two minutes. As he unlocked the front door, Sam decided to put thoughts of the canoe out of his mind. He had things to do. Sam had volunteered to deliver meals to shut-ins, an activity that provided much satisfaction. Each delivery made Sam proud, and the recipients were usually waiting, ready to bend his ear a little. Often, Sam was a shut-in's only contact with another human for a whole week, sometimes longer. He had heard some of their stories multiple times, but Sam patiently listened and asked them questions. Sharing tall tales was an integral part of the job. A few of the elderly ladies told him things that made him blush. Sam wondered where they came up with that stuff: soap operas, books, or gossip but hardly reality. They would have been wild to have had those experiences.

CHAPTER 2

The Island

Sam missed a day of his morning walks because of a dental appointment. His lips were numb for three hours, preventing him from drinking his extra morning coffee. He liked his coffee steaming hot but didn't want to burn his mouth. The pain in his mouth made him irritable, so Sam stayed home. He took a pain pill and tried to read a book but kept falling asleep. Those damn pills weren't supposed to make him drowsy. He only finished one chapter all day. Reading about religions didn't strike his enthusiasm button, but he had long felt the need to understand more than Christianity.

The next day, he resumed his routine. The weather was nice, the sun was out, and there was very little wind. There was no sign of clouds in the light-blue sky. When Sam could see the canoe, he noticed a for sale sign nailed to one of the trees that protected the sleek little boat from the weather. Sam had to assume the sign was with reference to the canoe. No one would be selling their garage, a part of the house, or the trees; they were thirty feet tall and stood like watch dogs over the property. Sam smiled when he considered using a chainsaw to make one of the trees into a totem pole.

Sam thought back several decades. William "Pinch" Miser and Sam had been buddies for about three years. Sam was thirteen. Pinch was two years older. Pinch was Sam's main resource for knowledge about the opposite sex. He got his nickname from being frugal because of his last name. Pinch wasn't smart measured by what he accomplished in school, but he was very practical. His family was not well to do. Kids said Billy squeezed pennies so hard Lincoln screamed. Sam had heard that joke about his uncle Lloyd.

One hot summer day in late July, Pinch came over to see if Sam wanted to paddle out to the island in the middle of the lake. It was to be a fact-finding trip. Pinch had heard many tales of the island from older boys. Sam and Pinch took the canoe off the garage wall and wiped off the dust and spider webs. The finish on the wood looked dried out and was starting to crack in several places.

"Dad told me we need to treat the wood before we put the canoe in the water," stated Sam.

"What do we treat the wood with?"

"Dad said we need to rub it down with linseed oil so the cracks will seal and the wood won't absorb water."

"How long will that take?" Pinch was a little impatient. He wanted to get the canoe on the water.

"I think about the same time it would take to wash a car," Sam replied. "But it will have to dry overnight. The oil has to soak into the wood. Dad said if we were going to use the canoe much we would have to sand it down and apply some new polymer finish."

"What's a polymer?" asked Pinch.

"Jeez, Pinch. Haven't you ever had a science class? Polymers are big molecules made out of a bunch of little ones hooked together."

"Isn't that chemistry? I mostly work with cars and plumbing—that kind of stuff. But it's getting more complicated all the time. There've been lots of new inventions, or should I say innovations? Some things were secrets during the war, but not now."

"Either word would work, Pinch. Let's get busy. We can do this in about an hour or so and then play pool and have a root beer float."

"Sounds good. We can check out girls downtown too," Pinch smiled, raising his eyebrows.

The linseed oil was applied liberally, and after nearly an hour of soaking into the wood, the excess was wiped off. The boys went to the pool hall and played pool for about an hour. They didn't see any interesting girls. After that, Pinch went home to do some chores for his mom, and Sam had to deliver newspapers to about fifty homes on his route.

The boat remained in the garage on sawhorses overnight. Pinch showed up at one o'clock after Sam had finished off the last of his lunch; a big, juicy, delicious apple. Sam saw Pinch walking toward the garage and went outside.

"Hey Pinch! Ready to go exploring?" quizzed Sam.

"Sure am. How's the boat look? Did we do okay with the oil?"

"Yeah, but Dad said it was only temporary. The canoe would have to be refinished pretty soon."

Sam went over to the trash can, lifted the lid, watched some flies zoom about, and dropped his apple core in the big container.

"Boy! Get a whiff of that!" Sam commented as he wrinkled up his nose.

Pinch said, "Come on stinky. Let's get this boat in the lake. We have an island waiting for us."

Sam and Pinch crouched beneath the canoe, inverted on two sawhorses, grabbed the sides, and stood up. Sam remembered when he was with Grandpa Bud, the canoe was very heavy, but now it seemed very light. The two teenagers walked the quarter mile to Lake Bliss and set the canoe on the shore. Sam pulled two life vests from a net bag in the canoe and dropped them on the ground. They untied the oars and slid the little boat into the water.

Pinch stepped in the canoe and nearly tipped it over. He quickly put one foot into about six inches of water to avoid falling. Sam told him to crouch down, move to the center, and sit down. Sam tossed the life-preservers beside Pinch, pushed off, and jumped in the boat. They drifted out into the water about twenty feet before they were ready to use the oars. Pinch had crawled toward the front of the canoe and they began to row.

"My grandpa told me a long time ago the island is called Handy Island," Sam volunteered.

"I've never heard that name. All the guys I know call it Hump Island."

"Hump Island? Oh, because of how it sticks up out of the lake?"

"Nope! You'll see when we get there. I'll show you," Pinch replied, grinning.

As the small island grew bigger, the boys surveyed the barren shoreline. Sam steered the canoe to a place where it would be easy to climb out onto land. When the boat touched bottom, Pinch jumped out and waded a few feet to shore, pulling the canoe beside him. Sam stepped out of the boat onto solid ground and gave the canoe another pull to get it completely out of the water. They didn't want to be marooned without a way to get home if the canoe floated off.

Sam looked up and down the shore but could only see gravel, sand, dirt and a few weeds. As they moved inland, more rocks were encountered, a few wildflowers, and bird nests were found, scattered randomly about. No trees, not even small ones, were there.

Pinch pointed to the high point of the sandy mound, and said, "Up there, I'll show you why this is called Hump Island."

It took less than a minute to climb to the top of the island. At the summit were a couple of eight inch diameter logs about twelve feet long, three large boulders, and a smaller rounded rock probably weighing two hundred pounds. Sand covered the ground to a depth of about four inches.

"Okay, Sam. What do you see?" quizzed Pinch.

Sam looked around and said, "Well, some broken bottles and a bunch of old water balloons lying around."

"You're only partly right," Pinch stated. "Those aren't balloons, they're used condoms! Now you know why this is called Hump Island."

"Jeez, someone should clean up this place. It looks bad," stated Sam.

"Yah, I know, but who wants to pick up those nasty old skins?"

"We could do it, Pinch," Sam suggested. "We can bring some bags, a rake and wear gloves. This place is a real mess. Let's clean it up."

"You think we should burn the condoms?" asked Pinch. "I don't want to take them home and put them in my garbage."

"I don't think we should burn them. They'd probably make a lot of black smoke. Someone would probably come out here to see what we're doing. We can't say we're burning rubber tires," Sam smiled.

Pinch said, "I know! We'll take them back with us and put them in old man Putnam's garbage cans. He leaves the cans near the street all the time. We can do it at night so nobody will see us."

"Good idea! That'll work. We'll do it tomorrow."

The boys completed the cleanup of the island in a few hours the next day. As they climbed back into the canoe to take the garbage back, Pinch commented, "We should get a merit badge for this, Sam. What do you think should be on the merit badge?"

The boys started laughing.

Sam and Pinch drifted apart during the next school year. Pinch had older friends with cars and they talked about sex and sports almost exclusively. Sam still rode a bike and continued to deliver papers. His interest in science took precedence over nearly everything else until he was a high school senior. His interest in the opposite sex blossomed when he began to plan for college. Sam still smiles and laughs about the Hump Island affair.

CHAPTER 3

College Days

The next day Sam had to postpone his walk; the morning was spent running errands. Sam set out on his walk after dinner, stopping to talk to a few neighbors. As he began the uphill part of his journey, Sam could see that the canoe was still there and so was the for sale sign. The canoe was becoming an old friend. He almost wanted to talk to it. Sam hoped no one would buy it, but he realized that was unlikely—the owners probably needed the money. Sam stopped and looked at the boat from the sidewalk and noted it was made of wood, not fiberglass or aluminum.

The canoe Grandpa Bud and Dad had owned was also made of wood. Previously, Sam had only stopped briefly to take a look at the boat from the sidewalk, but when he was having breakfast, he considered buying the canoe. But where would he store it, and how would he get it to water to make use of it? He didn't drive anymore, and he certainly wasn't going to carry it over his head. Forty years ago, he could have done that. Sam reluctantly dismissed the thought of buying it.

He still wanted to check out the boat so he walked over and put his hand on the sleek wood. Surprise! The canoe was made of aluminum! It was painted to resemble wood. He had sure been fooled. Sam put his hands under the side of the canoe and lifted, expecting it to be fairly heavy. Surprise again! The canoe was very easy to lift. Of course the other end was still resting on a sawhorse. He wondered what the price was, nothing was indicated on the sign. Sam resumed his walk and began to think back.

Early in the 1960s, Sam's family had moved from the upper midwest to Washington State, bringing the canoe with them. That little boat was part of the family, much like a dog or a cat. When they drove across country to their new home in Walla Walla, the canoe was mounted securely on top of the car. The boat had been refinished and looked new; the grain of the wood contributed to the beauty of the sleek lines of the canoe. Sam and his dad had sanded off the old, cracked finish and applied a new polymer coating over fresh mahogany stain. Both men were proud of their work. It was nearly a professional job.

Sam was ready for college at Washington State University, Pullman, Washington. One evening in August, a couple of weeks before fall semester was to begin, people were outside mowing lawns, washing cars, and sitting on porches enjoying the mild evening. New neighbors had moved in a week earlier and they had a college age daughter who was sitting on their front porch. Sam was checking out Fran Withers as he adjusted the sprinkler. She appeared to be sketching. He decided to introduce himself and find out what she was drawing.

Sam looked down at his clothes, making sure he wasn't unzipped. He would never recover from the embarrassment if that happened. He started across the grass, very slowly. He didn't want to be too enthusiastic and do something dumb, like stutter or spit when he began to talk. As he approached the girl, he noted how slim and trim she looked. There wasn't much fat, if any, on the sexy package he was observing.

"Hello, I'm Sam, two doors down," he announced and pointed to his house.

"I know. Hi, I'm Fran," she answered back. She hardly looked up as she continued to sketch. "Our mothers talked."

"What're you drawing?"

"Our neighbor across the street; the guy that's mowing his lawn," Fran responded, pointing with her charcoal pencil.

"Can I see?"

"Sure."

Sam stepped behind Fran, who was sitting on the elevated concrete porch. Her legs were dangling and barely touching the ground. *Nice legs.* He looked at the drawing and was surprised. The picture showed a man mowing his lawn; in addition, there was a large dog sprawled in the grass, and two young children were washing a car in the driveway. The boy held a hose and the girl was throwing suds at him with a large sponge.

"I like it. Why the kids and the dog?"

"Well, without them, the guy looked lonely. I thought he needed a family. It makes the picture tell a better story, don't you think?" she pulled her hair back from her face and smiled. She had little dimples, a straight nose and her eyes danced. She was good-looking, but not beautiful.

"Yeah. Good idea."

"Mom said you have a canoe."

"Uh-huh. We brought it from Wisconsin. Dad and I refinished it just before we moved. Why?"

"I've been thinking about doing a few watercolors of the Snake River terrain, but not the same old ones from the banks of the river. I'd like to try it from the water, say out in the middle of the river. Do you think we could take your canoe and float along in the river?"

"Hey, that might be fun! I can take my camera and you can do your watercolors.

But, before we go, you'll have to practice painting while wearing a life vest. The vest might cramp your style a little," Sam noted.

"I won't need a vest. I'm a strong swimmer," Fran replied.

"We can't do it then. You have to wear a vest, or we can't go on the water."

"Well, I guess if it's a requirement. Do you have one I can experiment with?"

"Sure, I'll get one for you right now."

Sam went to his garage and brought back a red life preserver.

"Have any other color?" Fran teased.

"I think I pity your boyfriend," Sam commented with a grin.

"Had one. He dumped me, I wouldn't put out," Fran said matter-of-factly.

"You should be proud of that, Fran. More power to you," Sam stated.

Fran had long auburn hair, pretty blue eyes, and Sam guessed she couldn't weigh more than a hundred and ten pounds. When she stood up, Sam was surprised; she was only a little over five feet tall, at most, five-four. He had expected her to be taller. She spoke with confidence and looked him right in the eyes.

Sam asked, "When do you want to go canoeing? We've only got a couple of weeks before classes start."

"How about tomorrow? I'd like to get some sketches and water-colors done right away."

"Sounds good to me. Let's leave about nine."

Fran came over to Sam's at 8:30 the next morning. Sam couldn't believe that she was early and had packed a lunch. Sam had the canoe on top of the car and the back seat had the life vests, oars and a small medical kit. He also stuck a hatchet under the seat and stuffed a pocketknife in the glove compartment. At the last minute, Sam tossed an old blanket in the back seat. It would be good to sit on while eating or wrap up in if they got wet.

In addition to the lunch basket, Fran had a box of charcoal pencils, watercolors, brushes, a muffin tin and paper. Sam took a final look at the map, and said, "We're off to Lyons Ferry. It'll take a little over an hour. When we get there, we'll find a place to launch the canoe."

Fran turned on the car radio and lowered the window on the passenger side. As they drove toward the river, Sam glanced occasionally at Fran. He liked what he saw. They didn't have much to say, but they seemed to enjoy each other's company. They talked a little about school. Fran gave Sam more information about the campus than the brochures did. She was going to be a sophomore at WSU and Sam a freshman. Fran was an art major, and Sam was going to major in math.

Time passed quickly. They reached the ferry at eleven-fifteen and found a place to back the car down to the water.

"You can help me get the canoe off the roof, Fran," Sam instructed.

"Are you too weak, or is the boat too heavy, or both?" Fran laughed.

Fran expected a smart comeback from Sam, but all he said was, "Both." Sam didn't even crack a smile. Sam was smiling inside, but he didn't want to divulge it to Fran. Sam thought most of the girls he knew could read his mind, but he didn't want to make it any easier for them. A poker face made him a little mysterious.

Fran put on her life preserver, as did Sam, and in a few minutes the new friends were rowing against the current. They paddled upstream about a mile and then drifted back to the ferry crossing. Fran got a good start on a watercolor and Sam took half a dozen pictures, mostly of the ferry and his dad's car, a 1958 blue Pontiac. Fran asked Sam to take a couple of photos at certain places in case she needed help to remember the colors of the landscapes she was painting. Sam almost joked he had black and white film, but he had color.

As they approached the ferry, which was in the middle of the river, people on the flat boat were yelling at them. At first, Sam couldn't figure out what the passengers were saying, but then he heard *dog*.

"Fran, I think a dog fell off the ferry. It will never make it back; the current is too strong."

Fran quickly put her art materials away as she said, "Let's rescue the dog!"

The two college kids grabbed their oars and started moving the canoe rapidly across the water downstream from the ferry. Fran watched the people on the ferry as they pointed to the dog. She scanned the water and saw a small white object thrashing about in the water.

"I see it, Sam! Go a little more to the left about thirty yards."

"Okay! I see it now. If it continues to move like that, it's going to go under. Let's hurry!"

The canoeists reached the frantic dog in about fifteen seconds. It was floundering and close to going under. Fran reached out, grabbed the dog's neck, and pulled the soaked furball into the boat. The little dog was shaking from fright and just sat in the bottom of the canoe for a moment. Realizing it was now safe, but all wet, the dog shook its entire body. Sam reached up and covered his face. With front paws on the side of the canoe, the little dog looked back at the ferry and barked. The owners were waving and applauding, happy to see their pet had been rescued.

Fran and Sam rowed to the ferry landing and returned the dog to its owners.

The owners, a vacationing couple from North Dakota, thanked the college kids profusely. They gave Fran twenty dollars for saving their little dog, Nikki. Everyone exchanged names and addresses, went their separate ways, and continued their activities. Fran and Sam had lunch and went back on the water for another hour before calling it a day. Both of them were sunburned after being on the river for over two hours. Sam's arms and shoulders were tired from all the rowing, but neither teen complained. They had enjoyed the day together and saved a dog. Fran and Sam stopped on the way home for pizza and cokes. What more could they have wanted? Sam told Fran to keep the left-over money.

CHAPTER 4

Sold

Fran and Sam dated during Sam's freshman year at the university, but Fran's father lost his job in Walla Walla, and the family moved to California. The college kids tried to keep in touch, but the time between letters grew longer and longer, and the letters finally ceased. Fran took a semester off, was working as an illustrator, and intended to finish school in California.

Sam met Sharon Durham during his sophomore year, and they married a couple of years after graduating from college. They didn't have any children but did a lot of traveling, visiting most of the European countries and parts of Asia. Sam worked as a mathematician for Boeing aircraft in Portland, Oregon. Sharon and Sam retired at sixty-five and continued to travel for two years. Sharon began having health problems, and a year later passed away from an autoimmune disease. Sam bought a house in Troutdale, Oregon, a suburb of Portland.

Fran finished college at USC and married a computer engineer. When the personal computer revolution hit, her husband, Eric Wilson, made a fortune. They retired to a small vineyard in northern California. Fran continued her art career, took over a struggling art studio and made it profitable. Her husband, Eric, took a trip to

France and Italy to visit vineyards and wineries. Wilsons were going to build a winery. His rented plane crashed in northern Italy, and everyone on board was killed. Eric and Fran had one son who joined the armed forces and was accidently killed in the Middle East. Fran had never remarried.

Fran wanted to escape the California area and haunting memories. After several months of searching the country for a picturesque place to live, she bought a home in the suburbs of Portland, Oregon. She loved the accessibility to the rivers, the ocean, and the mountains. She could find subjects for her artwork everywhere.

It was Monday and Sam missed another morning walk. There had been a downpour during the night, and it was still raining steadily when it was time to walk. Sam started a fire, did some push-ups and squats, and began to read the paper. He started reading the sports section but fell asleep for over an hour. When he woke up, it was lunchtime. The rain had stopped and there was a cool southern breeze. The overcast sky was beginning to be penetrated by the sun's rays. Water vapor rising from his neighbor's rooftop looked like steam in the sunshine.

After lunch, Sam sat down to finish reading the paper. When he opened the folded paper, some advertising brochures fell out. As he reached down to pick up the papers, he noticed a picture of an aluminum canoe for sale at a camping supply store. "Time for a walk," Sam muttered.

It was warm and humid outdoors, so he just wore a T-shirt and jeans. Sam locked the front door and began walking. When he arrived near the canoe site, he stopped and stared at the sawhorses. The canoe and sign were gone! He had grown to relish seeing that old canoe sitting there, reminding him of past experiences. In his disappointment, he just kept walking, not paying attention to the time or distance he had traveled.

When Sam's thoughts about the canoe ceased, he was on the main street of Troutdale, strolling down the sidewalk, glancing into the storefronts. He overheard two middle-aged women talking as they exited a shop with what appeared to be a painting. As Sam passed them on the sidewalk, he heard one woman say, "I think I got a good deal. This will fit perfectly above the mantel in the living room, and it was only one hundred seventy-five dollars."

"Do you know the artist, Helen?"

"No, I don't, but there are several other pieces of hers in the gallery. They are all very nice. Her name is Francine Wilson."

Sam thought, "*Could that be the Francine I knew years ago? What are the chances?*" He entered the gallery and a lady approached.

"May I help you?"

"I hope so," Sam smiled. "I just heard the name of an artist mentioned by some ladies outside. The name is Francine Wilson. Do you have anything else she has done?"

"Ah—yes! We have two other compositions, an oil painting and a watercolor. Please follow me."

Sam followed the clomping heels across the hardwood floor toward the wall at the back of the gallery. The buxom lady stopped and pointed at the pictures hanging from the wood paneling.

"These are both by Francine."

Sam looked at the watercolor and knew the artist was the Francine he had dated years ago. The picture showed a girl and boy in a canoe pulling a dog from the water of a river. *Rescue* was the title. Memories of the time Sam and Fran had gone to Lyons Ferry flooded his brain. He even remembered the pizza had Canadian bacon on it. He had dropped a piece of bacon on his shirt and it left a greasy spot. And on the way home, they had to stop to pee behind an old barn near the highway. Sam took the watercolor to the counter and said, "I'd like to buy this one."

The proprietor said, "That's a beautiful picture."

"It sure is! You might not believe this, but I'm the boy in the canoe, and the girl is Francine, the artist. That rescue took place about fifty years ago. We saved a little dog from the Snake River at Lyons Ferry in Washington State. That really happened." Sam couldn't stop grinning.

"You should get in touch with her. She doesn't live far from here, about a mile or so up the Sandy River. I'll give you her address. I don't think she would mind."

"Do you know if she's married?"

"She's a widow. Francine moved here from California about three or four months ago. You should get together and talk over old times. I'll bet she would love to see you."

Sam wrote a check for the picture and it was wrapped for him. As he was leaving the gallery, the lady said, "Thank you Mr. Kelly. Good luck!"

"You're welcome! Thank you for the address. Bye." Sam waved as he went out the door.

As Sam began his journey home, he couldn't believe what had just taken place. After all these years, he was going to meet with a former girlfriend he hadn't seen in five decades. It had all occurred because he missed seeing an old canoe in someone's yard. All kinds of thoughts were running through his mind. *Would Fran remember me? Had the years been good to her?* Sam had his health but had lost a good percentage of his hair and muscles. *Well, one step at a time.* But he was almost seventy and felt like there weren't many years left. He decided to try to contact Fran tomorrow. The address was on the old highway near the Sandy River about a half-mile from his house. *What a coincidence!*

CHAPTER 5

Found

Sam took another look at the watercolor before he got in bed that night. He climbed in his king-size bed early so morning would arrive faster. Sam knew he might be kidding himself, but he had to think positively, although being a bit nervous about the unknown. If he were asleep, no negatives would be creeping into his brain, except perhaps from a bad dream. Fifty-one years had been a long time since dating Francine; would she remember him? But Sam had dealt with other upsetting circumstances and lived. What did he have to worry about? Fran and he could still have a good reunion, even if no attraction existed. They certainly wouldn't run out of experiences to reminisce.

The next morning, Sam took extra care when shaving and put on clean clothes. After breakfast, he brushed his teeth and made sure he had breath mints in his pocket. He hoped he wouldn't get a case of dry mouth. Sam started toward the Sandy river at nine o'clock. He crossed the bridge on Stark and walked south on the old highway for about three minutes, checking the numbers on the mailboxes. Sam paused at the address he had gotten at the gallery, looked over the property, and started toward the front door. When Sam was about twenty feet from the door, a nice-looking woman stepped outside.

"May I help you?" she inquired.

"Fran?" Sam asked.

"Yes, I'm Francine. Do I know you?"

"I guess you don't recognize me or my voice. We haven't seen each other in fifty-one years."

"Oh, my God! Is that you, Sam?"

She opened her arms and rushed toward Sam. They hugged quietly for nearly a minute, stepped back, and tried to talk at the same time.

"You first," directed Sam.

"My gosh! It's so good to see you! Your eyes are just as I remember."

"Not much else though!" Sam grinned.

"Well, look at me! I'm a year older than you."

"You look great, Fran. You've kept in good shape. Do you exercise?"

"Oh yes. I walk along the highway and look for subjects to sketch and paint. Sometimes I walk along the river but there are places where the rocks are so big I can't climb over them. So, guess what I did?"

"Ah—you made stilts?" Sam laughed.

"Nope. I bought a canoe! Come and see it."

Fran grabbed Sam's right hand. Her hand felt soft and warm. She led him around the side of the house to the back yard, which bordered on the river. Just as they reached the back yard, Sam saw it. It was his canoe! Not his canoe, but the one that had started all his recollections.

"You bought the canoe!" Sam exclaimed. "I wondered where it went. I've been watching that canoe for some time. A few days ago I was remembering how we went to Lyons Ferry and saved that little dog. And guess what? I bought your watercolor called *Rescue*. That's how I found out that you lived here."

"I hope you got a good deal on the painting. That was the first picture I did after my husband was killed in a plane wreck. I was in my studio remembering good times from the past and that picture just happened. It just sprang forth from my pencils and paints as if something were causing my hands to move the way they did. It was a strange experience—magical. I almost didn't sell it to the gallery."

"Well, fortunately you did, and when I saw it, I knew you were the artist. I had to have it. The lady at the gallery gave me your address after I told her about the experience on the Snake River."

"Isn't it funny how things happen? I was driving around the other day and saw a man under a tree looking across the street. I glanced to see what he was looking at, and I saw the canoe. On impulse, I bought it."

"That was me! I stopped under a tree to get out of the rain for a few minutes."

"Oh yes, I remember it was raining pretty hard. I should have stopped and offered you a ride. Wouldn't that have been a kick?" Fran smiled. "But now I have a problem."

"What's that?" Sam asked.

"I can't row upstream by myself; I need a partner." She looked right in Sam's eyes.

"You've found one!" Sam replied. "This will be like old times! Maybe we'll rescue a dog." The tone of Sam's voice and broad smile revealed his excitement.

"Sam, have you ever thought something or someone is somehow controlling our lives?"

"I don't think I ever thought of it that way, Fran. I have always explained what happened to me was a result of hard work and being prepared. I assumed strange or bad things were because of probability or coincidence. Those things are hard to predict."

"Oh, that's right! You're a mathematician," Fran ribbed.

Sam ignored her teasing primarily because he didn't have any jokes about artists.

He focused his attention on Fran and said, "If you want, we could take a short trip now. How long will we be gone? It's almost eleven o'clock. I was thinking of taking you to lunch, but I don't know of any places to eat near the river," he sighed.

Fran thought for a moment and said, "Oh! I know of a place. There's a bar and grill about a mile or so south of us on the old highway. It's called MaD's. We can paddle up there, have a bite, and let the river bring us back."

"Sounds like a plan, Fran." Sam grinned when he heard the rhyme. "That was purely accidental, I'm no poet."

"I believe it," Fran grinned. "I'll lock up and we can set off on our second canoeing expedition."

"Okay, I'll get the boat ready. Do you have life jackets?"

Fran took a defiant stance with her hands on her hips and said, "*Yes, I have life jackets!*" Then she relaxed and laughed. "They're orange though, not red."

"Jeez, Fran! You had me scared for a second. I thought you were going to slug me. I guess you remembered what I told you before our first canoeing adventure."

"So, you remember that too," she replied giving a satisfied smile. "Wait 'til you see what else I have for our trip."

Sam approached the canoe and looked closely at it. He again experienced a twinge of disappointment that the canoe wasn't made of wood. He had loved that canoe his family had owned. Nearly thirty years had passed since Sam had seen that marvelous old canoe that was stored in his parent's garage. Maybe the canoe had been sold with the house. Sam couldn't remember what happened to it.

Sam wrestled the canoe from its location behind the house to the riverbank. The little boat wasn't very heavy; it was just awkward for one person to manage. Fran would have a difficult time getting the canoe in the water by herself.

Fran returned from the house with her arms loaded. Sam rushed over to help her and grabbed the biggest item, a twenty-two caliber rifle. Fran also carried a big knife in a scabbard, a one-gallon thermos bottle and a fairly large, multi-colored blanket. Sam remembered Fran always came prepared.

"Did you know Daniel Boone?" quizzed Sam, sporting a big grin.

Fran answered immediately, "No, but I *was* a boy scout!"

They both laughed and placed the gear in the bottom of the canoe. Sam pushed the canoe about halfway into the water and Fran jumped in. He was pleased to see how agile Fran was and how quickly her mind worked. Fran was quite a lady! His fondness for her was rapidly being rekindled.

Sam gave a giant shove and launched himself into the canoe without stepping in the cold water. They were off on a new adventure. Fran was already rowing when Sam picked up his oar. The current was strong enough that it required both of them to propel the canoe upstream at a significant rate. The shallow draft of the boat allowed them to skim through the water with relative ease. He dismissed his initial thought of their arms tiring out.

As Sam watched Fran rowing, he realized her perky appearance was primarily due to her short hair. Years ago her hair was long and hung down over her shoulders. Fran made comments about the scenery as they worked their way upstream. She was watching for places as subjects for future artwork.

CHAPTER 6

Trouble

The couple rowed for about ten minutes through sunny and shadowy areas of the river. The bottom of the river looked to be only two feet below them, but Sam had been fooled before when looking into streams. The water could be twice as deep and contain erratic currents and slick rocks. Aside from an occasional submerged beer or soft drink can, the river bottom was very clean, the water clear, and cold, in spite of the summer heat.

"There it is!" shouted Fran as she pointed to her left at a large log building. It was two stories high in the back with a balcony projecting toward the river. The top story fronted the highway. There was a makeshift dock, which apparently had not seen much use. The handrail was falling apart with one end hanging into the water.

As the canoe approached the dock, Fran grabbed the sloping rail and pulled the canoe against the wooden platform. A short length of rope was coiled on the dock which she used to tie to the forward canoe seat. Fran stepped onto the dock, got to her knees and pulled the canoe parallel to the planks.

Sam smiled and said, "Thank you, Captain."

"Scrape the barnacles off your butt and follow me, sailor!"

They were both laughing as they climbed the large flagstone steps leading uphill to the front of the building. Reaching the top of the slope, Sam could see the sign advertising Mom and Dad's Bar and Grill. A car and two motorcycles were parked in front. Fran was slightly ahead of Sam, reaching the entrance first. Sam reached over her head and pushed on the red, barn-like door, which swung open. Simultaneously, the couple noticed a man on the floor with his head in a large pool of blood.

Sam grabbed Fran, pulled her back outside and said, "Run for the boat!" Fran didn't hesitate. She ducked under his outstretched arm and moved quickly to the flagstones and descended the steps at a full run. As Sam tried to catch up with Fran, he yelled at her, "Grab the blanket and get into the water—head for the other side."

Fran picked up the blanket, and Sam grabbed the rifle and knife. As they dropped into the water they heard a call from the balcony.

"Help me! They shot my husband!" she screamed.

Sam looked at the lady and yelled, "Get down on the deck, slide over the edge and drop to the ground."

Just as he said *ground*, the lower floor screen door opened and a man appeared holding a pistol. Sam dropped the knife, swung the gun barrel up, and shot from the hip. His bullet struck the man's right thigh. The gunman dropped to the floor behind the screen door. Sam reached into the water and retrieved the wet hunting knife.

Fran yelled, "Hurry lady, we have to get away from here!"

The canoeists watched the lady slide over the edge of the balcony and drop to the ground in a heap. She rolled over, scrambled to her feet, and almost tripping, ran to the dock, She started to get in the canoe, but Sam grabbed the woman's arm and pulled her into the thigh-deep water.

"We're walking." Sam guided her into the deeper water. Fran was already halfway across the river and stopped to look back. Another man was exiting the door onto the balcony and Fran yelled at Sam, "Behind you on the balcony! There's another one!"

Before Sam could turn around, he heard a gunshot and a splash in the water beside him. Sam swung the twenty-two around, aimed, and pulled the trigger. The man on the balcony yelled out and grabbed at his shoulder, dropping his gun. Fran turned away from the building and continued toward the opposite shore, almost disappearing in water up to her armpits. As she dropped down, she extended her arms above her head to hold the blanket above the water.

"You okay, Fran?" Sam asked.

Fran was spitting out some of the river and said, "I'm okay, but watch out. There's a hole over here. It's pretty deep."

Sam had latched onto the woman's arm as she fell to her knees in the cold water. He helped her up and steadied her as they crossed the river. The deepest water they encountered got them wet up to their waists. When Fran was about ten feet from the shore, she sloshed through the shallow water and dropped to her knees in a sandy spot. Just as Sam and his companion reached shore, another shot rang out, and a slug ricocheted off the rocks a few feet away.

"Quick! Get behind those trees! Go!" Sam pointed about ten yards farther on the shore to a clump of shrubs, a downed tree, and tall evergreens. All three stepped gingerly around rocks, dead tree limbs, and shrubs to get out of sight of the killers at MaD's. They heard another shot and a bullet struck the ground near Mom's feet.

Once out of sight of the men, Sam inquired, "What's your name?"

The scared, wet lady answered, "A—Ada Hermon."

Sam said, "Well, Ada, we're Fran and Sam. What happened?"

"I was in the kitchen and Dan was at the bar. Two young men came in. pulled out guns and said to give them our money. They told Dan to give them all the money we had and he refused. The taller one grabbed me and said he would shoot me if Dan didn't give them all our money, so Dan opened the cash register and gave them the cash. The shorter ugly one counted the money and was mad. He said it wasn't enough and Dan told him we took our weekend receipts to the bank. That was all we had. Last night was a slow night; we only had four customers.

The taller one said he knew we had a safe, and we had to open it. Dan said we didn't have a safe and the ugly one, with all the tattoos, got real mad and shot Dan in the throat. Dan fell down and reached for his neck and then went limp. I knew he was dead," she sobbed. "There was so much blood! I thought they would shoot me too. After I heard you come in the front entrance, I told the boys I knew where some more money was, but it was in the back. The tall one said he would come after you, and the ugly one pushed me into the back room. I pretended to fall down, and when he tried to get me up, I pushed him, ran out the door, and yelled to you from the balcony."

"We need to get help, Fran. Do you have a cell phone?" quizzed Sam.

"No, I dropped it when I was getting away," she answered with disgust.

Fran pulled a cell phone from her pocket and punched in 911. Nothing happened. "Mine doesn't work."

"Okay, we're on our own. Those guys will be after Ada. She can ID them." Sam raised his eyebrows, grinned, and commented, "Let's outsmart them."

CHAPTER 7

Attack

"What do we know about them?" Sam asked.

Ada answered first, "The ugly one is shot in the shoulder, and he's the meaner one. He killed my Dan." Her eyes watered and she looked at the ground. Fran put her arm around Ada and said, "We're going to get even, Ada. You'll see. The tall one with the shaved head is shot in the leg. I hope he gets gangrene!" Fran grinned. She didn't really think that would happen, she just wanted to get some pent-up feelings out.

"The motorcycles must be theirs," Sam contributed. "Is the car out in front yours, Ada?"

"Yes. I have the keys."

"Did Dan have a set of keys, too?" quizzed Sam.

"No. He doesn't drive any more. He has cataracts. We were saving money so he could have an operation next summer. We don't have any insurance. I guess that's not going to happen." Ada sniffed and wiped her eyes with her apron.

"So the low life can't take the car," Fran commented. "Their only transportation is their bikes. They won't leave the building for fear of being shot. They don't know where we are now."

Sam said, "That's right. They know we have a rifle, but they don't know our positions. They'll probably call someone for help. I don't think they'll try to ride their bikes, but to make sure they don't, I'm gonna slice their tires. We've got a good knife for that." Sam held up Fran's big knife, still in the scabbard.

Ada said, "You're going back over there?"

"Sure. We have to do something, and that means we have to take some chances. I just thought of a plan. Tell me what you think."

"First of all, Ada, is there a shallow river crossing near us?"

Ada thought for a moment and said, "Yes, there is. It's upstream a ways though."

"How far, Ada?" Fran asked.

"About a city block from here, the river widens, and it's only about a foot deep. A long time ago logging trucks crossed there."

"That's perfect, Ada!" Sam responded.

"Fran will cross the river and work her way over to the highway. She'll stop a motorist and call for help. While she is doing that, I'll go over and puncture their bike tires. Ada, can you shoot a gun?"

Ada replied, "I sure can. My dad and I used to shoot his shotgun; a 12 gauge. I was a pretty good at clay pigeons."

"Great! Ada, you'll watch the river and shoot at them if they try to use the canoe.

What do you think, ladies?"

"I think it should work, Sam, but we have to be careful," Fran cautioned.

"I can shoot those bastards, no problem," Ada stated.

Sam verified that the rifle still had ammunition and handed the gun to Ada.

"Okay. Ada, get behind one of those big rocks near where we crossed the river. Keep your head down, but I don't think they can shoot you with their pistols; handguns aren't accurate enough at that distance. They're probably lousy shots anyway but be careful. Sam grabbed the knife. Ready?" Sam looked at the women and they nodded. "Let's go!"

Fran and Sam started moving upstream behind dense cover of bushes and trees. When they had traveled about 400 feet, they could see the shallow area of the river Ada had mentioned. Before Fran and Sam parted, Fran grabbed the front of Sam's shirt, pulled him toward her, and kissed him.

Fran said, "You be careful or I'll kill you!" She laughed as she stepped into the water and began crossing the river.

Sam grinned and responded, "All right—dear."

Sam undid his belt, threaded it through the slots in the scabbard and refastened it even tighter. He didn't want his pants to drop at the wrong time, especially if he were running for his life. He waded into the river a little distance from the shallows and crossed, getting wet up to mid-thigh. Sam worked his way down the shore to a position twenty yards from the dock at MaD's, withdrew the knife from its sheath, crouched, and started climbing toward the front of the log building, slicing through long grass, weeds, and wild blackberry vines.

Fran found an easy route to the highway and began the climb up the slope. She could hear a car but it was going the wrong way and very fast. Just as she reached the road, she heard a loud, rumbling, muffler and saw a dirty black pickup approaching. Waving her arms above her head, she stepped from the shoulder onto the asphalt, and the truck slowed down. She looked at the cab of the truck and saw a heavyset bearded man giving her the once-over. He slowed to a stop.

The window descended and the man said, "What's your problem, little lady?"

Fran quickly told the man what had happened, and he said, "Jump in and we'll take care of things. I've got a phone, but it's broke."

The truck was high off the ground and Fran had to grab the door and pull to climb into the seat. She slammed the door shut, latched her seat belt, and said, "I'm Fran."

The big man answered, "I'm called Boxer." His grin revealed his lower two front teeth were missing. His forearms were heavily tattooed with weapons and skulls.

Boxer stepped on the gas, and the big truck surged forward.

Sam exited the protective vegetation and sneaked along the side of the building. He moved to the front corner, ducked below the window, crossed the sidewalk to the motorcycles, and dropped to his hands and knees behind the bikes. The black and red motorcycles were painted with swastikas and German writing, including Heil Hitler. The tip of the big knife punctured the tires with ease. Sam enjoyed the hissing sounds. As he was celebrating a job well done, he heard a truck coming toward MaD's. Sam dropped to the ground behind one of the bikes, glanced through the spokes of the rear wheel, and saw a big pickup pulling up to the building. He couldn't believe his eyes. Fran was in the truck with a big slob driving. *Fran shouldn't be coming back here!* Sam rolled away from the bikes and slid under Ada's car.

Fran could see MaD's from the highway as they approached and expected Boxer to drive past the building and down the road to the recreation area. Someone there would have a cell phone. But, to her surprise, Boxer turned into the parking lot and stopped beside the motorcycles. He shut off the engine and said, "Get out, you old broad!" Fran hesitated, looking at his scowling face. Boxer pulled a gun from under his seat and waved it at her. "You heard me! Get out, bitch!" Scared, Fran climbed down from the cab wondering what was going to happen.

Boxer opened his door, stepped to the ground, and hustled around to the passenger side. As he was moving around the front of the truck, Sam threw a couple of pebbles at Fran's feet causing her to glance at Ada's car. She saw Sam pretending to bite his wrist.

When Boxer grabbed Fran's left arm, she realized what Sam had meant. She was to bite the man's arm as soon as she had a chance. As Boxer and Fran were moving toward the entrance of the building, Sam came from behind the car, closing the gap. As Boxer reached for the door, Fran bent down and bit Boxer's arm as hard as she could. He yelled and flung Fran aside just as Sam plunged the big knife into the fat man's belly.

Boxer dropped his arms to the side, staring at the knife handle sticking out of his guts. His expression was astonishment. He raised his gun, pointing it at Sam. Sam closed his eyes, expecting to be shot and killed. He just wished he had a chance to tell Fran how much she meant to him. Sam heard a shot but felt nothing. There was silence. *Am I dead?* Sam couldn't move.

"Sam!"

Sam heard Fran's voice and opened his eyes. He was standing beside the fat man. Boxer was on the ground with the hunting knife protruding from his belly. Blood was spurting from the fat man's neck and dripping from his arm where Fran had sunk her teeth, his eyes looking up at the sky. Ada stepped out from the corner of the building pointing the rifle at Boxer.

"I shot that son-of-a-bitch, right in the neck, just as they did to my Dan! I hope he's dead and rots in hell! She walked over, kicked the body, and said, "You piece of crap!"

A police siren could be heard coming from the old highway. Sam suddenly recalled there were two criminals still in MaD's. He grabbed the arms of both women and ushered them behind Ada's car for protection. Sam took the rifle from Ada and aimed it at the entrance of the building. About ten seconds later, a police car pulled up and skidded to a stop in the parking lot. Two officers jumped from the car with guns drawn. The driver slowly approached the entrance to the building and stood against the wall. The other officer went over to Sam, Fran and Ada. He took the rifle from Sam, removed the ammunition, and handed the gun back to Sam.

"What just happened here?" the officer quizzed.

Fran said, "The fat guy on the ground came to help the killers inside. I bit him, Sam stabbed him, and Ada shot him. I think he's dead. There are two more guys inside. Sam shot them. Ada's husband is dead, those guys shot him."

The officer motioned to his partner that there were two more men inside and then checked Boxer's body for a pulse, smiled, and said, "Looks like you people did a thorough job. You've saved the courts and the state some time and money. Another bad guy's off the streets for good."

The officer talked into a microphone on his shoulder, and in a couple of minutes, two more cruisers appeared in the parking lot. The police yelled into the building, and a minute later, the two thugs appeared at the door with their hands raised. They were handcuffed, placed in the cruisers, and taken to the hospital. The coroner's truck arrived and Boxer was pronounced dead. Ada's bullet had severed a carotid artery and scrambled his brain. Boxer's body was placed in the coroner's truck and Dan's body was taken to a mortuary in an ambulance

Sam asked one of the officers, "How did you know we needed help?"

"The canoe told us," he smiled. "Someone sent us a message that there had been a murder at MaD's Bar and Grill. We should rescue Fran, Sam and Ada."

Sam looked at Ada. "You wrote the note, put it in the canoe and let the canoe drift down the river. That was a very smart thing to do, Ada, *and* you saved my life!"

Sam and Fran gave Ada a big hug.

Ada spoke to Sam, "I had to do something—, like you said, take a chance. You were so good to help me, I couldn't let you and Fran do everything."

CHAPTER 8

Aftermath

The police taped off the restaurant so they could complete their investigation without intervention. A crew from the coroner's office cleaned up the bloodstains, and MaD's was restored to its original condition, except for a few bullet holes. Ada didn't want to be alone until the reality of Dan being gone had sunk in, so Fran invited Ada to stay with her for a few days. Dan's funeral was held on the next Saturday. More than a hundred people from the area were in attendance. Dan and Ada had made many friends.

The canoe and knife were returned to Fran. The officer and his partner drove by to see if the ladies were all right and returned the ammunition. Sam visited the women regularly. They discussed their adventure and the future of the bar and grill. Ada posed for a photographer as she worked in the kitchen at MaD's. She had decided to continue with MaD's and was going to use copies of the picture for advertising. Ada spent two weeks at Fran's before resuming her duties as the proprietor of the bar and grill. She hired a woman, Jamie Duncan, about twenty years younger than herself, to be the bartender.

After Ada had returned to her own home, Fran called Sam one evening. After a few minutes of conversation Sam said, "I have a little confession to make."

"Confession?" Fran responded.

"Well, not really a confession, but it was something I was thinking when all those policemen showed up at MaD's." Sam paused for a moment.

"Sam, are you going to tell me?"

"Well, I was going to ask the officers if they all came because they thought they were getting free coffee and doughnuts."

"Sam! Boy, you are so lucky!"

"What do you mean lucky?"

"If that officer hadn't taken the bullets, *I* would have shot you if you had said that!"

"I just thought about it, I didn't say it! I wouldn't do that. When I'm in a tense situation, I think of crazy things. Humor saves me from getting too shook up."

Fran said, "I can understand that. When you were almost shot, I nearly wet my pants."

"*That* would have been embarrassing."

"Well, if I had, I wouldn't have been embarrassed. It just would have happened."

"No, Fran. *I* would have been embarrassed."

"Sam!"

"Now you see, that was just a joke!"

"The main thing I called about was to ask you to come over for dinner tomorrow night."

"That sounds great. Thank you for the invitation. When should I be there?"

"You can come over whenever you like. I've got some things you can help me with. We'll eat at 6:00 p.m. And Sam—bring your toothbrush, some pajamas, and a big smile."

"I can do that."

Hidden Talents

The Coleman Family

Dr. Clay Coleman had just completed his internship at Harvard where he had been able to begin applying sports medicine in a university setting. Without a stethoscope, he looked like one of the athletes on the football team. He had plenty of opportunities to do some lifting in the weight room, but couldn't compete with the younger, more heavily muscled athletes. When no one else was around, Clay would sneak into the weight room and spend about thirty minutes exercising. He was slightly over six feet, weighed about one eighty soaking wet, and had a small scar, from his high school baseball days, over his right eyebrow. During the years in medical school, his tan had faded, and his brown hair appeared darker than it did when he lived in the small community of Melrose, New Mexico.

Clay had been hired by the Cornhuskers following their New Year's bowl game.

The athletic department at the University of Nebraska and the Big Red football team provided a great environment to develop his background in sports medicine. His contract was with the student medical center, but during football season and spring practice, he would be on the sidelines. For the away games, Clay would be flying around the country with a hundred topnotch athletes and a dozen coaches.

As he was growing up, Clay had few opportunities to travel, spending most of his time studying. His parents had sold him on the idea of getting ahead by being educated. They had never attended college, but Clay had made it to Harvard. His hard work was paying off.

The first five months in Lincoln passed quickly. Clay was immersed in the treatment of injured arms, legs, occasional concussions, and working with physical therapists to assist players during recovery. After Clay met Misty Ridgeway, a cute nurse at the medical center, devotion to his job began to decrease a little.

Misty hailed from Vermont, was five feet six inches tall, and wore her auburn hair in a ponytail. She carried herself with an air of confidence, and was quick to smile, her slight dimples not quite symmetrical. Misty's eyes danced, especially when she laughed or glanced at Clay. Her parents had been students at UNL in the early 1980s and loved the school. She was a year younger than Clay.

During spring practice that first year, Clay had accompanied an injured lineman to the hospital. Misty watched as the giant athlete limped into the examination room with two smaller men supporting him. She knew the orderly on the left but she had never met the other man. Then she saw the tag on his shirt. He was Dr. Coleman, the new doctor several of the nurses had talked about. They were right; he was good looking and apparently single. He didn't wear a wedding ring.

After the athlete was seated on the examination table, the orderly left and Dr. Coleman began examining the player's right knee. Misty watched as the doctor carefully applied pressure to the young man's knee and observed the athlete's expressions.

"I think I know what the problem is Chello, but we'll get some X-rays to check it out. We need to make sure nothing is broken."

Misty approached Chello carrying a pair of surgical scissors. He was the biggest man she had ever been this close to and his Afro hair style made his head appear enormous. He seemed to be nearly seven-feet tall and was nice looking, but not handsome. His grimacing indicated he was in pain, and she was unsure of how this man would react if she caused him some discomfort. His biceps were as big as her thighs. Misty had never met a black man and she was intimidated. She didn't know if Dr. Coleman could protect her from this giant.

The young man said, "Get away from me with those." He held up his massive hands to ward off any attempts Misty had to approach him with the gleaming, stainless-steel scissors.

Misty stepped back from Chello and said, "Take it easy seventy-three. I just want to remove part of your pants so we can get an X-ray. Your pads are in the way. If we pull your pants off, we'll hurt your knee. I won't remove any body parts," she grinned.

"Oh. I didn't know what you was going to do with those scissors. I don't like hospitals; they make me nervous." The lineman, a little embarrassed, looked sheepishly at the doctor and nurse. "Be careful where you cut."

Clay smiled, first at Chello and then slowly directed his smile to Misty.

She smiled back at the young doctor, and as she began cutting, she looked at the athlete and inquired, "So, seventy-three, what's your name?"

"Chello Fredericks, ma'am," he replied, wincing before Misty had even touched him.

"Well, Chello, my name is Misty. I'm going to be very careful with these scissors, so I don't cut off anything essential," she smiled. "Try to relax. Do you have any brothers or sisters?"

Clay placed his hand on the athlete's shoulder and explained what they had to do.

"I'll give you a shot to relieve the pain."

"No needles, Doc. I can take it," Chello grimaced. "What about aspirin? I have a sister. Name's Viola. She's twelve."

Clay replied, "I'll give you something better than aspirin after the X-rays."

Both men watched Misty remove the right leg of Chello's practice pants.

"Ah—nurse, you cut off the wrong pant leg," Clay commented with an irritated voice that was immediately followed with a smile.

"Oh! I'm so sorry!" Misty stepped back and looked in dismay at Clay.

"I'm just joking! You removed the correct one," Clay chuckled.

"So, you're a prankster!" She shook the scissors at Clay. "I'll have to be on my guard when you're around," she replied.

Chello said, "Hey, Doc, no joking around! My leg really hurts!"

"I think I know what happened. I believe you have some torn ligaments but no broken bones. The X-ray will tell us. If it's what I think, we'll give you some pain pills, a knee brace and some crutches. I'll give you some info about using ice, too."

The X-ray showed no broken bones so Clay gave Chello a page of instructions so the athlete could start the rehabilitation immediately. In a few days, Chello could begin no-load workouts in the swimming pool. A month later, the three hundred twenty pound lineman was back on the field but skipping contact drills until fall practices began.

During that month, Clay had the opportunity to see Misty again at the medical center and they began dating. Two years later, Misty and Clay were married, and a year after that, a daughter, Emma Jean Coleman, was born. Two years later, Eric John Coleman made his first appearance on the Lincoln campus. After Eric arrived, Colemans bought a little white cottage on 34th and M street, added a second bathroom, and a covered back porch. The house had been built in 1928. Shade in both front and back yards was provided by mature maple trees. The large back yard was surrounded by flower beds and a garden. Coleman's SUV was too big for their single car garage so the small building was used for storage and they parked the car in the driveway.

A decade zoomed by with both doctor and nurse immersed in work at the university medical center, attending conferences and caring for student athletes. The only other addition to the family was Warren. The Coleman family visited the animal shelter and fell in love with a male, Rough collie puppy. The puppy had been mistreated and was adopted when Emma was four. For all practical purposes, Warren was Emma's best buddy. Warren accompanied Emma everywhere. The friendly canine was Emma's watchdog. That was Warren's purpose in life.

The family dog grew quickly and loved to play with the children. One Saturday when Emma was about six, Warren came to the front door and began to bark. The door was open but the screen door was shut. Misty was doing some housework and the kids and a neighborhood playmate were in the back yard. Misty went to the door and opened the screen, but Warren wouldn't come in. He barked again.

Misty put down the dust mop and went outside with the dog and looked round. Seeing nothing out of the ordinary, Misty started back inside, but Warren blocked her path to the door.

"Warren, what are you doing?"

The dog nipped at Misty's jeans and began to pull her toward the side of the house. They moved around the corner and started down the driveway toward the back yard. Warren looked back to make sure Misty was following.

"Okay Warren, I'm coming with you."

Misty watched as Warren went into the backyard and started moving toward the children. When the dog was about ten feet from the children, he barked again.

"Be quiet, Warren!" Emma attempted to hush the dog.

"Emma, what are you kids doing?" Misty quizzed.

The three children stood up and faced Misty, holding their hands behind their backs. "Nothing Mama," Emma answered sheepishly.

"Eric, show me your hands please,"

Eric slowly brought his hands from behind his back with his fists closed. Misty walked over to Eric and said, "Please show me what you have."

Eric unclenched his little fists and looked at his hands. Both hands contained stick matches.

"Okay. Please give me all the matches." Misty held out her right hand, palm up and the children put their matches in her hand. "Thank you," Misty replied to their actions. Misty looked at the three kids and said, "Where did you get the matches?"

Eric raised his hand and pointed at Jason, their friend from across the street.

"Well, Jason, where did you get the matches?"

"A little box by the fireplace," Jason replied.

"You know, Jason, matches can start big fires, big enough to burn down a house.

You wouldn't want that to happen, would you?"

"N—No," the little boy answered quietly.

"Okay then. I don't want any of you to play with matches. If you find some matches, please give them to an adult, but don't play with them. Why don't you guys come in the house and I'll give you a cookie and some juice?"

Emma asked, "What about Warren, Mom?"

"Warren gets some fresh water to drink," Misty grinned. "And I think I can find him a dog biscuit."

A few years later, Clay came home from his office late. It wasn't really late, just an hour later than normal. The family had a pizza dinner. While Misty began cleaning up, Clay, the kids, and Warren went out to play in the back yard. The kids played badminton, and Warren ran around barking, chasing the kids.

After badminton, the family began watching a movie. Clay and Emma made popcorn that could be smelled throughout their little house. Clay had seen the movie so he picked up a map of Oregon, found Eugene, Interstate 5, the Portland area, and began to study it.

CHAPTER 2

Conference

With over twelve years' experience treating leg injuries, Clay had become a recognized expert in the field. He had been invited to the University of Oregon for a conference following bowl games during the holidays. After the conference, Clay was provided with a rental car to drive from Eugene to Portland to catch a flight home to Lincoln. His trip was supposed to have taken only a week, however, the travel gods had something else planned for Dr. Coleman.

"There's a credit card in the glove compartment to be used for gas, Clay," informed Dr. Markus, Clay's contact at the University of Oregon. "You'll need to get gas before you get on the freeway."

"Thanks Steve. I'll send you a copy of that paper you want."

"Okay. Have a good trip. Bye."

Clay said "Bye," closed the car window, and made a quick call to Misty at five forty-five. Unfamiliar with the roads, Clay got in the wrong lane and drove past a gas station but didn't want to turn around. Clay could see the freeway ramp so he turned to avoid the ramp in order to find another gas station. The fuel gauge was on empty, but he thought the reserve in the tank, probably about two gallons, should get him thirty to forty miles on Interstate 5 where he could find an easy-off easy-on place to get gas.

It was six o'clock and nearly dark. Clay had to be at the airport in Portland by 4:30 the next morning, so he decided to skip dinner, stop along the way for a burger, and perhaps some ice cream. He would also get gas. He turned the car around and tried to get on the freeway but missed the right turn to the access ramp and ended up on a maintenance road that paralleled Interstate 5. There were few markings on the two lane road, but occasionally he could see vehicle lights and hear the sounds of freeway traffic, no more than a few hundred yards away on the other side of a dense stand of fir. He reasoned that if he continued on, he should find another turnoff enabling a return to the freeway.

Clay passed a weathered, old wooden sign that indicated gas and lodging were available three miles to the right, so Clay turned down the road perpendicular to the maintenance path and drove for about ten minutes on the oiled gravel road. Nothing even resembling a gas station or a motel could be seen. He noticed there were weeds growing up through cracks in the compacted dirt and gravel. Clay had wasted time and gas. When he first missed the ramp, he should have retraced his path and returned to Eugene. There were no additional road signs so Clay turned around. He thought he had taken the wrong right. Maybe there was another path that led to the right farther down the road from where he had originally deviated.

Clay reached the T in the road and turned right. In a few minutes he saw some lights near the road and turned onto an oiled dirt road. If this wasn't the place, maybe he could at least obtain directions. He would need some gas before long. Fumes wouldn't take him very far. He had been advised there were several gas stations along the way, the easy access type. Clay had driven for nearly half an hour already, starting and stopping and retracing his routes. He certainly didn't want to run out of gas. Clay's friends in Lincoln would find out about it and razz him forever, plus, it was getting cold and dark.

As he neared the lights, he recognized that it was a farm, not a motel or a gas station. Clay saw a John Deere tractor under a carport attached to large white barn and a red pickup parked next to a two-story, light-yellow house. The interior lights were on so someone should be home. Clay stopped the car, went to the front door, didn't see a doorbell, so he knocked twice.

Clay could hear someone coming so he stepped back from the screen door but remained illuminated by the porch light. Someone parted the curtains and peeked out. Clay heard a woman's voice. "Hank, it's some feller."

The door opened and an obese woman of about fifty said abruptly, "What do you want?"

"Sorry to disturb you, but I wondered if I could buy some gas and get some directions. I'd like to get back on the freeway. I'm on my way to Portland."

A big man appeared behind the woman and said, "You can't get on the freeway near here. You'll have to drive back south about twenty-five miles along that there service road." He pointed behind Clay and waved his hand. "It's almost to Eugene. Come on in and take a load off. I'll sell you some gas. Three gallons for twenty bucks! It's out in the barn over yonder." He waved his other arm toward the barn. "Gotta git my shoes."

"Thank you. I don't want to bother you," Clay replied.

"No bother, just a minute."

"Where you been?" asked the woman as she wiped crumbs from her mouth with her wrist.

"I was in Eugene at a conference about leg injuries of athletes. I need to get to the Portland airport to fly back to Nebraska. My plane leaves in the morning."

"You a doctor or somethin'?"

"Yes. I'm a doctor," Clay replied and smiled.

"Okay! Let's get that gas for yah."

"Hank, he's a doctor!"

The big man looked at the woman, winked, opened the door, and went outside. It was getting chilly and Clay thought about getting his jacket from the car, but instead he followed Hank to the barn.

Clay felt small when standing beside the farmer. Hank looked to be six-six and weighed considerably more than three hundred pounds, bigger than most football players. The giant man slid back the barn door and turned on a light by pulling on a noose of twine hanging in midair. The light illuminated a fifty gallon drum of gasoline sitting on the floor against the wall just inside the door. The enormous cold barn reeked of gasoline and garbage. It felt colder in the barn than outside.

"Let's see yer money, if yah don't mind," Hank snickered.

Clay reached into his back left pocket and pulled out his wallet. Before he had a chance to open his wallet, the farmer grabbed it out of his hands.

"Hey!" Clay exclaimed as he reached for his billfold.

"Hold yer britches; jest checkin' yer money. Hell, you only got sixty bucks!

Where's the rest?"

"That's all I have. I don't need any money now. I'm on my way home."

"Yah sure got that right. Yah don't need no money!" the big man laughed as he folded Clay's sixty dollars and stuck it in the pocket of his overalls.

He held Clay's wallet out as if to return it, but when Clay reached for it, the farmer grabbed Clay's wrist and gave a jerk. Clay stumbled forward and the big man grabbed Clay in a bear hug. Clay tried to escape but Hank had overpowered the doctor. Clay looked for a weapon, but if he had located one, he probably wouldn't have been able to pick it up. Hank was squeezing life from him. Clay continued to struggle, trying to breathe.

"Stick him, Clara!"

Clay turned his head to see the fat lady lunge toward him with a big kitchen knife. Clay couldn't get out of the way but he twisted as violently as he could. Clay's cell phone fell from his shirt pocket. A crunch could be heard during the struggle. Hank had Clay firmly in his grasp, but Clay continued to squirm. He didn't want to die in this stinky old barn.

Clay felt pain as the knife cut through his shirt and entered between his ribs. At the same time, Hank yelled, "Son of a bitch, woman, you cut me!"

Clara let go of the knife and stepped back from the two men. "Sorry, Hank!"

Hank suddenly released Clay and grabbed at his arm. Clara was bending down to retrieve the knife for a second plunge when Clay took advantage of the only chance he might have. Clay stepped to the side, pushed Clara to the ground in front of Hank, and scrambled from the barn to his car.

He jumped in, started the car and spun the tires as he started back on the road that had led to the farm. Clay remembered what the man had said, so he drove back along the route he originally had taken. In about ten minutes, Clay stopped to assess the damage to his side. He didn't want to take too long; Hank and Clara might be following him. He didn't bother to pull over.

Clay turned on the dome light and pulled his shirt up so he could see the wound. He had to twist his body and look at his back but he felt no more pain. There was a one inch wide cut in his side but the knife blade probably hadn't penetrated through his rib cage. Clara was so fat she hadn't been able to swing the knife hard and had not completely punctured Clay's ribs. She had probably done more damage to Hank's arm than Clay's ribs. Clay theorized that most of the blood on his shirt had come from Hank. The big man's arm might have saved Clay from a much deeper, more severe wound. Clay stripped off his shirt and T-shirt, tore the T-shirt into several strips and tied it around his chest to keep pressure on the wound. He was surprised at the lack of blood on his T-shirt.

Clay put his shirt back on and donned his thin gray jacket. He was getting cold. The temperature was about forty degrees. The gas gauge was pointing below empty. Clay would drive until he ran out of gas, then walk to get some help. He drove for another ten minutes and decided to stop to rest a little. Clay looked back down the road, but no one seemed to be following him. He wondered why he had stopped at that farm. Had he gone there on a house call? There weren't any sick children and the adults were eating dinner. Why had he wrestled with that farmer?

Clay sat in the driver's seat for about ten minutes trying to make sense out of what he was doing. His mind was stuck on two thoughts. Find the airport and a gas station, but what should he do first? Clay climbed from the car for a minute to clear his head. The temperature had dropped several more degrees and a southwest wind was blowing. The wind chill made the effective temperature below freezing. He looked around trying to figure out what road he was on. His mind seemed to clear for a second and he calculated it was another ten to fifteen minutes to the Interstate. Clay looked at the dash and saw that he was almost out of gas. He resumed driving at a slow speed trying to get every mile from the remaining fuel. Clay kept watching for a gas station. As he passed the ten-minute mark, he felt the car beginning to vibrate.

"Damn it! A flat tire!" he yelled angrily. He stopped and circled the car looking at the tires. The passenger side back tire was going flat. Clay popped open the trunk and looked for the spare. There wasn't one! He rarely got mad but this finally set him off. He slammed the trunk, kicked the fender, denting it, stuffed his fists into his jacket pockets and began to walk. In his anger, he had forgotten about his suitcase in the back seat.

As Clay walked, he began to hear vehicle noises coming from beyond the trees. The sounds of traffic were not all suppressed by the vegetation, especially the noises from big trucks. Lights began to appear, seeming to dance between the trees, first moving to the right and then the left. He continued to walk but couldn't remember where he was going. Walking was requiring more and more effort. Lifting his legs was becoming very difficult and he was getting colder by the minute. He began to lurch, nearly tripping over his own feet. The swoosh from passing vehicles was the last thing he heard before collapsing in a silent still mass.

Clay felt a hand on his shoulder shaking him and a male voice saying, "Looks like you need some help. Can I give you a ride?"

"I—I guess so. Wh—Where am I?" inquired Clay.

"You're right outside of Eugene. Are you all right?"

"I—I think so. My side hurts."

Clay twisted to look at his side. He lifted his jacket and shirt and pulled the strips of cloth away from his side and saw a cut. "Seems like I got cut somehow. Maybe I was in an accident." He looked up at the elderly man and quizzed, "Eugene?"

"Yes. Eugene, Oregon. Where would you like me to take you?"

"I don't know, mister. Where are you going?" Clay asked.

"I'm on my way to Portland. You want to go there?" the man asked.

"I guess so," Clay replied as he stood with the man's assistance.

"I'm Orin Wright. What's your name?" he asked Clay and stuck out his hand.

Clay reached out and shook hands with Orin.

Clay thought for a few seconds. "I—I don't know," Clay replied.

"Well, check your wallet. Your license will tell us who you are."

Clay reached back to his left-hand trouser pocket but didn't find a wallet. He checked his other pockets but found nothing.

"I guess I don't have a wallet, Mr. Wright. Maybe I wasn't driving."

"Son, you can call me Bud or Orin. Looks like you're married."

Clay looked at his left ring finger and saw a gold wedding band.

"Remember your wife's name?"

Clay thought a minute and said, "No, I can't remember. I bet she won't like that!" He gave Bud a tired smile.

Bud responded, "You've got a good sense of humor. I guess you haven't lost that."

"I wouldn't bet on it. I might not have had a good sense of humor," Clay stated, "maybe that's something new."

"I'm going to take you to a hospital in Portland and they'll check you out. Okay?"

"Okay, Bud. Thank you. I guess I need some help. I don't remember much of anything. I must have amnesia from bumping my head. I don't remember how I got cut."

The doctor at the emergency room recognized Clay's wound immediately and reported it to the authorities. Clay had been stabbed. As a dressing was being applied to the wound, the police arrived and began to question Clay.

"What's your name, sir?" the officer asked.

Clay thought a moment and said, "I don't know, officer."

"You don't look like you're homeless. Where do you live?"

Again, Clay thought and said, "I don't know, officer."

"Have any ID?"

"No. I've checked every pocket. I don't have a wallet. Sorry."

"Why are you in Portland?"

"Bud brought me here," Clay replied.

"Bud?"

"Yeah, the man that drove me here from Eugene, Bud Wright. He found me beside the interstate near Eugene. He's out at the nurse's station waiting for me. Can we finish this? I think he has places to go."

The officer grinned and said, "You mean Bud Lite? You were drinking?"

"No. I'm not kidding, his name is Bud Wright." Clay spelled out Bud's name.

"Okay. So you were in Eugene? Where were you before that?"

Clay was getting frustrated with the questions, but remained patient with the officer. "I don't remember being anywhere. My memory starts when Bud gave me a ride."

The officer commented, "There was a stabbing in Corvallis and the suspect escaped on I-5 heading north. Maybe you're that man. Let me see where you were stabbed, please," the officer asked but it was more of an order. Clay raised his shirt but the policeman could only see the bandage. The doctor talked with the officer and sketched the cut on the officers report pad indicating the dimensions and shape of the wound.

"I need to get an address for you, sir."

"I don't have an address. I guess you'd better put down the hospital address."

"I need a name, too. What should we call you?"

"What's your name, officer?"

"Dave," the officer replied.

"Okay. My name is Dave," Clay smiled. "You're Dave and I'm Dave, too." Clay held up two fingers.

The officer and the doctor both laughed at the double meaning of the sound of too. The officer suddenly got serious and said, "Well, Dave, I suggest you keep in touch with the police, about once a week. Make sure you check in with us. You are a suspect in the Corvallis knifing. Another man ended up in the hospital with severe injuries."

Search for Clay

Over a week had passed since Clay went to the west coast. Misty received a call from her husband just after the conference ended in Eugene. Clay was going to drive to the Portland airport, PDX, and fly back home. He would arrive in Lincoln about noon the following day, but Clay didn't return as planned. The next day the university hospital called to see if Clay was sick and couldn't come to work. Misty informed the hospital that Clay had not returned from Oregon and she didn't know where he was.

Misty called the airline and asked if Clay Coleman had been on the flight to Lincoln from PDX. Clay's plane ticket hadn't been used. No record of Clay boarding the plane existed. Now she began to worry. *What if he was in a traffic accident between Eugene and Portland?* Misty called the Oregon State Patrol.

"Can you tell me if there were any accidents between Eugene and Portland in the last week?"

"Let me check. One moment please." About fifteen seconds elapsed and the male voice returned. "No ma'am. No accidents have been reported."

"Thank you, officer. Bye."

"Goodbye."

Within a few minutes of making the call to the State Patrol, Misty's phone rang. She thought the police were calling back.

"Hello?"

"This is Doctor Steve Markus from the University of Oregon. Is Clay there?"

"No, Doctor. I'm his wife, Misty. We haven't seen Clay since he left for Eugene more than a week ago. I had one call from him right after the conference. He said he was on his way to Portland. I was going to call you and ask if you had seen him recently."

"No. The last time I saw Clay, he was getting into a rental car. He must have called you about then. I just got a call from the rental company and they want their vehicle back. I was calling to find out what Clay did with the car. He should have left it in one of the airport parking areas, but no one has seen it. One moment, please—"

The phone went silent for ten to fifteen seconds and Dr. Markus said, "Mrs. Coleman?"

Misty answered, "Yes?"

"I just received a call from the rental company. The car Clay was driving was found on a Department of Transportation access and rural road just off Interstate 5 near Eugene. There was no sign of Clay, but his suitcase was in the back seat. The car was nearly out of gas and had a flat tire. I remember the gas tank was almost empty when he left the campus. He was going to get gas before getting on the freeway. This is very strange. I'll file a missing person report and the police will contact you for more information about Clay. They'll need a complete description. Maybe you can fax them a picture."

"All right, Doctor. Please call if you hear anything. Thank you very much. Goodbye."

"I'm sure Clay is all right. The police will find him. Bye Misty."

The silence of the phone left Misty with an empty feeling. The sounds of placing her phone back on the charger seemed louder than normal. She sat by the phone for a few minutes staring at the wall. She refused to consider that Clay would not come home. Misty had to set emotion aside. She had to take care of the kids and the house.

Logical thinking returned. *I'd better keep some notes. I'll use that spiral notebook I take to the medical seminars.*

She went to the desk looking for the blue notebook and opened the top right drawer. Misty found her notebook under some envelopes and Clay's Day Minder book in which he kept his off campus appointments. *Hmm, maybe there's a clue in here.* Misty opened the little book and looked at Clay's scheduled meetings. She saw the note for the Eugene conference and turned the page. Two days after he would have returned from Oregon, there was to be an appointment with Sheila at 1:00 p.m. *Who is Sheila? Clay has never mentioned that name.*

Misty found her blue notebook and dropped Clay's little appointment book back in the drawer. She grabbed a pencil from the Nebraska mug on the desk and returned to the dining room table. *Could that be the reason Clay hasn't come back? Is he leaving me for Sheila? I don't believe it! I'm sure he loves me and the kids. Besides, the notebook wasn't hidden, so the entry wasn't a secret.*

She grabbed the phone book and called the police. Misty asked for missing persons and was transferred to a secretary. After answering a seemingly endless number of questions, she hung up the phone and sighed. *Now what?*

A loud knock on the front door brought her attention back to her everyday reality.

She looked at the clock. *Oh! The kids are home from school. I didn't think it was so late in the afternoon.* She hurried to the door, almost tripped over Warren, and let Emma and Eric in the house.

Emma asked, "Hi Mom! Have you heard from Dad?"

Eric added, "Yeah, Mom. When is he coming home?"

"Let me tell you what I did today."

Misty told the kids about the various phone calls and the missing person reports she submitted to the police in Lincoln and Eugene. Emma and Eric both hugged their mom. Emma, almost crying, said, "What are we going to do to find Dad?"

Misty had to be strong for the kids and said, "Don't worry, the police will find him for us. I'm sure he's just fine. If he's in the mountains somewhere, he probably just can't get to a phone." However,

Misty was getting very worried. The rental car had been found, but there was no sign of Clay, just his suitcase. She kept that to herself.

A week went by, then two. Misty and the kids were getting more concerned. Emma suggested they go to church and pray, which they did. Misty had never been a church goer, but Emma and Eric seemed to benefit. Even Misty felt more at peace after the experience. She wasn't worried or afraid anymore, just concerned. Misty had called the police after the first week. They had no new information, but investigators were working on the case.

In the middle of the third week, there was still no word about Clay. Misty was tired of waiting. She decided to hire a private detective in Portland to carry out an investigation. Misty thought someone closer to where Clay had last been seen would be more successful. Besides, the police had many other activities to tend to and probably wouldn't attach much importance to finding a highly educated doctor.

Misty logged on the computer, with the kids watching, and did a search for detective agencies in Portland. Fredericks-Alexander Investigations was the second name on the printout. Misty thought Fredericks sounded familiar so she put in a call to them.

"Fredericks and Alexander Investigations. How may I help you?" a baritone male voice inquired.

Misty began explaining her problem and suddenly the voice said, "Are you a nurse from UNL? I'm Chello! Remember me, number seventy-three? You cut off my pants."

"Oh, my gosh! I remember you Chello. You were so big, I was afraid of you. Oh, I hope you can help me find my husband. You remember Dr. Coleman, don't you?"

"Sure do. So you two got married. Any children?"

"Yes. We have two kids, Emma, thirteen, and Eric, eleven. I need to find their dad. I'll send you all the information that I sent the police and maybe you can track him down. I think he must have been hurt. Please call me as soon as you have any information."

"Will do, Mrs. Coleman. We've solved all our cases so far. We don't want to ruin our record. We'll get right on it. We'll go to

Eugene and work forward and backward. We'll find your husband. Keep your chin up! I'll call you tomorrow evening. It was nice talking to you. Bye now and don't you worry."

"Thank you Chello. Please find Clay for us. Bye."

Misty hung up with hope for a change. Now she should get some results! *Chello sounded like he has a way of finding out things from gentle persuasion to downright intimidation. I'll bet his associate is as big as he is.* Misty smiled as she looked at the phone. *What a fortunate thing to have happened. Maybe going to church helped more than I thought.*

CHAPTER 4

Chello Investigates

Chello hung up the phone and went to Rod's office. Sandy-haired Rod Alexander was an inch shorter than Chello and had always had a crew cut. Rod had played football for the Oregon Ducks. They became good friends when they were studying to be investigators. After receiving their investigator's licenses, they decided to team up. F and A Investigations, Inc. was born.

Much of the work Fredericks and Alexander accepted was locating missing persons, although they did deliver summons and subpoenas. Covert surveillance work was difficult; both men weighed three hundred pounds and were six and a half feet tall. It was hard for them to sneak up on anyone without being noticed, but they had some success using cameras.

"Rod, we have a new client. We need to find Dr. Clay Coleman. He has been missing about ten days. I know Clay and his wife. Let's drive to Eugene and see what we can dig up. As soon as the faxed material arrives, we'll hit the road."

The company car was a large, silver-gray, gas-hog Hummer. Both men felt comfortable in the spacious vehicle, plus they had room for any equipment they might need. Rod preferred driving and

Chello worked on notes, planning the strategy for the investigation, as they drove south on Interstate 5.

The Hummer moved to the right lane and slowed to thirty-five mph as they approached Eugene. Chello had thought of several things to check, but first, they needed to see the police report about the rental car. Cops would have checked it out when the Department of Transportation crew found the vehicle.

"Where to, Bro?" asked Rod.

"The police station."

It took about ten minutes to find the station. The two giant men walked into the lobby and approached a balding, overweight sergeant shuffling papers at a large, metal desk.

"May I help you gentlemen?" the seated sergeant asked as he looked up over his glasses.

"We're PIs from Portland. We'd like to see a report about a car found by the Oregon Department of Transportation on the freeway access road about a week to ten days ago."

"I need some ID, please, both of you."

The PIs flipped open their wallets exposing their picture ID cards. The officer looked at the photos and looked back at Chello and Rod.

"Okay. One moment."

Sergeant Kopf took a couple of steps to a cabinet, pulled out the top drawer and grabbed a manila file. As he stepped back to his desk, he opened the file.

"That's a rural road as well as an access route for road crews. Not much here, actually," he commented.

Chello scanned the report and handed it back to the officer. Chello grinned. "Thanks Sarge."

Chello turned and headed for the exit. Rod followed him to the car. They mounted their seats and Chello pulled a map of Eugene from the glove compartment. He unfolded the multicolored paper on his lap and traced the freeway with his finger.

"What are you thinking, Chel?"

"How'd the car get on that rural road, and why was it pointing south?"

Rod thought a moment and said, "What time of day did Dr. Coleman leave Eugene?"

"He called his wife about the time it was getting dark, or at least the sun would have been going down," Chello replied.

"The doc doesn't know the area. Right?" quizzed Rod.

"Ah—I got it! He missed the turn to the freeway and got on the access road!"

"That's what I was thinking, dude," Rod smiled.

He rarely got ahead of his pal when deep thinking was involved, but Rod wasn't driving, he was just standing looking at a map. Rod admitted not being very good at multitasking.

"So, let's take the access road," Chello stated.

Just as Rod turned the key, Chello's cell rang.

"Hello. Chello speaking." A few seconds later, "Hi Mrs. Coleman."

Chello listened for nearly a minute, taking notes on a clipboard. Rod watched as his buddy printed the letters CLMM across the paper, followed by a question mark.

"All right, Mrs. C. We'll check it out. We're in Eugene now, so it won't take us more than three hours to get to Crater Lake. I'll call you with the results in the morning.

You're two hours ahead of us so it will be too late to call you tonight. Bye."

Rod looked at Chello and said, "We're going to Crater Lake?"

"You got it. Someone used Coleman's credit card three days ago for gas at CLMM."

"What the hell is CLMM?" quizzed Rod.

"How about Crater Lake Minimart?" Chello smiled. He looked at the map and said, "We take Route 58 to Route 97, south to 138 and follow the signs. Should take about three hours with you driving all the way, longer if I drive," Chello grinned.

"What if we stop for a burger? I'm gunna be very hungry in three hours."

"Yeah—me too. We'll stop for something at Oakridge. It's less than an hour from here."

At Oakridge, they inhaled some burgers, fries, and milkshakes and hit the road. Two hours later they were on the outskirts of Crater Lake. As they approached the town, the PIs could see about a dozen bright lights in a cluster, so they headed for that area. There were big signs advertising the multi-services available at Crater Lake Minimart. Smaller signs used only the letters CLMM.

"We found what we were looking for, dude," Rod announced.

Chello was snoozing and quickly sat up, rubbed his eyes, and looked around.

"Great! Find the office and see if we can discover who used Doc Coleman's credit card. They should have some tapes we can look at."

"I see it. Over on the right, behind those pumps."

Rod pointed his massive index finger at the brightly painted building illuminated by banks of glaring fluorescent lights. He guided the Hummer up to the building and the two men stepped to the asphalt. They slammed the car doors and walked into the minimart adjusting their clothes as they approached the main cash register near the middle of the building.

Chello spoke to the pimply-faced, male clerk, "We'd like to see the manager, please."

"The manager ain't here," replied the clerk defiantly.

"Well, where is he?" asked Rod, as he stepped toward the wimpy clerk a little more aggressively than Chello had been.

"She's at home. I'm in charge of the night crew," the ruddy-faced young man stated as he moved back from the counter.

"When will she be back? In the morning?" asked Chello.

"She's usually here around 6:00 a.m. What do want her for?"

Chello and Rod flashed their photo PI licenses and Chello said, "It's a matter of life and death . . . maybe yours," he grinned.

Rod and Chello turned away from the young man and moved toward the exit. Rod turned back toward the kid and said, "Make sure she's here in the morning. Don't tell her we were here, and I mean that."

The kid saluted. "Yes sir!"

Rod commented to Chello, "That little pipsqueak better watch out, someone's going to pants him and paddle his butt."

"You wouldn't do that, would you RA?"

"Nope. Too many cameras around," Rod grinned.

The two PIs rented a motel room and Chello lay down on a bed to relax. Rod went to get some snacks. It had been over three hours since they had eaten. When Rod entered the room, Chello saw his partner had harvested a half dozen Twinkies from a vending machine. Chello reached out and Rod tossed him two of the cakes, paused, and then tossed him a third and laughed.

"I'm beat. Let's skip dinner and hit the sack. We can get a big breakfast in the morning." Rod looked at Chello. Chello had eaten only one Twinkie and was falling asleep.

"Okay," Chello mumbled.

The PIs got up at 6:00 a.m., ran a razor through their stubble, and were out the door. As they returned the key to the motel office, they each grabbed a doughnut, a small Styrofoam cup of black coffee, and headed to the minimart.

The manager was expecting them. Rod's mini-threat hadn't been taken seriously. The badge pinned on the manager's blouse said Lorraine. She had shoulder length, wavy, brunette hair and was good looking. Rod gave Chello an elbow in the ribs when they first saw her.

"What can I do for you gentlemen?"

Chello responded, "Good morning, ma'am. We'd like to see the tapes of your customers from three days ago. Somebody charged forty-three seventeen for gas—used a stolen credit card."

"May I see your credentials, please?" Lorraine requested.

The PIs flipped open their wallets and displayed their picture IDs.

"Please come with me. Sylvia, take the counter for a few."

Lorraine was about five-ten and walked with a purpose. As they followed her, Rod noticed her nicely shaped legs. Chello, grinning, looked at Rod. Rod raised his eyebrows and grinned at Chello, acknowledging Lorraine's sexy legs.

The back room was rather small, but they crowded into it with Lorraine. She wore just enough perfume to suggest femininity; however, the scent wasn't necessary. She had just enough room to sort through the DVDs. She stuck a disk in the player and they watched the monitor. As the disk began to turn, Lorraine keyed in $43.17 and the monitor flickered as the search began.

The picture flickered and then a clear view of the main counter appeared. Legs covered with work pants were seen first as a customer approached the counter. A plaid shirt covering a large belly, then the head of a man about fifty years old appeared. An obese woman in a flower print dress, more than a foot shorter than the man, stood beside him. They talked and she handed him a credit card. He swiped the card, signed on the pressure sensitive pad, and they left.

"Well, Rod, now we know who we're looking for. They should know what happened to Doc Coleman, but we might have to pressure them a little."

"I think we can handle that," Rod grinned. "He's a big dude though."

"Lorraine, could you please print a copy of those two animals for us," Chello asked.

"Sure can. Just a moment."

In ten seconds the PIs had a copy of the thieves. They thanked Lorraine for her cooperation and headed for the exit. As they walked toward the door, Rod said somewhat loudly, "Man, she has some nice equipment." Chello knew what Rod meant. He wasn't talking about the electronics. Rod looked back at Lorraine and winked as they went through the automatic door. She threw him a kiss, a big smile, and waved goodbye. Rod waved back and held up his hand like a phone to indicate he would call her.

CHAPTER 5

The Farm

The PIs were going to be on the road for three more hours, so breakfast was a necessity. They drove to Denny's and sat in a booth savoring the smell of coffee and bacon. After eating pancakes, bacon and eggs, and talking about Lorraine, the PIs started the return trip to Eugene with Chello driving. On the way, they discussed the options for approaching the man and woman whose images had been captured by the store camera.

"Let's start going north on the access road and check each house we come to along that route. Without much gas, Doc Coleman wouldn't have gone far from the access road."

Rod added, "Let's not tell them initially that we know they used the credit card. Let's just say we are looking for Dr. Coleman. We'll see how many lies we can catch them telling. You said the police report mentioned a blood spot on the driver's seat. If one of them is injured, we can use that against them. We'll tell them we know they got blood on the doctor because we found it on the car seat. They won't know whose blood it is."

Chello said, "I'll call Mrs. Coleman and tell her what we've found. She'll be interested to hear that it wasn't the Doc using his card at Crater Lake." Chello was on the head set for about two minutes telling Misty of their plans. He said he would call her again in the evening with more information.

The PIs arrived in Eugene at 11:20. They gassed up the thirsty Hummer and found the access road where Clay's rental car had been found. Rod took over the driving so Chello could refer to his notes about the location of the abandoned vehicle. Near the three mile marker, Rod stepped on the brakes and cut the engine. The PIs walked a quarter of a mile north and south along both sides of the road looking for clues the police might have missed. They found nothing but trash along the road.

Back in the Hummer, they drove slowly northward. After traveling about ten miles they turned to the right and followed a dirt road a couple of miles to a small farmhouse. They knocked, but no one came to the door. Chello and Rod returned to the access road and made a right. The next turn was another right. They followed the dirt and gravel road about fifty yards to a house, a large white barn and some farm equipment. There was a rusty, green pickup parked in front of the house.

The Hummer moved slowly in a circle as the PIs investigated the surroundings.

"Let's check the house, Rod. It looks like there's a floor lamp on in the front room."

Rod parked the Hummer and the PIs stepped to the ground. Chello reached back into the front seat and grabbed his clipboard. He showed Rod the picture Lorraine had given them so they would have the couple's image fresh in mind.

Clara and Hank were watching the Hummer as it drove around in a circle in the graveled parking area. Hank could see two men in the front seat.

"What do you think they want, Hank?"

"I dunno. Let's wait and see. Looks like they're comin' to the door."

Clara said, "Look at the size of those guys! They're as big as you, Hank. That black man looks like he could crush rocks with his fists. We'd better be damn careful."

Chello stopped about three feet from the door, extended his right fist and knocked, hard. Rod stood back about ten feet. Chello could hear someone coming to the door and stepped back. The door opened slowly. A large woman appeared, nearly filling the doorway.

Rod uttered, "Yup!" He recognized the woman as the one in the minimart photo.

"Yes?" the fat lady inquired. "If yer sellin' somethin', we don't want any."

"Good afternoon, ma'am. My associate and I are PIs from Portland."

Chello held out his wallet ID, as did Rod. "We're trying to locate a man named Clay Coleman. He's a doctor. His family has reported him missing. Here's his picture."

Chello held out the clipboard containing Clay's faxed picture on top.

"I ain't seen him." She turned away from Chello and said, "Hank, you seen this here man?"

A big man, apparently Hank, appeared at the door behind the woman. He squinted as he tried to see Clay's image.

"Nope! Can't say I have."

Chello extended the clipboard toward Hank and the man reached for it. Chello could see that the man had been cut on his arm recently. There was a scab forming and the immediate area around the wound was red and slightly inflamed.

Rod asked, "Have you been to Crater Lake in the last week, sir?"

"Nope! Clara and me don't get out much. Farmin's a lot of work. I just come in from the barn to get a drink, been weldin' all mornin' on a plow."

Chello held up the copy of the camera image from Lorraine and said, "Who do you think these people are, your twins?"

"Well, okay. We was at Crater Lake the other day."

"And you used a stolen credit card belonging to this man, Dr. Coleman," Rod added.

"We didn't steal it, he dropped it when he run away," Clara stated.

Hank added, "That guy tried to take some gasoline and I stopped him. He pulled a knife and cut me on the arm."

Chello said, "What kind of knife, a scalpel, like doctors use?" Chello was leading Hank into a trap.

"Yeah. It was a sclalpel. That's what it was. I grabbed him and he dropped it. Clara heard me wreslin' with him and came a runnin'. She picked up the sclalpel and stuck 'im in the back. He was scared an run to his car an drove off."

Chello asked, "How did you get his credit card?"

"When we was fightin', it came out with his billfold."

"Well, the police will be here to get the wallet and the money for the gas, unless of course, you can pay for it now. You owe the doctor's wife $43.17."

"Clara, git that cookie jar. We throwed away the wallet and I dropped the card in the trash back at that store where we got the gas."

Clara came to the door and shoved the money at Chello, two twenties and four ones.

"Thank you. We'll tell the police you paid for the gas. We might just come back, so stick around. Don't leave the area on any long trips, okay?"

Rod and Chello turned and walked toward the Hummer. Chello looked back at the house and saw Clara watching them from the window. Chello and Rod both waved to her and she disappeared from sight. They heard the door slam shut as Hank went back in the house.

"Now, those are some real nice people." Rod said sarcastically. "I wonder what she eats."

Chello said, "I have no idea what a hippopotamus eats, but I think elephants eat hay and peanuts." They both laughed and climbed in the Hummer.

As the PIs drove back toward Eugene they discussed the farm animals.

"Hank is lying through his teeth. He outweighs the doc by more than a hundred pounds. The doc wouldn't be wrestling with that dude. And why would he have a scalpel with him? He had been at a conference. That story is a bunch of hogwash!"

Rod said, "I agree. They must have taken his wallet and tried to stab him, and he escaped by driving off. He retraced the path that took him to the farm but was running out of gas. And to compound his problems, he got a flat as he escaped. That's when he abandoned the car."

"I'll bet he tried to walk to the freeway but he was cold, hurt, and didn't make it. Somebody might have given him a lift, maybe to Portland. He didn't return to Eugene. He was supposed to fly back to Lincoln the next day," contributed Chello.

"Yeah. That sounds probable. Let's head back to Portland and check the hospitals."

"Okay. We'll check in Tualatin first," directed Chello.

"I'm hungry," informed Chello. "Let's get some chicken and we can eat while we drive."

"Sounds like a plan. We don't want to deprive ourselves of brain food."

"Brain food, that's a good one," Chello snickered.

Two hours later they arrived at the hospital in Tualatin and checked the emergency room records for the past two weeks. Nothing was found.

Back in the Hummer, Chello said, "Let's go to Providence on Glisan and 50th."

There were other hospitals in Portland but Chello reasoned the ones with easy access from the freeways should be checked first. Providence was just off Route 84. They parked the Hummer on the street and walked to the main entrance. Their big Hummer wouldn't fit very well in the parking garage.

A young lady at the desk directed them to the emergency wing. The PIs showed their IDs and asked to talk with any doctor that had treated a stab wound during the last two weeks. There had been several stabbings treated by the same emergency doctor.

"Where can we find Dr. Lunce?" Chello asked the receptionist.

"Let me page him for you sir. One moment please."

The young lady entered a code on her console and a green light flashed twice.

"He'll be here in a minute or two, gentlemen."

Rod said, "Thank you very much."

"You're welcome," replied the receptionist and gave Rod a big smile.

"I can't understand why the ladies like you," Chello stated.

"I think I look very healthy, clean cut," Rod grinned. "Maybe they would like to take a handsome man home to meet their parents." They both chuckled.

A couple of minutes elapsed and a doctor came to the desk and spoke to the receptionist. She said something and pointed at the two PIs. The label on his coat said Dr. Fred Lunce, M.D. He was nearly six feet tall but the two PIs dwarfed him.

"I'm Dr. Lunce, how may I help you gentlemen?"

Chello spoke first, "Rod and I are PIs trying to locate this man." Rod held out the clipboard with the picture of Dr. Coleman on top.

Chello added, "He's Dr. Clay Coleman, an expert in sports medicine from the University of Nebraska. He gave a keynote address at a conference in Eugene a couple of weeks ago, and he hasn't returned home or been heard from."

"Yes, he was here. He had a stab wound in his back which I sutured."

Rod asked, "Was the wound made by a scalpel, or could you tell?"

Dr. Lunce laughed. "Not a scalpel. The wound was too jagged, probably done with a kitchen or pocket knife."

"Was the wound severe?" quizzed Chello.

"No. I only used two sutures. The cut is probably closed by now and will only leave a small scar. There was no internal damage. I called the police because it was a suspected stabbing. An officer interviewed Dr. Coleman."

"What did he tell the police," Chello asked.

"Nothing."

"Nothing?"

"Yes. Dr. Coleman has amnesia. He doesn't know his name or where he's from."

"Amnesia?" Chello questioned.

"Yes. He had a traumatic experience and he has forgotten many things except his medical training. That's not uncommon is cases like this. He will probably begin to remember things provided there are the proper stimuli. We just don't know how long it will take."

"Did he have a name?" asked Rod.

"He took the name of the officer. It was Dave."

"Doc, did he say where he was going?" Chello inquired.

"He didn't say much of anything. Oh, he did say to use the hospital address when the officer asked him for an address. Sorry, gentlemen, that's about it. I hope you can find him. Reuniting with his family just might stimulate the complete return of his memory."

Rod said, "Well, thanks Doctor. We appreciate your help. We'll have to try a new approach and see if we can discover where he went."

The PIs shook hands with the doctor and left the hospital. When they got to the car, Chello called Misty.

"Hello Mrs. Coleman, this is Chello. We found out Dr. Coleman was injured but not severely. He was treated at Providence Hospital in Portland. We know why he hasn't contacted you. He has amnesia and doesn't know his real name or that he's a doctor. I'm sorry we haven't found him yet, but we'll continue to search for him. We're still optimistic. At least now you know why he hasn't returned. Oh, you're welcome. We'll be in touch."

CHAPTER 6

The Search Continues

Back in their office, the two men sat and looked at each other in silence. Chello was fiddling with a pencil as he was thinking. Rod was the first to comment.

"Where do we look next? The doctor has no money and no place to live, but he's extremely resourceful. What would we do in his situation?"

Chello replied, "We might be in the same situation if we don't do some work we'll get paid for. Let's spend a few days earning some money. In the meantime we can fabricate a plan to locate the doctor. Okay?"

As Rod stood up he said, "Yeah. What if we spend one day a week on the Coleman case? If we get some good leads, we can devote more time searching for the doctor. I've got to eat and get some rest. See you later."

"Later, partner. We can devote Fridays to the Coleman case. Let's see what else we can come up with in the next two days."

Chello heard the outer door close and lock. He leaned back in his chair and closed his eyes. *The doc has no money, no friends, and no place to stay. Where would he go?* Chello thought about it for a few minutes, picked up a pad and began to write. His page of notes would be reviewed on Friday when they continued the search. Before he left for his apartment, Chello made thirty copies of Clay's picture Misty had faxed to the PIs.

There was steady rain on Friday. The closest YMCA to the Providence hospital was on 60th, ten blocks farther east, so they stopped there first. No one remembered seeing Dave. They left several of the pictures, some business cards, an offer of a fifty dollar reward and asked to be called if anyone saw Dr. Coleman.

Their next stop was the YMCA on 79th. Inside the building, Chello shook the water from his baseball cap and asked the receptionist if she had seen Clay. Rod held up a copy of the fax. The older woman looked at Chello, back at the picture and inquired, "What'd this gentleman do?"

"Nothing. We're trying to find him for his wife," Rod answered.

"Ran out on his wife, did he?"

"Nope. He has amnesia and doesn't know where he lives or who his wife is."

"Oh my!" the elderly gray-haired black woman responded. "Let me look at that picture again."

Rod turned the picture so the woman could see it clearly.

"I think so—maybe. Billy?" She called to a middle-aged black man sweeping the floor. He shuffled over to the woman and she asked, "Have you seen this gentleman, Billy?"

Billy rubbed his beard and commented, "Yes ma'am. He was here 'bout a week back. Stay one night. Help me clean second floor toilets. He got a beard."

"There you go! Billy remembers every face he's ever seen. I'd bet on him being right."

Billy smiled and turned away to resume sweeping.

Chello said, "Thank you, Billy."

"Yessir. He real smart—name Dave."

Rod and Chello looked at each other. There was no doubt the doctor had been there. Finally, the PIs had some good luck. The trail hadn't grown cold.

Two weeks elapsed before the PIs could resume their hunt for Dr. Coleman. They were required to do some work in Vancouver and Battleground and couldn't get free on the previous Friday to resume the search. Since the doctor had apparently been drifting eastward, Chello and Rod decided to leapfrog farther ahead to the east. Thinking Dave would be trading aluminum cans for cash, they drove to the redemption center at 233rd and Halsey. When they arrived at the recycling center, Rod started to get out of the Hummer, but Chello stopped him.

"Hold on! Let's watch for a few minutes and see who comes to turn in cans and bottles."

Rod sat back in his seat and shut the door. During a period of about fifteen minutes, several cars drove up, and the occupants pulled plastic bags of cans and boxes of bottles from the trunks. The vehicle activity lulled, and a young man and woman with a baby entered the building carrying two large bags of aluminum cans. Chello motioned for Rod to get out, and the two men approached the couple.

The man stepped in front of the woman and baby, not knowing what these two big men intended. His face displayed some anxiety, and Chello noted he was making fists, presumably preparing for a fight.

"Don't worry, man, we're just looking for information. We're PIs." Rod and Chello flashed their IDs to the couple.

"You scared me for a minute. You guys are so damn big, but I guess you don't look mean."

"Thanks," Chello grinned. "Have you seen this man?" Chello held out a picture of Clay and the couple looked closely.

"James! I think that's Dave, but he has a beard. Yeah, I'm sure of it. He has kind blue eyes. He fixed my baby's tongue; she was tongue tied and couldn't stick out her tongue. Dave borrowed some finger-nail scissors and removed some tissue from under Sarah's tongue. You should have seen him! He checked her mouth, borrowed some scissors, burned them with some matches and snipped out a little triangle-shaped piece of tissue. It only took him a minute or so. It was amazing. There was hardly any bleeding. Sarah cried for just a minute—until I gave her something to suck on," she smiled.

Chello said, "I'm sure that was Doctor Coleman. Your baby was in good hands. Do you know where he is?"

The young woman answered, "No. We haven't seen him in the last—." She looked at her husband for support. "ten days or so?" Her husband nodded. "What did he do? I hope it wasn't something bad. He was a nice guy."

"He didn't do anything wrong. He has amnesia. His family is looking for him. He lives in Nebraska," answered Chello.

Rod added, "And Dave doesn't know he's a doctor."

The PIs thanked the couple, gave them a twenty dollar bill for the information, and climbed back in the Hummer.

Rod looked at Chello and said, "Next stop?"

Chello looked at his watch and said, "That's enough for today. I've got to get some rest. I'm really beat. I'll go to the truck stop in Troutdale tomorrow afternoon and see if I can find someone that's seen him. Maybe I'll spot him, who knows?"

CHAPTER 7

One Step Ahead

At the time the PIs were at the redemption/recycling center, Dave was wandering through the truck stop off Route 84 in Troutdale. He had to be observant to avoid being run over by a semi or cars changing lanes to either get into Shari's restaurant, or back on the freeway after eating and gassing up. The activity seemed unrelenting.

Dave watched as a vagrant held up a sign trying to get handouts from occupants of cars. Few people that stopped at the traffic light even acknowledged the man. His sign said, "We're hungry. Anything would be appreciated." The sign referred to the man and his dog. A small, apparently well-fed, brown mutt was on a leash beside the beggar.

Unfortunately, only two vehicles stopped during a fifteen-minute period, and Dave later found that the sun-tanned, bearded beggar had received just a one-dollar bill. The other car was a police cruiser, and Dave turned away so the officers couldn't see his face. Dave hadn't checked in with the police since being interrogated at the hospital. He didn't want to get involved in something he had no recollection of, so he deliberately avoided the police. He couldn't imagine being in a knife fight.

Drivers were not generous because of recent television and radio reports that the beggars were running a scam. The man folded his sign, waited for traffic to diminish, and began walking across an overpass that carried traffic over a half dozen railroad tracks to the old scenic highway and downtown Troutdale.

Dave hurried to catch up with the man and his dog. Before the beggar had gotten to the other side of the viaduct, Dave caught up with him. The dog turned and snarled, baring its fangs. The man stopped and turned around.

"Don't come up behind me, mister. My dog'll take a chunk outta yer leg."

"Sorry, but I noticed you have a bit of a limp. Looks like you have a bad knee."

"You got that right. A car almost run me over the other day. Twisted my knee trying to git outta the way. You don't look like a doctor or nuthin. Who're you?"

"I'm Dave. I know about things like that. I don't know why, I just know. Is there a place we can sit down? I'll have a look at your knee. Maybe I can help."

"I'm called Truk 'cause of where I work. Glad to meet you, Dave."

They shook hands and continued across the arched concrete structure.

"How long have you been around here, Truk?"

"Let's see now—about three years, I guess. I moved down here from Seattle. Not quite as wet here and a little warmer. I've got a place up on Buxton. Nobody knows where I live. They think I'm homeless," he laughed, "but I'm not. I'm kind of tricky."

Dave walked along the Old Columbia River Highway for three blocks with Truk and his dog. They made a right turn and kept moving slowly up the steep hill on Buxton. Four blocks of walking was enough to make Truk weary. He was walking noticeable slower, and more bent over, undoubtedly because of the bad knee.

The two men and the dog turned down an alley and trudged another twenty yards or so and stopped.

"Well, look around, Dave. Can you see my house?"

Dave scanned the shrubs, berry vines, and trees but couldn't see anything but the back of a garage behind the next house on Buxton.

"No, Truk. Is it below ground?"

"Damn! You're a smart cookie!" Truk smiled. "Let me show you my mancave."

Dave could see the older man was missing three of his front teeth, two on the bottom and one on top. Dave reflected that Beav would be a better name for the man than Truk, since his central incisors, both uppers and lowers, were still present. Dave smiled back.

Heinz, the dog, pulled on the leash and assisted Truk up the incline between two overgrown shrubs. Dave followed and was surprised at what he saw. It looked like a storm cellar from the Midwest where people sought refuge from tornadoes. Truk moved a large stake, which operated as a lever, and the door opened. The old post looked like it was a fence post marooned amongst the vegetation.

Truk ducked his head slightly as he descended below ground. Dave moved toward the opening and saw a light come on. Heinz ran down the three steps and disappeared.

Truk called out, "Come on down, Dave. Take a look."

Dave went down the steps, ducked his head and entered into a small cavern. Surprised at what he saw, Dave smiled and said, "Wow!"

Truk chuckled, proud of the room he had dug out of the hillside. There were two small chairs, a table, a bookshelf, a bed, and a kitchen area with a hotplate. Three sheets of plywood made the floor. The space was being used to its optimum. However, the ceiling was less than six feet high so Dave had to bend over.

"Have a seat, Dave." Truk motioned for Dave to sit down in one of the chairs.

"Where did you get all this stuff, Truk?"

"I been dumpster divin' for years. People throw things away that can be fixed and I get 'um and fix 'um. Most of my stuff was free."

"What about electricity?"

"Well, that's donated by the family that owns the garage, but they don't know it," Truk grinned. "I buried an extension cord and hooked up to the electricity in the garage. They've got a freezer up there and I tapped into the line. I don't use much power unless I have a feast, but that ain't often. Say, Dave, what do you do, I mean, for a living?"

"I'm looking for work. I'd like to find a job."

Truk laughed, "Work? That's a dirty word! You must be crazy."

Dave responded, "How do you make ends meet? You only made a dollar today. You can't live on that, can you?"

"Oh, hell no. I get social security and a small pension. I could live in a big house if I wanted, but I don't need all that crap. I like nature! Heinz and I have a great time, except now. My leg is pretty sore, hard to get around very much."

"I think I can help you with that, Truk. I know about knees and joints."

"You a nurse, or maybe a doc?"

"I don't know, Truk. A doctor told me I have amnesia. I don't remember lots of things. I don't even know my name."

"It's not Dave?"

"I don't think so. I took that name from a policeman. I don't have a last name."

Truk said, "Why not Buxton? That's the street out there and it's a good last name. Dave Buxton sounds good. The names seem to go together."

"Yeah, that'll work," Dave smiled. "Thanks, Truk. Let me take a look at your knee."

Truk carried out specified movements with his leg and Dave watched Truk's facial expressions for signs of pain. After about five minutes, Dave said, "Okay, that's enough. I know what's wrong. You need some support and some over-the-counter pain pills. Don't walk on it for a couple of days."

"Jesus, I can't do that. I have to be at my spot or somebody will take it from me."

"You don't even need that place, Truk. Why do you go down there? Do you like the dirty looks you get?"

"I meet some interestin' people, get fresh air, some exercise and time goes by faster than if I was sittin' around in this hole. I just sleep here so I'm protected from bad people that're out there at night. No rain in here, either," he smiled.

"Well, I'll get you some tape and some pain pills and we'll get you fixed up. Where's the nearest drug store?"

Truck replied, "You'll have to go to 257th and up the hill. It's a good mile and a half from here. You'd do that for me?"

"Sure. I can use the exercise, and I can check out the surroundings. I think I'll hang around here a while. I need to find a place to live. This is a nice area."

"Well, you can stay here as long as you want, but no more than a week," Truk laughed. "You can sleep on the floor. I've got another sleeping bag and an air mattress you can use. Do yah snore?"

Dave thought a few seconds and said, "I don't think so. You can always kick me if I do but use your bad leg."

Truk responded with a chuckle, "That's a good one Dave."

The week passed quickly and Dave was ready to move on. The men parted company with a handshake and a hug. Dave continued up Buxton to Stark Street and made a left turn. He walked to the park on the Sandy River and stayed there a few days while he investigated the surroundings. The police made him leave the park on the third night. Dave left the area after that first warning, not wanting to attract any more attention. A law prohibited staying in a park overnight.

Dave had taken several walks along the old Columbia River Highway to see where nearby residents lived. During one of those walks he discovered an old building about the size of a single car garage. The structure was overgrown with blackberry vines, weeds of all types, and some downed limbs from tall evergreen trees surrounding the shack. He decided to clean up the place and stay awhile. Dave wouldn't be evicted from the park again. There was no indication of the building's owner.

CHAPTER 8

Dirty Old Man

Julie, a young lady with short blonde hair, had just turned thirteen. Now, a full-fledged teenager, her chest had begun to lose its flatness. She was self-conscious about her body and wore loose clothes to conceal the changes. Spring vacation had started a week ago. Julie had just read an article in one of her mother's magazines while she ate breakfast. The essay, written by a registered nurse, mentioned that poor diet and lack of exercise were messing up the lives of today's girls.

Julie usually had one piece of toast with the crust cut off and a small glass of orange juice, but not today. A glass of milk and two scrambled eggs had been added to her breakfast and she left the crust on her toast. Saturday was a good time to start a new routine. Julie wanted to take control of her diet and exercise immediately.

Robert Walser, Julie's dad, was an electrician and had gone to work at 7:00 a.m. at a new housing project. He was lucky to have the job; construction of new homes had nearly halted because of the slow economy. Her mom, Marcia, was doing laundry and house cleaning. During the week, Marcia was a teller at a branch of U.S. Bank.

Julie was riding her balloon tire bicycle north along the right shoulder of Troutdale Road. Most of the shoulder was covered with asphalt, but once in a while there were spaces of dirt, gravel, and of course, weeds. There was one particular spot where she had to be careful not to steer off the edge of the road. An abrupt slope was terminated with a cyclone fence about five feet high. She was well aware of the danger that section of the road possessed for someone on a bicycle. The drop-off extended about twelve feet from the road to the bottom of the fence. She had ridden past that spot many times and looked down at the trash against the bottom of the wire barricade.

Suddenly, a cyclist in a racing uniform rocketed past her at about thirty miles per hour. The swish as he passed surprised her, distracting Julie from watching where she was going, and her front wheel turned enough to skid in the gravel. She abruptly started down the steep slope. Julie reacted quickly, slid sideways off the bicycle seat, and pushed the bike down the slope. She hit the ground on her hands and knees and clawed at the weeds to keep from smashing into the wire fence, sliding in the dirt and trash. The wire fence put a stop to her movements.

Her bicycle had continued on about twenty feet, stopping with the right hand grip poking through the fence. As the dust cloud settled, Julie stood up and wiped the dirt from her hands. Her fingers were only slightly scraped, sore but not bleeding. Stepping over rocks, weeds, and broken glass, she cautiously picked her way through the debris to her bicycle.

The bike was resting on top of some rags; something probably discarded by a resident of the house on the other side of the fence or tattered material that had fallen from a passing vehicle. When Julie pulled on the rear fender of her bike, she saw the rags move and heard a groan. Someone was under the rags! Holding onto the bike seat and backing up, she kept the bike between her and the moving rags. She had used her bike before to protect herself from barking dogs, but this time it was a man.

He looked old. His clothes were dirty and rumpled. He turned over and sat up, leaning against the fence, shielding his eyes from the morning sun. A scraggly beard concealed his features. He had a bloody gash over his left eye. Dried blood and dirt were mixed in his beard, so his face looked distorted. His appearance reminded Julie of a picture she had seen in a storybook about a hermit that had fallen from a horse into a mud puddle.

"My gosh!" Julie exclaimed. "You're hurt."

The man squinted, reached up to feel his forehead, and said, "Emma, is that you? Where's the kitten?"

"I'm not Emma, I'm Julie Walser. What kitten? And how did you get down in this ditch?"

The man sat in silence, blinking his eyes, and then cleared his throat. "Well, young lady, it's a pretty short story. I was walking along the road late last night and heard a quavering meow. It sounded more like a whine than a meow, and then I saw it, a tiny black and white kitten. I was afraid the kitten would get run over, so I picked it up. I wrapped the kitten in the hood of my jacket to keep it warm. A speeding car, radio blaring, was approaching and I turned to look at it. Something hit me and I was falling. I must have ended up here. I guess whatever hit me must have knocked me out."

Using the fence to steady himself, the elderly man rose to his feet. He looked around on the ground and found an unopened, dented beer can with a trace of blood on it. He opened the beer and surprised Julie. Rather than drinking it, he poured the beer on the ground, held up the empty can, and said proudly, "I don't like beer, but here is five cents!"

He reached for a wadded up dirty gray windbreaker on the ground a few feet from where he had been. There was a tiny meow, more like a squeak, and the jacket moved. A little black and white face appeared from under the material, and then the entire kitten wobbled out from under the coat.

"There you are."

"Oh! What a cute little kitten! What's your name, mister?"

"Ah—Dave."

"What's your last name?"

Dave replied after thinking a second or two, "Buxton."

He bent over and picked up his jacket, shook it out, put the empty beer can in a pocket, and scooped up the kitten with his right hand.

Julie thought it was a little strange the man had to think about last name. Maybe it was because he got hit on the head. Julie wanted to help the man, but she had been warned many times about strangers, especially men, but Dave was hurt and trying to care for a tiny kitten. Her mom would understand.

"I'll bet you and the kitty are hungry."

The man blinked his eyes a few more times, looked at the kitten and said, "We sure are."

"I live several blocks from here on Kibling. Why don't you come with me, and my mom will fix you breakfast. You can get cleaned up and she can cut your hair. Mom's pretty good at fixing cuts, too; she worked for a doctor before she married my dad."

"She's a nurse?" Dave asked.

"Not really, but she fixes up my dad and me all the time. Let's go. Okay?"

"Okay. You climb up first, and I'll hand you the kitten, then I'll bring up your bike."

Julie scrambled up the steep incline, braced herself with one foot on the asphalt and reached back down the slope. Dave handed the kitten to Julie and brought her bike up to the road. The handlebars were twisted so she couldn't ride. They walked slowly toward Julie's house.

"What are you going to name the kitten?" asked Julie.

Dave grinned, "I was thinking Catastrophe. The end sounds kind of girlish, don't you think?"

"I think that's too complicated. The kitten would have a hard time spelling that," Julie laughed. "How about Beacon?"

"Why Beacon?" Dave frowned.

"I was thinking B-can for beer can, but Beacon sounds nearly the same and makes a better name," Julie grinned.

"That's very clever Julie. Beacon it is!"

"Julie, do you have a younger brother?" Dave inquired.

"Nope, but I have a dog named Nittie. She's a German shepherd. Why?"

"Oh, no reason, I guess. I just thought you should have a brother and a dog."

"Well, I do have a dog. About a year and a half ago, before Christmas, Mom and Dad took me to the animal shelter near Halsey. Nittie had just been cleared for adoption and we all fell in love with her, so we brought her home. At first, we thought she should have a different name but I kind of like Nittie, so we kept it. I think she likes that name. If I ever become a rapper, there are plenty of words that rhyme with Nittie," Julie grinned.

Five minutes later, Julie pushed the bicycle up the driveway on the right of a light-yellow, ranch house trimmed in white. The siding near the foundation was dirty from rain splashing mud from the flower beds.

"We're home!" Julie announced as she leaned the bike against the house. "Come on Dave, I'll get my mom." She motioned for Dave to follow her to the front door.

Dave ran his fingers through his hair trying to comb it into place but without much success. He hadn't seen or used a comb in several weeks. Dave pulled at his beard and walked a little hesitantly toward the door. He hoped he wouldn't scare Julie's mother. Dave stood on the porch trying to straighten his wrinkled, dirty clothing as he looked at the knocker on the front door. The knocker was in the shape of a little monkey.

Dave watched Julie open the door and yell, "Mom! We have a visitor."

A nice looking, curly-haired blonde, approximately forty, and a little taller than Julie, approached the door, but stopped suddenly when she caught sight of the disheveled man standing on the doormat.

Julie stood beside her mother and said, "Mom, I'd like you to meet Dave. Dave, this is my mom, Marcia Walser."

"Hello, Mrs. Walser. Sorry I'm so dirty," Dave said apologetically. "Your daughter found me unconscious, or maybe asleep, beside Troutdale Road. She invited me to come over to get something to eat and clean up a little bit. I don't want to be any bother, so I'll leave." Dave turned away from the front door.

"No, don't leave. I'll make you a sandwich and some coffee. We taught Julie to be kind, but cautious, so come in. Sit down over here and we can talk," Marcia motioned to a chair next to an arched doorway, and she went into the kitchen.

"Thank you Mrs. Walser."

"Please call me Marcia."

"What do you do for a living, mister—ah, Dave? What is your last name?"

"Oh, it's Buxton, same as the road down the hill to the highway. I take care of some property across the Sandy River from the Stark Street Bridge. Mr. Stenos, the owner, has a small shack where I live. The electricity doesn't work but he pays me $125 a month." Dave grinned. "It's a good deal. I only have a few duties, a roof over my head, and I don't have to sleep in a park and evade the police. I've got a wood burning stove, too."

CHAPTER 9

Clean Up

Marcia, Julie, and Dave sat down at the breakfast bar. While Dave ate his sandwich and drank coffee with a little artificial sweetener added, Marcia and Julie had some tea. Beacon was lapping sugar water from a saucer on the ceramic tile floor. The Internet said not to give cow's milk to kittens, so Julie had prepared some sugar water for Beacon. Dave finished his sandwich and wiped some crumbs from his beard.

"How about an apple, Dave?" Marcia asked.

"Sorry, I don't have any apples," Dave grinned.

"I mean—would you like an apple?"

"I know, Marcia. That was just a joke and not a very good one," he smiled. "Yes, please. Do you have anything around the house that needs to be fixed? I'm pretty good at repairing things. I seem to have a knack for figuring out how things work, or don't."

"Ken, my husband, said the lawn mower needs to be fixed but he hasn't had time yet. He's got a housing project job that's keeping him busy these days. He's an electrician."

"That's what Julie told me. I'll take a look at the lawn mower. I'd like to trade something for your kindness."

"Why don't you take a shower, and I'll trim your hair afterward. You're pretty shaggy. We wouldn't want your hair caught in the mower!" Marcia laughed. "Leave your clothes outside the bathroom and I'll wash them. You're about the same size as my husband. You can borrow some of his clothes to wear."

"That's very nice of you. I'd like that."

Beacon was wandering around with drops of sugar water on her whiskers and nose, curious about the new environment. Marcia wiped the kitten's face with a paper towel and put the little kitty back on the floor near Dave.

Marcia looked down at the kitten. "Beacon is so cute. I'll get the clothes for you. I'll be right back."

"Mr. Buxton, do you think you could help me fix my bike?"

"Sure Julie. All we'll need is a small crescent wrench or a pair of pliers."

"Okay. I know where that stuff is. We have a tool drawer in the kitchen."

"You get the tools and we'll fix it right after I take a shower."

"I have a shirt, some pants and some underwear for you while I'm washing your clothes, Dave," announced Marcia. "Here you are." She handed him a pile of folded clothing and pointed down the hallway to the bathroom.

Dave entered the bathroom, placed the clean clothing on the toilet seat and turned on the fan. The stripped off filthy clothes were tossed in a heap outside the door as he was instructed. He turned on the hot water and stood under the showerhead watching the brownish water disappear into the drain. The baths he had taken in the cold water of the Sandy River hadn't been enough to remove all the grime and odor that had accumulated during the past few months.

He washed his hair and stood trance-like in the hot water cascading over his body. After enjoying the experience, he turned off the water and stepped out of the shower to dry off. He borrowed a little deodorant, donned the clean clothes, and looked in the mirror.

"Well, that's some improvement," Dave mumbled as he sniffed his armpits.

Dave opened the medicine cabinet and scanned the shelves. He picked up a tube of antibacterial ointment, placed some of the gel on the gash in his forehead and covered the cut with a Band-Aid. The shaving cream was within easy reach, as well as some disposable razors. He spent ten minutes deftly guiding a razor through his three-month-old beard. He inspected his shaven face to see if there were any nicks, but none was found.

"Pretty good job," he whispered.

After straightening up the bathroom, Dave stepped into the hallway and encountered Julie coming from her bedroom.

"I'll be right back, Nittie," Julie commented, looking into her bedroom. Dave observed a shocked look on Julie's face when she saw him.

"Dave, you aren't an old man! I'll bet you're about the same age as my dad!"

"You mean he's sixty-years-old too?" Dave smiled.

"No, he's thirty-nine, not sixty! You're pretty funny."

Dave grinned. "So you think I'm about forty?"

"Uh-huh. You have kind eyes, too. I have to get some water for Nittie, and then we can work on my bike. Okay?"

"Is there something wrong with your dog?" Dave inquired.

"We have to take her to the vet; she can't walk. Something's wrong with her right front paw," Julie answered.

"Can I take a look?"

"I guess. She's in her bed on the floor. She doesn't want to get up. I think her paw really hurts."

Dave followed Julie to the dog. Nittie raised her head and looked at Dave, then Julie, and dropped her head back on the blanket. Dave knelt beside the dog and spoke softly to the Rough collie.

"Nittie, you are a very pretty girl," Dave said as he stroked her neck and back.

"Julie, please come over here and pet Nittie while I look at her paw." Dave moved so Julie could take his place. As soon as Julie was in position and was stroking Nittie, Dave lifted the dog's paw and looked at it closely. Dave began parting the pads on Nittie's right front paw and found a lump between two pads. Nittie growled and pulled her paw back from Dave's hands.

"Well, Julie, I think Nittie has a thorn or sliver stuck between the front pads of her paw. I'll bet it's from a blackberry vine; there are a lot of them around here. I can get it out, but we'll have to hold Nittie tightly so she can't bite us. Let's ask your mom to help."

"Mom! We need you!" Julie yelled.

Marcia stuck her head through the doorway and said, "Dave, you look human! I heard you talking about Nittie. Have you figured out what the problem is? What do you want me to do?"

Julie replied, "Dave thinks Nittie has a thorn in her paw."

Dave inquired, "Marcia, do you have any xylocaine? We can deaden the area where the thorn is and I can extract it without hurting Nittie. The thorn is stuck deeply in her paw."

Marcia responded, "My husband has a big medical kit in the garage. Let me check."

Dave looked at Julie and asked, "How about a pair of needle-nose pliers?"

"I'll get them. I know just where they are," she answered enthusiastically.

Marcia returned to the bedroom with a medical kit, opened it, and pulled out a vial.

"Here's some lidocaine. Will that work?"

"Good. That's the same as xylocaine. Xylocaine is the trade name for lidocaine," Dave instructed and smiled. "Do you have a small syringe?"

"Yes. There are some disposable syringes, too," Marcia replied. "Here's one."

Julie returned with the pliers and handed them to Dave.

"Okay! We're all set, except for a blanket or a big bath towel."

Marcia retrieved a large bath towel from the hall linen closet and handed it to Dave.

"Now, you ladies are going to hold the towel with your hands and knees so Nittie won't be able to move. She won't like it when I poke her paw with the needle to administer the pain killer."

Dave placed the towel over Nittie so when Julie and her mom were kneeling on it, Nittie couldn't get up or bite anyone. Julie and Marcia got on the towel and Dave injected some anesthetic into Nittie's paw. Nittie yelped for a second when Dave inserted the needle but she calmed down immediately. The lidocaine was working.

"Okay, I'm going to extract the thorn with the pliers. It will only take a second."

Dave parted the pads on Nittie's paw, grasped the thorn with the pliers and pulled. "I've got it." Dave showed the bloody thorn to Julie and her mom. He wiped the bloody pus oozing from Nittie's paw, applied some antibiotic ointment, and wrapped the paw with gauze and applied some tape. "The operation is over and the patient will be fine!" Dave smiled. "I would like to thank you nurses for a job well done. You can let Nittie up now."

Marcia and Julie moved back so they were kneeling on the floor. As soon as the weight was removed from the towel, Nittie stood and began licking Julie's face. They all began petting the dog.

Dave said, "Good dog, Nittie," and stroked Nittie's back.

CHAPTER 10

Beacon's New Home

"How did you know what to do, Dave? Are you a veterinarian?" quizzed Marcia.

"I don't know, Marcia. It seems I just know about broken bones and things like that," Dave replied.

A high-pitched hissing came from the kitchen. Marcia and Dave looked at each other in surprise. Dave grinned and said, "Oh-oh, I think Beacon and Nittie just met."

Julie rushed into the kitchen, the adults not far behind. There was Nittie, looking a little bit afraid of the tiny ball of black and white fur. Beacon had her back up and was standing her ground next to Nittie's water bowl. Beacon's nose and whiskers were wet. Nittie had surprised the kitten as she was getting a drink. Beacon didn't know that bowl was for Nittie's water.

Julie picked up Beacon, handed the kitten to Dave, and refilled the water bowl for Nittie. The thirsty dog stuck her nose to the water and began lapping noisily. Dave could feel Beacon shaking, her little heart racing.

Dave held the kitten up and said, "What a surprise! You didn't know there was a dog in the house, did you? Say, Marcia, do you have a pet carrier? I'd like to put Beacon somewhere safe."

"Sure, we have a small one in the garage. I'll get it for you."

In about a minute, Marcia returned with a small gray plastic pet taxi. Dave placed Beacon inside the carrier on a layer of foam rubber.

"Thanks Marcia. She should fall asleep now."

"Well, Dave, I think I should give you a haircut. What do you think?"

Dave smiled and quipped, "Can I trust you with scissors?"

"What do you mean scissors? I'm going to use a chainsaw." Marcia laughed.

"I guess I deserved that," Dave grinned.

They went outside on the covered back porch, and in fifteen minutes, Dave had a near professional haircut. He was surprised and amused at the amount of hair Marcia had snipped off. Julie watched as the transformation took place.

Julie remarked, "You are very handsome, Dave."

He looked in a mirror Julie had brought from her bedroom dressing table.

"Thank you Julie! You are a good judge of manly elegance," Dave smiled.

"I agree with Julie, Dave, but let's not get carried away!" laughed Marcia. "I see you're wearing a wedding ring. Where's your wife?"

"*That*, I don't know. I'm still hoping she is looking for me," Dave answered soberly. "I've given that some serious thought. I've decided to stay where I am with the hope she can find me. If I keep moving around the country, she might never find me. I think I have a daughter, too. I think her name is Emma, and I have a dog, but I don't remember the dog's name."

Julie said excitedly, "Emma's the name you called me when I found you in the ditch. I'll bet your daughter's name *is* Emma. Oh! Thank you for removing the thorn from Nittie's paw."

"You're welcome Julie. Thanks for bringing me to your home. That was very nice of you. Let's fix your bike and then we'll check out that lawn mower."

"Julie, we'll need a small wrench."

Julie dropped to her knees on the kitchen floor in front of the cabinet next to the slider that led to the porch. She pulled out the bottom drawer, reached in and grabbed a six-inch crescent wrench. She held it up for Dave to see.

"That'll work."

Julie stood, grinned, and said, "Follow me, Mr. Fixit!"

The operation of the bicycle only took a few minutes. Dave loosened the handlebar, rotated it about twenty degrees, and tightened the bolt. He sat down on the cement driveway, looked at the rest of the bike and said, "I think that's all we need to do. Everything's lined up. Okay, where's that lawn mower?"

Julie grabbed Dave's left hand and helped him to his feet.

"Come on, Dave, I'll show you! I hope you can fix it!"

Dave followed the teenager into the hot garage. The mower was hanging on a big metal hook attached to a stud a few feet from the garage door. Dave lifted the mower from the hook and placed it on the floor. To enable them to see better, Dave opened the two-car garage door from the inside. He familiarized himself with the engine, stepped back and gave the starter-cord a jerk.

Nothing happened. There was no sign of life from the engine. Dave noted a voltmeter on the workbench and checked the spark plug. It was functioning, so he had one last thing to try. He removed the cover on the air filter and discovered it was plugged with oily dirt. After putting the cleaned filter in the mower, the motor started easily.

"Hey! It works!" exclaimed Julie. "Dad will be glad you fixed it! I'll bet you can fix anything, Dave."

"Thanks for the vote of confidence, but there are some things I can't seem to fix. I can't fix my memory, but I'm working on it all the time," he grinned.

Dave cleaned up the garage floor where he had been working and shut the door.

"Julie, tell your dad it was just a dirty air filter."

Dave looked around the yard but couldn't see any other projects to work on so he walked toward the back door with Julie following. Nittie, her tail wagging, was watching through the screen door. The dog backed away from the door as Dave opened it for Julie to enter. Nittie followed Dave into the living room where Marcia was sitting watching TV.

"Marcia, I've got to be going now. Thank you for everything. If you have my clothes, I'll change and be on my way."

"You can forget about your clothes; I threw them away. They wouldn't even make good rags. You can keep the clothes you have on as payment for Nittie and the lawn mower. You saved us time and money," Marcia smiled.

"And Dave fixed my bicycle, Mom," added Julie.

Dave thought for a moment and said, "Well, all right. But I'll return the carrier in a few days. You might need it again. Another bearded guy with a cat might come by."

Dave grinned, knelt beside Nittie, stroked her neck, and scratched her ears. Nittie licked his face and stuck her nose in his hand. "You're a good dog, Nittie. Take care of Julie and Marcia. Okay?" When he stood up, Nittie gave a little bark. Dave smiled and said, "I like you, too, Nittie."

Julie handed the pet carrier to Dave. Beacon was curled up in a back corner sound asleep. It had been a scary but rewarding day for the tiny kitten. Marcia and Julie escorted Dave to the front door and said goodbye. When Dave reached the sidewalk, he turned toward the house and waved.

"I'll see you in a few days. I want to meet your father, Julie. Thanks again."

The handsome young man with the pet carrier made his way to Stark Street, turned left and began the half mile walk to the Sandy River Bridge. Traffic on the Old Columbia River Highway was pretty heavy. Teenagers and some younger children were being dropped off to spend the afternoon playing in the cool, clear water of the Sandy. The bridge could carry only one lane of cars, and traffic had to alternate crossing the river. Dave walked beside cars as they slowly moved across the narrow bridge.

About fifty yards south of the bridge, Dave climbed a steep bank and disappeared from view of the revelers. Climbing the slope was awkward with the pet carrier in one hand, but Dave was able to hold onto trees and pull himself nearly twenty yards farther up the hill to an old dirt road nearly concealed by vegetation. The single lane route was no longer used and had become overgrown. Spots of gravel defined where the old road had been. It might have been a private road on the property long ago.

Avoiding blackberry stickers and rotting fallen trees, Dave advanced another forty to fifty yards back toward the bridge to a small cabin, about the size of a single car garage. No longer looking like a hermit, Dave felt empowered. He had done some good for others today, and he felt pretty sure he had a daughter named Emma. *Perhaps if I think less about my name, it will magically come to me.*

Dave placed the pet taxi on his cot and looked inside at Beacon. The kitten was sitting up looking at him. Dave imagined the kitten to be slightly afraid of the new surroundings.

CHAPTER 11

Misty

"Well, Beacon, you've got to learn all about your new home. I'll let you out so you can investigate. While you check out the room, I'll make you some kitty litter."

Dave took Beacon out of the carrier and watched her walk around, a little wobbly at first. When Dave rolled a golf ball across the floor, the kitten began to wrestle with it, rolling over several times. Dave laughed and left the cabin. He picked up a bucket and headed toward the Sandy River. Some baking soda had been left in his house by previous occupants. Sand was the only other thing needed.

When Dave had found the concealed cabin, he had foraged for things along the Sandy. A Home Depot bucket, a couple of towels, and two pairs of old shoes found their way to Dave's house during his early hunts along the riverbanks. The shoes were too small so he cut most of the upper leather away and made sandals out of them. He laughed when he thought about having lace up sandals.

Mr. Stenos had confronted Dave a week after he first arrived. Stenos told Dave he was trespassing, and Dave said he was just looking for a temporary place to stay while he regained some important parts of his memory. Dave told old man Stenos he had been in some kind of traffic accident and had been injured. Dave really thought he had been hit by a car and tossed from the road. When he woke up, he discovered the cut in his side. He bound the wound with his undershirt and passed out beside the highway. Dave wasn't sure his story was true, but it seemed to make sense. He continued the explanation to Mr. Stenos.

A Good Samaritan had taken Dave to a hospital where a doctor cleaned the wound, sutured the incision, and gave him some antibiotics. The doctor said Dave had been stabbed. Dave couldn't remember his name, where he was from, or where he had been. The doctor said Dave's amnesia was probably only temporary. After a couple of days in a shelter, Dave felt an urge to go east, so he started traveling parallel to Interstate 84, sleeping under motel and apartment stairwells, or in parks. He stayed overnight with some homeless people a couple of times and at a YMCA.

When Dave reached Troutdale, he decided to explore the scenic area and found the building at the edge of Mr. Stenos's property. The little house was not being used but had a wood burning stove and a few household items, so Dave became a modern day squatter.

Stenos had no reason to think Dave was lying. Dave looked Stenos in the eyes as he related his story. Stenos offered Dave a job for the summer. All Dave had to do was move some irrigation sprinklers, run off any coyotes, and make sure no kids from the Sandy River recreation area got hurt in the woods. Stenos told Dave he could have six eggs and one chicken each week from the farm and $100 per month.

During the first two weeks at the little house, Dave collected aluminum cans, which he sold. He used the money for special purposes. A package of disposable razors would be his next purchase, along with some shaving cream and a stick of deodorant. His haircut and shave had decidedly improved his self-image. When he recalled how he must have looked when Julie found him, he was surprised Julie hadn't run away frightened.

Dave threaded his way through the trees and undergrowth down to the highway and descended to the riverbank. He walked upstream, found a sandy area, and put roughly a half cubic foot of sand in his bucket. The sand originated from the volcanic rock around Mt. Hood about twenty miles away. The gray-black sand was warm and dry; it had been exposed to the sun all day. After climbing the riverbank, he crossed the winding old Columbia River Highway and began ascending the steep hill to the remnants of the archaic abandoned road.

The climbing was difficult. He carried the sand bucket with one arm and then the other as he picked his way through the weeds and gravel. Dave slowly opened the cabin door. He didn't want to hit Beacon or let her out until she realized this was to be her home. There were also some hawks in the area and tiny Beacon might be carried away as lunch for the big birds. Dave would have to be with Beacon when she was outside until she grew much larger and was able to fend off winged attackers.

Beacon was sound asleep, curled up on the cot. She didn't wake up when Dave entered the shack. Dave cut down a cardboard box, added the sand, about two cups of baking soda, and mixed the components together. He placed the kitty litter behind the wood stove where Beacon could enjoy a bit of privacy when taking care of business. A scoop was made from an old piece of metal window screen. Dave wondered if Beacon would find the litter box and know what it was for.

The wood-burning stove provided plenty of heat to warm the shack in the mornings and late evenings. The nearly unfurnished room looked pretty bleak when Dave woke up around 6:00 a.m., but now he had a companion to talk to about the new day's activities. Beacon had joined Dave on the cot sometime during the night and was curled up under the blanket. Her little head was the only thing sticking out.

Dave started a fire, made some coffee, cooked some eggs and made French toast on the top surface of the stove. He used a cedar shingle to flip the toast over to brown it on both sides. Dave had purchased a small bottle of syrup for his toast and pancakes. He only bought foods he didn't have to refrigerate. As he was finishing up his French toast, he watched Beacon emerge from under the covers, stretch, jump down to the floor, and slowly move behind the stove.

"I guess she found the litter box," Dave uttered.

Dave visited a veterinarian on Stark Street, picked up some milk replacer formula, and asked when to feed Beacon solid food. The round trip only took forty-five minutes. The veterinarian sold Dave enough cat food for a couple of months for only ten dollars. Dave was very grateful for the generosity.

A strange thing happened as Dave was returning with the pet food. When he crossed the bridge on Stark Street, he glanced upstream and noticed a mist above the river. Just as he cleared the bridge he smelled smoke and realized he hadn't seen a mist of water, but smoke drifting across the river. A resident on the east side of the river was burning weeds and trash, creating a hazy cloud. A driver of a car passing over the bridge leaned out the window and said to Dave, "Kind of misty, huh?"

Dave smiled back at the driver and said, "Yeah, I think it's smoke." Dave suddenly realized Misty was the name of his wife. A warm feeling spread over his entire body as he smiled and said aloud, "My wife's name is Misty!" Now Dave knew it was just going to be a matter of time until he recalled all of his past life. His brain was healing!

CHAPTER 12

Julie

Following lunch, Dave had to work for Mr. Stenos. Almost an hour was spent moving hoses and sprinklers from one of the pasture areas to another. Then, he walked the perimeter of the farm and checked for fence breakages and signs of coyotes. The last thing on his work list, before he had some free time, was to check for children in the woods next to the old highway. Mr. Stenos liked to keep the woods free of trash and damage. In the past, kids had cut down some young trees and damaged much of the ground cover.

When Dave finished his inspection tour, he went back to the cabin and checked to see if Beacon was all right. The kitten was sound asleep on top of a stool Dave had made from cedar shakes and tree limbs. Dave added some syrup to a piece of toast and had an afternoon snack. He rinsed his sticky fingers in a bowl of water from the sprinklers and put on a pair of his homemade sandals.

The swimming area on the Sandy south of the bridge was part of a park that was the hub of recreational activity on the river. Two lifeguards were assigned to watch swimmers at all times. Rescues were not uncommon; kids underestimated the strength of the river's current and were swept away. People needed help if they were not strong swimmers or tried to swim against the current. Lifeguards gave frequent lectures about the dangers of the river, but the warnings were not always heeded.

Dave descended the slope to the highway, crossed the road and noticed a commotion about a hundred yards upstream. A canoe had overturned and onlookers were yelling for help. Dave watched from the bridge as one of the lifeguards grabbed a floatation device and began running along the riverbank toward the disturbance. Almost everyone's attention was drawn toward the accident, and when the first lifeguard arrived on scene, he waved to the other lifeguard that he needed help. Dave noted the concern of the second lifeguard for the swimmers in his area. Dave yelled at him. "Go! I'll take over here. I'm trained as a lifeguard. I'll watch the swimmers."

The second lifeguard ran to aid his coworker; Dave crossed the bridge and worked his way down to the lifeguard facility. The plywood shack had large open windows on three sides enabling a full view of the area where swimming was allowed. But Dave didn't enter the facility; he didn't really belong there. Standing next to the little building, he watched the activities of the kids and noticed someone he knew.

It was Julie Walser and her dog, Nittie. Julie must have ridden her bike to the river, or perhaps her mother had dropped them off. It was a long walk from her house. Dave looked around but didn't see anyone with whom she might be associating. Julie didn't see Dave; she was on the other side of the Sandy playing with Nittie. She had a stick and was throwing it for Nittie to retrieve. They seemed to be having a good time; Julie was laughing and Nittie was barking at Julie to throw the stick.

Dave shifted his attention to two boys about ten years old who were kicking a soccer ball around in the sand. One kick sent the ball over the head of the other boy. The ball dropped in the center of the thirty-yard-wide river and started floating downstream. Julie had been watching and yelled, "I'll get it!" Julie ran down the bank of the river as the ball gained speed. Dave noted that the water was much deeper where the river narrowed and traveled under the bridge.

It appeared if Julie entered the water she might get in trouble so he yelled at her, "Julie! Don't go in the water!"

It was too late. Julie had kicked off her shoes and dived into the deep swirling fast moving water. Dave watched as she disappeared beneath the surface. Nittie had followed Julie and was standing on the riverbank barking. The dog was standing in the sand, watching, expecting Julie to surface, but she didn't reappear. Nittie continued to bark as if to say, "Come back, Julie!"

As soon as Julie hit the water, Dave said, "Damn!" He ran as fast as he could, stripping off his shirt. He hadn't the time to remove his sandals; there was no time to stop and unlace them. Dave dived into the clear water and scanned for Julie but couldn't see her. As Dave surfaced, he yelled out, "Julie!"

"Over here, Dave! I'm over here!"

Dave looked under the bridge and could see Julie standing on the other bank holding the soccer ball. She was waving to him, jumping up and down. Nittie had seen her climb from the river and had run to greet Julie as she emerged from the water. Nittie was barking at Julie, wanting her to throw another stick.

"Stay there, Julie. I'll let the current carry me to you."

Dave could feel the water swirling below his feet as he drifted to the other side of the bridge. His feet banged into some logs and boulders as he moved through the water beneath the bridge. The submerged logs and boulders presented a real danger. Someone could get caught under water and not be strong enough to work free and surface. He would suggest a net be placed upstream from the bridge to prevent any disasters.

A strong swimmer, Dave still had to fight the current to reach the other side of the river downstream from the bridge. Julie extended a dead branch and Dave grabbed it when he was a few feet from her location. Julie leaned back and pulled Dave to the shore.

He crawled out of the water and stood up.

"Thanks Julie. That current is treacherous. How did you make it to shore?"

"I don't know. I was underwater and then all of a sudden I was tossed on the shore. It was like someone threw me. It was magical!"

"I guess some things happen without an explanation," Dave noted. "Let's get back to the recreation area. We've got to climb up to the road and cross the bridge."

CHAPTER 13

Closing In

More than a week after Dave left Truk and continued his journey up Buxton to the park, the PIs visited the Troutdale I-84 Truck Stop. They had missed a week of looking for Dave because of court appearances and gathering paperwork for their income taxes. Some things just couldn't be ignored; the extension on their taxes had just removed the tension temporarily.

The Hummer exited the freeway, had to stop for a red light, and then continued toward McDonalds. They pulled up outside the restaurant and surveyed the bustling truck stop.

"Over there, Chel," Rod said as he pointed to the disheveled man standing at the corner with a sign requesting money or food.

"I don't think that's our man."

"Me either, but we can ask him if he has seen the doc."

"Good idea, but don't get hit," Chello responded with a grin. "I don't want to pay for damage to a vehicle."

"Thanks a lot. Jesus, do I have to do everything? Okay, be right back!"

Rod looked back against oncoming traffic and hustled across two lanes of asphalt to the corner island. Truk saw Rod approaching, scowled and yelled at the intruder. "Hey! This is my corner!"

"Calm down old timer. I just need some information. Have you seen this man?"

Rod unrolled the picture of Dr. Coleman and held it so Truk could get a good look.

"Well, what'd he do? Why's he wanted?"

"His family is looking for him. He's got amnesia. My partner and I are trying to find him so he can return home to Nebraska. He's Doctor Clay Coleman."

"Yeah, I seen 'im."

"Great! Where is he?" asked Rod.

"I dun no."

Rod reached into his pocket, pulled out his wallet and held out a sawbuck. Truk looked at the ten-dollar bill and looked away. Rod put the ten back in his wallet and pulled out a twenty.

"Now yer talkin'! He stayed with me fer about a week and then took off walking up Buxton. Ain't seen him since. His name ain't Clay Coleman; it's Dave Buxton. You say he's a doctor?"

Truk reached out and snatched the bill from Rod's fingers.

"Yeah, he's a doctor. Thanks dude." Rod ran back across the road to Chello.

Chello looked questioningly at Rod and said, "Well?"

"He was here. He left a week ago and started up Buxton. Got the map?"

"Yeah, in the dash. The paper one's in the glove compartment. Let's go."

Rod turned the key and the Hummer's engine sprang to life. Chello punched in some information for the dash computer and a map of the area popped up.

"There's Buxton. We go over to the old highway, three blocks left, make a right, and go up the hill! Let's find Doctor Coleman!"

Chello was excited about their chances of converging on Dr. Coleman. Chello wondered if the doctor would remember him, they hadn't seen each other in over ten years. But, if Dr. Coleman had a beard, the PI might not recognize him, but Chello would remember the doctor's voice and mannerisms.

Rod could hear the excitement in Chello's voice. He wanted to get moving as fast as possible, but they had to avoid cars and trucks trying to get back on the freeway. He finally was given the opportunity; the tires spun and the Hummer lurched forward. Other drivers heard the squealing tires and stopped, letting the big Hummer have its way.

The two lights they encountered were both green, so they were on Buxton in less than a minute after leaving the truck stop. The speed limit was twenty-five but the Hummer was nearing forty when the PIs reached the top of the hill.

"Hey Rod, slow down, a minute more or less won't make any difference. And where are we going anyway?"

"There's a big park up here, I remember seeing it on the map back at the office. We make a left on Stark and the park is right where the bridge crosses over the Sandy River. We're only a few minutes away. Maybe someone has seen Dr. Coleman."

"I hope so, but with our luck, he has been there and gone," Chello replied.

Dave and Julie had been out of the water for less than fifteen minutes. Their clothes were almost dry. The lifeguards were still upstream where the boat had overturned and were tending to the three people that had fallen into the river. When Dave had resumed his position at the guard station, he could hear a siren approaching. An ambulance had been called for the injured boaters.

Julie and Dave were talking as they watched the kids playing on the shore and in the water.

"I need to return the pet carrier, Julie. Beacon doesn't need it now. She's used to staying in the cabin and I don't let her out alone."

"I know you want to meet my dad. He'll be home this weekend for a change. His job is almost finished, so he'll have a week or so off."

"Good, I'll come over and return the carrier."

The two boys that were kicking the soccer had just kicked it into the water again. One of them was wading in to get the ball. He suddenly disappeared from view. His friend yelled, "Help! Ruiz slipped and went under. He can't swim!"

Dave grabbed the inflation needle from the air pump and yelled for Julie to follow him. As he ran to the river, he put the needle in his pocket. Dave couldn't see the boy but had anticipated where the current had taken the kid.

"Julie! I'm going after the kid. Get the ball and bring it to me. If anyone has an inner tube, bring that, too; anything with air in it."

Dave scanned the river as he ran but couldn't see the boy. After Dave's earlier experience with the logs and rocks under the bridge, he felt the boy might be caught underwater. He had no time to lose.

He dived into the deep water and scanned for the boy. Previously, Dave had only seen logs lying on the river bottom, but now a log was sticking up at an angle toward the surface. The orientation of the waterlogged tree sections had changed from a half hour earlier. Their positions had shifted in the swirling water under the bridge.

Dave saw what he first thought was a tree branch but looked more closely. It was a boy's leg sticking up from near the bottom of the river. Dave fought the current and grabbed the tree above the boy. Dave saw the frightened look on the boy's face and knew he had to get air to the kid. The boy couldn't hold his breath much longer.

Dave was directly above the boy now. He wrapped his legs around the log and rose up. Dave's head was just above the surface. Julie was standing on the shore holding the soccer ball.

"Throw me the ball Julie!"

Dave was taking a big chance that Julie would be able to toss the ball accurately enough so he could catch it. Her toss was perfect. Dave grabbed the ball out of the air and disappeared beneath the surface of the churning water. He jammed the ball under his shirt so it couldn't get away and pulled the inflation needle from his pocket.

Dave rotated his body farther down into the water, extracted the ball from under his shirt, and inserted the needle into the valve using his finger to prevent air from escaping. The boy was nearly to the point of giving up; he couldn't hold his breath any longer. Air was escaping from his mouth and nose. The poor kid would start breathing water in a few seconds.

Dave held the ball close to the boy's mouth and released his finger. Bubbles shot from the needle and Ruiz realized what to do. The kid grabbed the ball and put his finger over the needle and into his mouth. Ruiz released the air and was able to take a breath. Dave signaled he would have to go up and the boy nodded.

When Dave took the ball underwater, Julie was yelling for help and people were coming to her aid. Chello and Rod had just driven up and were watching the commotion on shore beneath the bridge. They both jumped from the Hummer and ran to Julie.

Rod yelled, "What's going on?"

Chello was removing his shirt and shoes.

"My friend Dave is trying to get a boy from under the water. I think the boy is stuck. Can you help him?"

Rod said, "Damn! I can't swim."

"But I can!" Chello said as he waded into the water and submerged to see what was going on beneath the surface. He could see a man motioning to a boy that he had to go up.

Chello stood up, bracing himself against the swirling water.

Dave's head appeared. He gulped air to refill his lungs. Dave saw a very large man standing a couple of feet from him and instantly recognized him.

"I know you. You play football. You're Chello."

"Doc, what can I do?"

"There's a kid trapped between two logs and I can't get him out by myself. Help me lift the top log and I'll pull the boy out. Okay?"

"You got it Doc! Be right there."

Chello let the current carry him to the logs. He gulped some air and dropped beneath the surface. Dave gulped some air and joined Chello about five feet down into the whirling water. Chello could see the problem and moved to get his shoulder under the top log, his feet on the river bottom. Dave got between the logs holding the boy and motioned for Chello to lift. The two men pushed together and the upper log lifted off the boy's leg. Dave grabbed the boy and shoved him toward the surface. The soccer ball acted as a flotation device and Ruiz shot to the surface.

When Julie saw the boy appear above the surface, she jumped into the water up to her waist, grabbed the boy's shirt collar, and dragged him ashore. The youngsters were climbing out of the water when a loud roar of yells and clapping could be heard. Dave and Chello broke the surface of the water simultaneously and swam ashore after drifting under the bridge. The crowd of onlookers added more applause and cheers when they saw the two rescuers emerging from the river.

The boy, on his hands and knees, was crying and coughing. He rolled over onto his back and looked up at Julie standing over him.

"Oh! Thank you! Thank you!" he called out between coughs as he shivered from being in the cold water.

"You need to thank Dave and that big guy over there."

Julie pointed at Dave and Chello. The two men were emerging from the water fifteen feet farther downstream. Dave joined Julie, dropped to his knees next to the boy, checked his pulse, and skin color. Satisfied with the youngster's condition he stood up.

Dave looked at Julie and said, "Get some bath towels or a blanket and warm him up. You, too."

Chello addressed Dave, "Dr. Coleman, you remember me!"

Dave, a little confused, turned and looked at Chello.

"You're Chello Fredericks, but you don't belong here. You called me Dr. Coleman. Is that my name?"

Chello hugged Clay and said, "You're Dr. Clay Coleman. I've been looking for you for several months. Your wife contacted me to help find you. She's waiting to hear that you're all right and are coming home. Misty and the kids want you back home in Nebraska."

As Chello continued to talk with Clay, a helicopter was landing about a hundred yards upstream in an open area. The chopper was from a Portland TV station. Two people were running toward the bridge, one carried a camera, the other a microphone. They arrived at the bridge and began asking questions. In less than a minute, Clay, Chello, Julie and Rod were being interviewed about the harrowing experience.

As the reporter was talking with Clay and Chello, Julie walked over to Ruiz and escorted him to the reporter.

The boy told the reporter what had happened, and how the two men had freed him from the logs that were holding him underwater. He went to Clay and Chello, shook hands with the men and gave them each a big hug. He began to cry but was able to say, "Thank you for saving me." Clay put his arm around the boy and held him until he quit crying.

Julie told the reporter how Dr. Coleman had used the soccer ball to supply air for Ruiz while he was submerged for so long. Rod mentioned that he wasn't able to help because he couldn't swim. He recommended that everyone learn how to swim.

Following the interview, the reporter and cameraman worked their way upstream to the location of the boat accident to conduct a second interview.

Chello pulled his phone from his pocket but realized it had been underwater and wouldn't work. He wanted to call Misty. Chello, Clay and Rod walked to the Hummer to use the car phone. Rod got in the passenger seat and started talking on his cell phone.

"Who are you talking to, Rod?"

"Lorraine. I told her we'd be in the news tonight. She thinks I'm kidding."

Chello took the phone from Rod and said, "Lorraine, he's not kidding. We should be on Channel 8 at five o'clock." He grinned.

Call Home

Misty had just gotten home from the hospital. After the first month of Clay's disappearance, she had realized she couldn't simply sit at home and wait for the phone to ring. She had house keys made for the kids and gave them instructions for being home alone. They would be alone for only a couple of hours each day.

Eric was watching the five o'clock network news and Emma was setting the table for dinner. Eric suddenly saw his dad on the screen.

"Mom! Emma! Come here! Dad's on TV!"

Misty dropped her purse and keys on the floor and rushed to the TV set. Emma ran from the kitchen to see if Eric was right. They dropped to their knees in front of the screen but were having trouble understanding what was going on.

Emma yelled at Eric, "Turn it up!"

Eric pressed the sound button several times. The speakers were blasting the room full of strange voices, except for one.

They were transfixed watching Clay talking to the reporter. So happy to see Clay again, they began hugging each other. Misty began to cry and didn't hear a word that was said. Emma had tears running down her cheeks and Eric, tears in his eyes, was hugging Warren.

The phone rang once, then again and again. Misty heard the third ring and answered the phone.

"Hello?" She motioned to Eric to turn the sound down so she could hear the voice on the phone.

"Oh! Hi Chello! Yes, we just saw you and Clay on TV. Tell me what was going on. We were so excited to see Clay, we couldn't figure out what happened. Did he save somebody from drowning?"

The PI told Misty the whole story, how Clay had used the soccer ball for air and how he and Clay had gotten the boy out from under the logs.

"Can I talk with Clay, Chello?"

"Yes, but he doesn't remember some things yet. Keep it simple."

"Okay. Oh, it is you Clay. It's so good to hear your voice! I love you! When will you be home, sweetie?"

Clay didn't quite know what to say except to answer Misty's questions. How could he say he loved her when all he could remember was her name?

"I'll be home in a few days. I have to take care of a few things here before I can leave. I'll call you and let you know when I'll be at the airport. You and the kids can come and get me. How are Emma and Warren?"

"They're fine, Clay. Eric is fine too."

"I wasn't worried about the dog, Misty."

"Warren is the dog, sweetheart. Eric is your son."

"I'm sorry. Things are a bit confusing. I'll get it right when I get home."

"Don't worry, Clay. We'll help you get back to normal."

"You'll have to be patient with me. I'm a little hazy right now. I'll tell you everything when I get home. Okay?"

"All right. I love you. Bye for now Clay."

"Bye Misty. Tell the kids I'll see them in a few days, Warren too."

The next day, Clay began preparing for his trip home. He faced some tough decisions for ending this part of his life, a part he knew more closely than his previous one. Beacon had to stay in Troutdale.

Clay felt as if he was deserting his tiny kitten in her time of need. He put Beacon in the carrier and began the walk to Julie's house, carrier in one hand and a bag of cat food in the other.

What if Walsers didn't want the kitten? He held the carrier up and looked at the wide-eyed cute little ball of fur. Clay felt his throat tighten as tears came to his eyes. The little cat had been his for a short period but he had grown to love her. She had slept beside him on the cot at night for more than a week. Clay had enjoyed the company Beacon had provided, but sometimes things had to be done whether he liked them or not.

Mr. Walser's pickup was in the driveway. Clay had told Julie that he wanted to meet her father. This was the last chance he would have to do that. Chello was going to take Clay to the airport in the early afternoon.

Clay went to the door and pressed the doorbell. Two tones sounded and, after a short pause, the door swung open. It was Julie.

"Come in Dr. Coleman! I want you to meet my dad."

"That's one of the reasons I'm here, Julie. Would you take care of Beacon? She needs a good home."

"Oh, Dr. Coleman, that would be wonderful! Thank you."

Julie took the carrier and the bag of food and asked Clay to follow her into the kitchen. Mr. and Mrs. Walser were sitting at the kitchen table drinking coffee. They both stood when Clay entered the room. Mr. Walser extended his hand and Clay felt the grasp of a man that worked with his hands day in, day out. Marcia introduced the men and commented, "Ken, Dr. Coleman is wearing some of your old clothes."

"They seem to fit the doctor better than they did me," he laughed. "I'm glad they were put to good use."

"I want to thank you for your kindness. I'll be going back to my family this afternoon. I was fortunate to meet your family, Ken. Marcia and Julie are wonderful ladies."

Ken said, "I think so too. We'll miss you, Doctor. You've done some good things for our city."

"Well, I've got to be going. I have to see my employer about some things before I get on the plane. I'll send you a card when I get home. We'll keep in touch. I'd like Julie to meet my daughter, Emma. Maybe our families can get together sometime soon. Goodbye."

The Walser family, including Nittie, followed Clay to the door and said goodbye.

Clay waved and wiped away some tears as he started the return trip to his shack.

His temporary home looked very lonely standing under the pines, isolated from the main farm buildings. Clay took a few minutes to clean up and then walked to the farmhouse to talk to Mr. Stenos. Stenos understood Clay's desire to get back to his family and wished him good luck. Clay offered to refund some of his first month's salary but Stenos refused. Stenos told Clay he deserved a reward for saving the boy from drowning. They shook hands and Clay returned to the shack one last time.

Clay entered the tired little building and looked around. There was nothing there but a few memories and they would wane as his new life grew in importance. The few things Clay had assembled for his life there were left for the next occupant. Clay's Timex read 10:15 a.m. It was time to get down to the highway to find Chello.

As Clay approached the bridge, he could see the big silver-gray Hummer arriving to take him to the airport. Chello and Clay had planned to meet at 10:30, but Chello had come a little early. Clay climbed into the Hummer and they drove slowly away from the bridge.

"I see you don't have luggage, Dr. Coleman."

"Please call me Clay, Chello."

"That seems strange to me. How about Doc?"

"Okay, Mr. Fredericks," Clay chuckled.

"I'll bet you're excited about going home."

"Yes, but a little nervous, too. I don't remember what my family looks like."

"Well, let me tell you. Misty is a gorgeous woman and although I haven't seen Emma and Eric, I'll bet they are very nice looking kids. You are very lucky in a way."

"What's that?" Clay replied.

"You get to fall in love with a beautiful woman a second time. Plus, you will love two kids and a dog all over again! You should be looking forward to all that."

"I hadn't thought of it that way, Chello. You are a very intelligent PI."

"Thanks, Doc! I never thought I would be called intelligent by a doctor," Chello grinned.

Clay called Misty from the airport and gave her his flight number and arrival details. The plane landed in Lincoln right on time. Misty and the kids waited at Gate 12. To Misty, each minute seemed like an hour. The kids watched intently as the passengers deplaned and entered the waiting area. Misty saw him first, pointed at Clay and said, almost yelling, "There he is!"

They had to wait for Clay to clear the crowd. He stood with a blank look on his face, not knowing what to expect. Misty and the kids ran to him and they had a group hug. Misty stood on her tiptoes and kissed Clay. Clay wasn't sure how to react, but he grabbed Misty around the waist and kissed her, then hugged Emma and Eric again.

He looked at all three smiling faces and knew he was home. The ordeal was over, and Clay was right where he was supposed to be.

The Pumpkin Tree

Mission to Grandma's

"Joey! Time to get up! I have to be at the bank at eight o'clock." Marion Wilson, Joey's mom, was calling to her seven year old son at 7:14 a.m. Marion, a bookkeeper, had to drop Joey off at school and continue on to Western State Bank. She could have worked at the other bank, Western National, but the commute was longer. That extra half-mile every day would put more strain on their old, gray '39 Packard.

"Okay Mom! I'm up!" Joey yelled back.

Joey tossed back the sheet, changed his underwear, and wiggled into his white corduroy pants. The belt Grandma had given him for Christmas didn't hold up his pants 'cause his hips were small, so he wore suspenders and a belt. Grandpa said Joey needed to wear suspenders, but hardly any of the boys wore them anymore. Grandma said Joey didn't need to have plumber's butt. Joey laughed when she said stuff like that. He pulled a yellow T-shirt over his head and stuck his arms through the holes. He liked the bright yellow shirt with red stripes around the waist.

Joey dug three white socks out of the top bureau drawer, checked for holes, tossed the worst one back, and shoved the drawer closed.

He sat on the floor, pulled on his socks and slipped into his brown oxfords. As he pulled the left shoelace up tight, it snapped.

"Mom! My darn shoelace broke!"

"That's okay. I have some spares, but only black ones. What color do you need?"

"Brown, for my brown shoes."

"Well, black will have to do for today. Why don't you wear your old black shoes? I'll get some more brown laces today on the way home."

Joey thought about putting on his old shoes, but he would have to shine them. It would take too long; he'd get polish on his fingers, and then he'd have to scrub his fingers. He would wear his newer shoes with a black lace on the left foot. Joey removed his left shoelace and put on the shoe. After putting on the right shoe and tying the lace, he clomped down the hallway and went downstairs to the kitchen for breakfast.

Joey could hear his dad backing his recently purchased brown Ford pickup down the driveway and into the street. Joey looked out the side window and watched the pickup move out of sight. Joe Sr. was pretty proud of his new pickup. It was 1949 and most everyone was still fairly conservative after living with few excesses during the war. Joe Wilson needed the pickup for his furniture business. Senior had tried to find a used pickup, but veterans had bought up all but the ones that nobody could fix. Marion and Joe Sr. had discussed buying a pickup last December.

Joey remembered hearing his mom and dad talking about buying the pickup. A couple of weeks before Christmas, Joey heard his parents talking about the little truck. A grating in the living room ceiling opened on the second floor in Joey's bedroom near the door. Following Thanksgiving, as soon as Joey was ready for bed, he crouched down above the grating and began listening to conversations, hoping to hear some Christmas secrets. He knew eavesdropping wasn't right, but Joey couldn't help himself. Most of what he heard was of no interest to Joey, but he remembered one conversation because of his dad's promise to his mom.

"Joe, you have to promise me not to use our emergency fund to make payments on the pickup. What if one of us, or Joey, gets sick?"

"I've already thought of that. I'm going to put a note on the bulletin board down at McKuehen's grocery store to find out how much customer interest there would be in making deliveries. I think I can make the $37.91 monthly payments from selling firewood, delivering groceries and newspapers, and taking trash to the dump outside of town. So, I promise. Anyway, it will be a few months before I buy the truck. I've got to be sure I can make the payments."

Six months of the three-year truck contract had passed, and Joe Sr. hadn't missed a single payment. But Joe was already feeling the strain of the extra work. However, Marion steadfastly refused to dip into the family emergency fund in order to make loan repayments. She wished Joe had borrowed a pickup for his furniture business deliveries.

Christmas orders were already coming in, and Joe Sr. started going to work an hour earlier, around 7:00 a.m., the day Joey started the second grade. That gave him five more hours of work per week. Wilson's furniture store was next to the post office on Main Street. Sewicholah, Washington was a town of around 1,400 people twenty miles northwest of Yakima. Having the post office next door to the furniture business was pretty handy most of the time, but there were a few exceptions. Occasionally, someone would enter the furniture store, interrupt Joe Sr., and ask for postage stamps.

Joey sat at the kitchen table and looked at the empty bowl in front of him. Would it be Corn Flakes or Cheerios today? The Corn Flakes were crispy and crunched when he chewed even though he had added plenty of milk. He would rather have them crunchy than soft though. When the flakes were gummy, they stuck to his teeth.

"Finish up, Joey. We have to lock the doors and leave. Do you have to take anything to school today?"

"Nope, just my lunch box." Joey finished his orange juice with two big gulps and picked up his lunch box from the counter near the back door.

"Joey, your hair's a mess. Go in the bathroom and fix it."

Joey went to the bathroom, leaned over the sink, and looked in the mirror. His long brown hair was mussed up, so he got both hands wet, ran his fingers through his mop, and used his dad's big comb to straighten his unruly hair.

"Joey, let's go. You can put on your shoelace in the car."

It was two weeks into September. Joey had started the second grade on the 3rd. That was last Monday, over a week ago. Today was Thursday. The elementary school was only five blocks from Joey's house, so it was an easy walk home from school. As usual, Joey's mom dropped him off a few minutes before the first bell rang. Students were late after the second bell, which rang ten minutes later.

One day last summer, Joey asked his mom what she did at the bank. She told him she had to enter lots of numbers in big books called ledgers. Joey admired his mom's beautiful handwriting and her numbers were something to behold. Joey hoped to be able to write like that someday. His mom said it just took practice and pride in doing a good job. She was pretty good with numbers. Marion showed Joey a few tricks that would help him find errors in his arithmetic.

School let out at 2:00 p.m. for first and second graders. Buses didn't arrive until 2:30, but Joey walked. He would be home in ten minutes. His grandparents lived three blocks from the school but on a different street than the one he normally took. Today, Joey would pay them a visit. He stopped in to see them about once a week, but the time of the week he stopped by varied. Joey walked with his classmate and friend, Zachery Conners, a block farther than his normal turn to go home. Zak was slightly shorter than Joey and wore dark, plastic-rimmed glasses. Zak had a crew cut and his glasses seemed to stick out from his head, 'cause his ears were small. He resembled a smooth melon with glasses attached. Zak had to travel three more blocks to get home, so they said, "See yah tomorrow," and continued on their separate ways. Joey turned right and walked about a block and a half. Grandma's was the third house on the left side of the street.

The mailbox had Bertelson and the number 621 painted on it. Harriet and Claude were Joey's grandparents. Joey had only one set of grandparents; his dad's parents had passed away before Joey was born, so he never knew them. They had lived in Canada on a farm near Lethbridge. His dad's four sisters had all lived in Canada at some time. Two of them still lived there; one had died of pneumonia when a teenager and the other one lived in Pasco, Washington. The two Canadians had trained their little dogs to hide under the car seats when they came to the U.S.-Canada border. They didn't have any papers from the vets saying their dogs were disease free. Fortunately, the little dogs were never sick. Joey's dad was born in Oregon and was the youngest of the five Wilson children. He had been a handsome man when younger, but had aged noticeably during the war.

Grandma and Grandpa were about the same height. They weren't very tall. They were about the same height as Joey's mom. Marion was five feet four, wore glasses, had black hair, and big bosoms. Grandma had big bosoms, too, but over the years they had sagged. Grandpa was a little taller, maybe an inch or two. Both had white hair, Grandpa's was wavy and Grandma's was curly. Joey noticed Grandma's hair was a little more gray than white and she made jokes about going bald. When she wanted to look real nice, she wore a hairpiece, so her hair had two colors. It made her a little taller. She wore gold-colored, wire-rimmed glasses and had all her teeth.

Grandpa was retired and had false teeth. He had been a Sheriff's deputy and a prison guard for many years. As a young man, he had served in the U. S. Army during the Spanish American War. Grandpa had been a pitcher on a minor league baseball team. He used to tell Joey that his index finger on his right hand was longer than the one on his left hand 'cause of throwing a baseball so much. Joey liked to believe Grandpa's right index finger was his trigger finger and was stretched from shooting lots of bullets. Joey didn't know if Grandpa ever shot a prisoner or anybody during the war. Grandpa never said.

Bertelson's home wasn't very big, but the nice front porch had some rockers and a little three-legged table for snacks and a Bible. Grandma would sit on the porch and write letters to her friends in Tennessee. Grandma was born and grew up in Tennessee. Saturday morning was usually her day for writing. Joey once asked Grandma why she looked in the Bible when she was writing letters. She told him she didn't have a dictionary so she looked up words in the Bible. She knew where the words were from reading the Bible for many years. She hadn't had much education, but Joey thought she was pretty smart. Her cookies were delicious, especially the chocolate chip ones.

As Joey approached the house, he could see Grandpa sitting on the porch doing something on top of the little white table. When Joey stepped on the first of three steps up to the porch, Grandpa looked up.

"Well, hello Junior."

"Hi Grandpa. Whatcha doin'?"

"I'm sharpening my pocketknife. It needs to be real sharp so I can get the corn off the cob at dinner time."

"Oh. Is Grandma inside?"

"Nope."

"Where is she?"

"Out back in the garden."

"Can I go see her?"

"Yep. Make sure you latch the gate."

"Okay. I'll leave my lunch box here. See you later."

Joey went to the side of the house where the gate was. The fence was painted light blue, not white like all the others. Grandpa had gotten the paint on sale. Someone didn't like the color and had returned the paint, so it was cheap. Grandpa said he liked to be different; why should all fences be white? Was there a law?

Joey opened the gate and could see Grandma on her hands and knees in the garden. She was picking weeds out of the vegetable area. Near the garage, Grandpa had some raspberry plants. The garden areas took up most of the back yard. Grandpa had also planted some corn next to the garage but it hadn't done very well. But corn was cheap at the grocery.

Joey remembered watching Grandpa cut the corn off the cob with his pocketknife at a family dinner. Grandpa said the table knives weren't sharp enough to do a good job; they just mushed up the corn. Grandpa cut the kernels off the cob and ate them with a fork. He couldn't bite the corn off the cob; his false teeth would come loose.

Joey closed the gate behind him and heard it latch. Grandma looked up.

"Hello Joey!" she said with a smile. Grandma always smiled at Joey. When he tipped over some milk one time, she smiled and said, "No matter, we can wipe it up." Joey liked his grandma's eyes. They kind of danced behind her glasses.

"Hi Grandma. Are you gettin' all the weeds?"

"I sure am. I wish the vegetables would grow as fast. I think your dad and grandpa are going to have to put up chicken wire to keep the turtles and rabbits from eating the vegetables."

"Turtles and rabbits?"

"Uh huh. I can see on the plants where they've been having dinner. Got any news from your mom for me?"

"Yes ma'am. She wants to know if you would like to go to the fruit stand out at Washburn's farm on Saturday."

"That sounds like fun. I should make some pies. Tell her I'd like to do that. Have her call me, so I'll know what time to be ready, and if I need a box."

"Okay, I'll tell her."

"How's school?"

"It's okay. We're doing cursive in our tablets and some arithmetic. In the first grade we could only print. The teacher said we have better coordination now so we're learning to write longhand."

"That sounds right to me. I hope you work hard in school, Joey. These days, good jobs require a good education."

"I'm try'n hard, Grandma. Activities are the most fun though. I like to draw stuff and listen to stories."

"Your mom used to like to draw and color. I think I still have some of her pictures from grade school. I'll show them to you sometime. Did you see your Grandpa?"

"Uh huh. He was on the front porch sharpening his knife."

"Well, he does more sharpening than cutting, if you ask me. He used to do some woodcarving, but arthritis in his hands prevents that now. How's your dad's furniture business going?"

"Okay, I guess. He told Mom about some orders he got the other day. Some people ordered rocking chairs for Christmas."

"Well, in my opinion, your dad has magic in his hands. He does beautiful work."

"I'll tell him you said that, Grandma."

"You do that. Let's go out front and see what Grandpa is doing." Grandma struggled to her feet, removed her gloves, and wiped her forehead with the back of her hand. "I need to wash up."

They walked toward the gate. Joey suddenly darted ahead, unhooked the latch, and held the gate open for his grandma.

"Thank you Joey."

Joey closed the gate and made sure it was latched. He didn't want to see Grandpa's mean face. When Joey was younger, Grandpa's mean face made Joey cry, his eyes looked like he wanted to shoot someone.

Grandpa was still on the porch, but he had put his knife away.

"Claude, I'm going in to clean up. Can you talk with the boy?"

"Sure can. I've got a story to tell him."

"Remember what I told you about your stories."

Grandpa hooked his foot around the leg of the other wicker chair and pulled it out from the table so Joey would be facing him.

"Sit right here, Junior." Grandpa pointed at the chair.

Joey climbed into the chair and slid his butt back.

"Are you comfy?"

"Yes sir."

When Joey sat back in the chair, his feet didn't touch the floor. They stuck straight out.

Grandpa looked into the house through the screen door and then back at Joey.

"Do you know what grows on trees? I mean besides leaves and branches."

"Yes sir. Apples, peaches, oranges, and…"

"And some others. Okay. Those are all fruits. What about pumpkins?"

"Umm, I don't think so. They grow on the ground. I think they're too heavy for trees."

"You are correct except for one kind. They are small and have colored spots on them."

"Where do they grow, Grandpa?"

"They grow on trees."

"No Grandpa, I mean where in the world do they grow?"

"Oh! They grow on the Philippine Islands out in the Specific Ocean. I saw them in pictures during the War. The tree is called a Pumpkin Pine. The locals make pie from the pumpkins, pumpkin pine pie. My buddies called it 3-P dessert. Whipped cream from goat's milk goes on top. It's pretty tasty. My Army buddies told me they had some after dinner one night."

"Gee, do you think Mom could make some for us?"

"I think she's too busy. There's a lot of preparation of ingredients and there's a special oven temperature. If the recipe isn't followed exactly, it tastes terrible. Over the years, the native people figured out how to take the bad taste out, but they kept it a secret. Let's keep the story between you and me, okay? That will be our secret. Next time we talk, I'll tell you how the pumpkin pine pumpkins got their spots."

The conversation was interrupted when Grandma came out on the porch.

"Well, I'm ready to walk you home Joey."

Grandma had put on a blue dress, white shoes and a white hat. She looked nice, almost like she was going to church.

"Here Joey, take my hand."

Joey reached out, took Grandma's left hand in his, and they took the three steps down to the brick pathway. Grandma took one step at a time. She was afraid to lose her balance.

"Oops. I forgot my lunchbox."

Joey released Grandma's hand and grabbed his lunchbox from the top of the porch. Grandma had walked a little farther so Joey ran to catch up. He took her right hand in his left.

As they approached the city sidewalk Grandma turned and said, "Claude, I'll be back in about a half hour or so."

"See you later Grandpa," Joey waved his lunchbox.

"Okay," Grandpa answered.

CHAPTER 2

Credibility Questions

Joey looked up at his grandma and said, "Shall we cross the street here Grandma?"

"No Joey. Let's wait 'til we get to the corner. We don't want to be jaywalkers. In some places the police can give you a ticket if you jaywalk."

"What's jaywalking? That's a funny word."

"That's when you cross a street in other than proper places for walking. Lots of people don't pay attention to the rules anymore, but you should learn the right way to do things. There's less chance of being hit by a car if you cross in the right place, usually at the corner."

Joey and his grandmother crossed the street at the corner and continued walking on the concrete, but on lawns where no sidewalks existed.

"What did you and your grandpa talk about, Joey?"

Joey remembered Grandma telling Grandpa he shouldn't tell anymore stories. Joey didn't want to lie so he said, "Fruit trees and vegetables."

"When we get apples on Saturday, I'll make some pies and applesauce. Your grandpa likes whipped cream on his pie. I like to use red delicious apples for my pies because they don't need much sugar."

"Boy, there sure is a lot to learn, Grandma."

"That's why you go to school Joey."

"Where did you go to school, Grandma?"

"Tennessee. Do you know where that is Joey?"

"I think so, but I can look at a map to make sure."

"When I was a girl, school wasn't so important. After we learned to read and write, we found a job to help with the family or we got married. I quit school after the eighth grade."

"But you're smart, Grandma!"

"Life teaches a person a lot of things Joey."

"Look! There's our car. Mom is home from work."

"It must be after three o'clock. You can go the rest of the way by yourself Joey. My legs are sore. Remember to tell your mom to call me."

"I will Grandma. Have a nice walk back home."

Joey walked and skipped about a block to his two-story yellow house. Joey walked up the six steps to the screen door on the covered porch spelling encyclopedia, two letters for each step. He opened the front door and yelled, "Hi Mom! Where's the encyclopedia?"

Joey's mom was in the kitchen putting groceries in the cupboards. She came to the living room, looked around, and said, "Joey, we don't have an encyclopedia. Where's your grandma?"

"She said her legs were tired, so I walked the rest of the way by myself."

"I wish mother had come to the house. I could have given her a ride home."

"Mom, what's that big book with the maps called?"

"That's an atlas."

"Oh. Where's the atlas?"

"I think it's on top of the piano. Do you want me to get it for you?"

"No thanks, I'm big enough. I can get it."

Joey climbed on the piano seat so he could see on top of the upright piano and spotted the red, white, and black atlas cover. He moved the artificial flower arrangement, lifted the big atlas off the top of the piano, and jumped to the floor. Joey paused to think for a second or two and took the atlas to the dining room table. If necessary, he wanted to be able to ask his mom some questions.

"Oh! Grandma said you should call her. She wants to get some apples for pies. She needs to know what time and if she should have a box."

"Thank you, Joey. I got you some brown shoestrings." She held out the shoestrings, and Joey put them in his pocket. "Thanks Mom."

Joey found the Glossary and ran his finger down the page to Philippine Is. It said page 19. He turned to page 19 and began looking. *There it is, Philippine Is.* He inspected the shapes of the green islands and then looked at the large expanse of blue ocean east of the islands. The ocean was labeled Pacific Ocean, not Specific Ocean as Grandpa had said. Joey wondered if he had heard correctly, or perhaps Grandpa's false teeth kept him from saying Pacific. Or maybe Grandpa was just making it all up? Grandpa was known for being a little tricky. He liked to tell funny jokes and embarrass family members. Joey looked up from the atlas at his mom.

"Mom, was Grandpa ever in the Philippine Islands during the war?"

"No. He was in Cuba during the Spanish-American War of 1898."

Joey thought for a moment. *So Grandpa was in Cuba during the war, not in the Philippine Islands. I'll have to ask him if he said he was in the Philippine Islands. If he says yes, then I'll know his story was just made up.* Joey knew from past experience he had to be careful about what Grandpa told him. One time when Joey was chewing bubble gum and the family was about to eat dinner, Grandpa told him to put the gum behind his ear. The gum got in Joey's hair and Mom got mad at Grandpa.

"Mom, when will Dad be home?"

"He said he would get here about six o'clock Joey. Why?"

"We're s'posed to play catch before dinner."

"Well, when he gets home, give him a chance to relax a few minutes before you remind him about playing catch. I'm sure he will want to though, maybe after dinner."

"Okay."

After dinner, Joey's mom called Grandma and they set the time to get apples at 9:00 o'clock Saturday morning. Dad had to work so Joey would have to stay with Grandpa until the women came back with the fruit. Joey and his dad played catch for a while after dinner. Joey had a catcher's glove to catch the hard ball. The gloves with fingers cost more. Big Joe used his bare hands.

"Dad, Grandma said to say you have magic in your hands. You do beautiful work."

"Is that right? I'll have to thank her. Thanks for telling me that."

"You're welcome."

After playing catch, Joey and his dad went in the house and listened to The Lone Ranger on the radio in the living room.

When he heard he had to stay with Grandpa on Saturday, Joey began thinking of things to ask the former soldier and deputy. Joey had all day Friday to think up some good questions.

Saturday with Grandpa

Joey woke up at 8:00 a.m. Saturday morning to a beautiful, clear-blue sky. The sun was out and it looked like the day was going to be nice and warm. The dew on the lawn would be gone before long. Mom and Grandma would have a great day to shop for fruit, and Joey was looking forward to spending the day with Grandpa and listening to his story. Dad had already gone to the shop to work on furniture.

Joey pulled on his jeans and a white T-shirt. He pulled the neck of a sweatshirt over his head, worked it over his ears, and then slid his hands through the arms. Even though the sun was out, it was cool. Mom suggested the sweatshirt to prevent goose bumps. Joey added milk to a bowl of cereal, sprinkled on a bit too much sugar, and poured some orange juice. After eating the Cheerios, he picked up the bowl and drank the leftover sweetened milk. The juice went down in five big swallows. The orange juice tasted funny after eating the sugared cereal.

Joey put his dirty dishes on the counter next to the kitchen sink and went to his bedroom to put on his tennis shoes. Mom told him to put on white socks but he liked the softer gray ones. So, he put on one gray sock and one white sock. Joey didn't like to disobey his mom, but if she checked his socks, he would show her the foot with the white sock. He was pretty sure she wouldn't check both feet. Joey just had to remember which foot had the white sock.

"Joey, we have to go now," Mom yelled from downstairs.

Joey ran down the stairs, out to the car, and climbed in the front seat. He had to wait for his mom to lock the kitchen door and get in the car. She carried a couple of empty apple crates and put them in the trunk. In a couple of minutes, they arrived at Bertelsons'. When they pulled over in front of the house, Grandma was standing on the parking strip by the curb. She had been pulling up dandelions as she waited. Joey jumped out of the car, held the door while Grandma backed toward the front seat, sat sideways, and swung her legs into the car.

"Okay Joey, you can close the door now," his mom instructed.

Joey slammed the door and stepped away from the car toward the house.

"See you later, alligator," Grandma said with a smile and a wave of her black purse as the car pulled away from the curb.

"Grandpa! Where are you?" Joey yelled. Joey could barely hear, "I'm out in back in the garden." Grandpa rarely yelled, so Joey had to listen carefully. The only words he heard clearly were *back* and *garden*. Joey walked to the gate and went into the backyard.

"Did you close the gate?"

"Yes Grandpa."

"Good boy!"

"What are you doing?"

"I'm getting some raspberries to put on my cereal."

Grandpa was picking raspberries and putting them in a cereal bowl. Joey looked in the bowl and could see about a dozen berries, tiny bits of leaves, and some dirt.

"That's enough berries, I just need a taste. Let's go inside."

Grandpa rinsed his little cluster of berries and tossed them on a paper towel to remove most of the water.

"Joey, take a seat at the table. Do you want to eat something?"

"No thank you, Grandpa. I just had some cereal and orange juice."

"Well, I'm having some cereal with raspberries and a few raisins. Keeps me regular."

"Regular, Grandpa?"

"Yep. In a few hours I'll go in the bathroom with the newspaper and do my duty."

"Don't you use toilet paper Grandpa?"

The old man laughed. "You don't understand. I read the newspaper while I'm sitting there," smiled Grandpa.

"Oh, I get it." Joey smiled back.

As his grandpa ate, Joey asked some questions.

"Were you ever in the Philippines, Grandpa?"

Joey was ready for his grandpa to say yes, but he was surprised.

"Never was, Joey, but I was in Cuba."

That confirmed what his mom had said. Grandpa had been in Cuba during the war.

"How did you get there, by airplane?"

"Nope. We went in a large ship with our supplies. We didn't have airplanes then."

"Really? That must have been a long time ago." Joey thought he would kid his grandpa so he said, "Were there any dinosaurs around then?"

Grandpa smiled and laughed, "Good one, Joey."

How did those friends of yours get to the Philippines?"

"Same way, big ships. That war took place in 1898, Joey. It was a long ocean trip to the Philippines. Lots of the guys got seasick."

"Didn't you get seasick going to Cuba?"

"Nope. It was a short trip and the water was calm." He slid his chair back and stood. "Well, I've finished my cereal. Let's go out on the porch and I'll tell you about those pumpkin trees in the Philippines."

Joey and Grandpa took their favorite places on the front porch and Grandpa started his story.

"It was about 400 years ago. At that time, the only visitors to the islands in the South Pacific were from islands nearby or from Mainland China. But new explorers came from Europe. They had guns and other things the natives hadn't ever seen. The explorers had something else that was very bad for the natives, sickness."

"What kind of sickness, Grandpa?"

"Pox, Joey."

"What's pox?"

"Well, I know of chickenpox and smallpox. They cause fever, vomiting, and sores on the skin."

"I think I had a vaccination for smallpox, Grandpa. See, I have a scar on my arm."

Joey put two fingers in the neck of his sweatshirt and pulled the shirt over his shoulder so the scar on his upper arm was visible.

"Probably for chickenpox too, Joey." Grandpa continued, "A little native girl got sick with pox and the tribe doctor didn't know what to do. After the sores appeared on her skin, the doctor made a creamy mixture from pumpkin seeds, flower seeds and chicken fat. He smeared the mixture on the sores. In a few days the sores were gone and the girl recovered."

Joey was giving Grandpa his rapt attention and was leaning forward in his wicker chair. Grandpa leaned back and ran his fingers through his wavy white hair. As he leaned back, Joey leaned farther forward as if to keep the same distance between them. Suddenly Joey jumped up and shook his right leg.

"Pins and needles, Grandpa!"

"Your leg fell asleep. It better not snore!" Grandpa grinned.

"Grandpa! Not that kind of sleep."

"I know, Joey. I'm just kidding. The edge of the chair shut off the circulation in your leg. Stand up and move around for a minute."

Joey jumped up and down a few times and sat back down with his rump on the edge of the chair so his leg wouldn't do that again. Using both hands, he rubbed his legs. He looked at Grandpa and said, "Did the little girl have some scars?"

"Sure, pox always leaves some scars when the sores heal. After several days in the heat, the leftover creamy mixture started to stink, so the native doctor buried it with some garbage and old pumpkin seeds. The garbage contained some of the used mixture that had been wiped from the girl's body. Well, about two months later, the natives noticed a new plant growing in the vicinity of the little girl's hut."

"What did the plant look like?"

"It was about your size with small green and yellow flowers that had spotted seeds the size of raisins in their centers. The flowers looked like little sunflowers. The people harvested many seeds from the plant. They tried to eat the dried seeds, but the seeds tasted terrible. The natives spit them out on the ground. In another few months, there were small trees growing everywhere a person spit. With all the heat and rain in that area, several crops can grow in one year, Joey."

"Did the little trees have leaves or flowers?"

"No flowers. As the days passed, the trees grew fairly tall, over ten feet, and buds appeared on the limbs along with some leaves. At first the buds grew in the shape of a pickle. After a week or so, the end of the pickle grew round and started expanding."

"I know! I bet they looked like little pumpkins," suggested Joey.

"You're right, Joey, and they had spots on them. Those spotted pumpkins were about this big." Grandpa made a fist with one hand and put the other hand over his fist.

Joey thought for a few seconds. The only food he knew of with pumpkin in it was pumpkin pie. "Did they make pie from the pumpkins?"

"They tried, Joey, but the cooked pumpkin pies tasted real bad, just like the seeds from the flowers. They tried cookies, too. They tried putting sugarcane in the pies and cookies but they couldn't overcome the bad taste. So, they just used the pumpkins for decorations at their festivals. It took many years before someone figured out how to take the bad taste out of the food made with those pumpkins. The natives didn't write down how they did it but they knew the secret. A few years ago some chefs in France figured out how to treat the pumpkins so they wouldn't taste bad."

"I don't think I'd like being a chef. I like to get my food from a box, like cereal. And I don't need to be a chef to make pancakes or waffles. Mom and dad do that all the time."

"Chefs usually work at big hotels and restaurants, Joey. They make good money there."

"Grandpa, the only chefs I've ever seen are fat."

"Yep! They have to taste their food to see if it's okay for others to eat. They munch all day long. Hey Joey, do you want to help me put together a jigsaw puzzle? I just got a new one and it looks like it's going to be a doozie. It's a sailing ship on the ocean and the white caps are going to be tough."

"Okay. Where can we start the puzzle?"

"We'll set up a card table and put the pieces on it. Let's go inside. It's cooler in there."

Joey and Grandpa spent nearly an hour working on the puzzle. They assembled the relatively easy outside edges first. Then the real work began. They checked the picture on the puzzle box to help them find some pieces that would fit together. Joey began working on the sails of the ship and had some success. He was growing tired of the puzzle but he kept trying pieces. While Grandpa worked on the ocean waves, Joey was able to find most of the pieces of the ship. He wondered what it would have been like to sail the ocean long ago. He probably would have gotten seasick, so sailing wouldn't have been much fun.

CHAPTER 4

Zak Visits

Saved by the bell! Joey heard the car horn, ran to the front window and looked out. Mom's Packard was pulling into the driveway. Joey yelled, "They're back, Grandpa!"

"Take it easy, boy. I'm not deaf!"

"Sorry Grandpa. I'm goin' out and help them with the fruit."

"Okay. Me too."

Grandpa slid his chair back, put his hands on his knees and rocked forward. He straightened out his back and walked slowly to the door. Joey was already helping Grandma from the front seat. She was a little stiff from riding in the car. She swung her legs out, held onto the car door, and stood up. Joey held his hand out to help steady Grandma when she let go of the door. Marion had gone to the trunk and opened it.

"Thank you, Joey. You'd better help your mom with the apples. The box is too heavy for one person."

"Okay Grandma."

Joey walked to the trunk and looked in. There was a wooden apple box heaped with Red Delicious apples and two medium sized brown paper bags full of bright reddish-purple cherries. When Joey saw the cherries, his mouth began to water.

Joey's mom said, "You can eat some cherries, Joey, but try not to get stains on your clothes. Don't eat too many."

Joey started to grab a fistful of cherries but thought better of it. He took just one, pulled the stem off and popped it in his mouth. He worked the cherry pit around in his mouth until the fruit was removed and he spit the seed on the grass. Joey couldn't stop with only one, so he grabbed two more fat cherries. One went in his mouth and the other was ready in his left hand.

"Could you help me with the apple box, Joey?"

"Sure Mom," he answered and grabbed the box with his left hand forgetting that there was a cherry ready to eat. The cherry squished and the juice started dripping from his fingers. Joey cried out, "It's going to slip, Mom," and he lowered the box to the edge of the trunk. He quickly wiped his dripping, juice-stained fingers on his shirt. He suddenly realized what he had done and looked at his mom. "I'm sorry."

She looked a little dismayed and then smiled, "That's all right, Joey. I'll just use a little more bleach when I do your clothes tonight while we listen to the radio."

Before Joey could take hold of the box again, Grandma and Grandpa came to the back of the car with some large cake pans. Grandpa put his pans down and as Grandma held her pan with both hands, Grandpa filled it with apples. They didn't need to move the big box of apples. Joey noticed Grandma's fingers had big bumpy knuckles.

"Why are your fingers bent and bumpy, Grandma?"

"Well, Joey, that's because I have arthritis in my fingers."

"Same as Grandpa's fingers?"

"Same thing, Joey. We rub Ben-Gay ointment on our fingers and it seems to help. We also take an aspirin each day so our fingers don't hurt so much."

Joey thought for a moment and said, "That's why your house smells funny!"

"That's right. It's because of the ointment. I'll take these apples in the house. Maybe you can help Grandpa with more apples and some cherries. Put the cherries in the small pan, please."

"Okay, Grandma."

Joey took the smaller of the two pans Grandpa held and filled it with cherries. When Grandpa had his pan full of apples they walked into the house and put the pans on the kitchen counter. Marion was already peeling apples. Grandma was going to make two pies, one apple and one cherry, for Sunday's dinner. Joey was already thinking of which kind he wanted for dessert. He hoped there would be whipped cream for the pie. His mouth was watering just thinking about it. Grandma's pies were even better than his mom's. That made sense: she had made a lot more pies because she was much older than Mom.

"Joey! There's someone here to see you!" Grandpa called from the front porch.

Joey walked to the front door and looked out through the screen. Zak was out at the curb on a bicycle.

Joey pushed the screen door open and yelled, "Hi Zak! Whatcha doin?"

"I went over to your place to see if you could play for a while. No one was home so I figured you might be here. I was at the park."

"You have a girl's bike, Zak."

"Yeah. It's my sister's. My brother's bike is too big. I can't reach the pedals. Greg says the top bar below the seat is a nut-cracker."

"Nut-cracker?" quizzed Joey.

Zak pointed at his crotch and said, "You know."

Joey laughed, "Oh, I gotcha. That hurts just thinking about it."

Zak continued, "I'm waiting to get my own bike when I get a little bigger. My dad said I could be big enough by Christmas, but we would see."

"Hey! Want some cherries?"

"Sure!" Zak dropped the bike on the sidewalk.

Joey pointed at the car. There was a bag of cherries still in the trunk and the boys leaned against the rear fenders of the Packard as they munched on the fruit. Zak suddenly stopped chewing and listened.

"I think I hear my Mom's whistle. We live over that way." Zak pointed toward the back of Bertelson's house. Zak looked at his wristwatch and said, "Mom said to be home by four. I'd better go or I'll be late."

"Your mom must be able to whistle real loud."

"No, she has a whistle like the referees use, you know, on a string around their necks."

"Oh yeah."

Zak straddled his sister's bike, righted it, and pushed forward with one foot on a pedal. The bike wobbled a little as he got on the seat. As Zak picked up speed, he turned his head and waved to Joey.

"Bye Zak!" Joey yelled.

"See you Joey. Thanks for the cherries!"

Joey watched Zak disappear behind some shrubs at the corner.

CHAPTER 5

Church and Sunday Dinner

Sunday was another nice day. Joey woke up and could hear birds chirping and a dog barking. Joey stretched his arms as he climbed out of bed and pulled on his jeans. He had worn his underwear to bed and didn't use a blanket, just a sheet. He couldn't hear anyone else up so he sat on his bed and looked around for something to do. The bag of marbles on the bookshelf gave him an idea. He poured the marbles out on his bed. There were some clear ones of various colors and a lot of cat's-eyes, about two dozen in all.

If Joey was going to try out his idea, he had to wash the marbles. He took them in the bathroom, closed the sink drain, turned on the hot water, and put the marbles in the sink. He got some Ivory soap from the shower and dropped the bar into the water. He turned off the water, put the bar of soap back in the shower, and swished the marbles around. After about a minute, he pulled the plug and watched the soapy water vanish down the drain.

Joey rinsed off the traces of soap from the marbles and got a fresh bath towel and laid it on the bathroom floor. Using both hands, he transferred the marbles from the sink to the towel. After folding the corners of the towel together, he picked up his makeshift bag, took the marbles back to the bedroom, and opened the towel on his bed.

Standing on the floor at the foot of his bed, he popped a marble in his mouth and spit it toward his pillow. The marble dribbled out of his mouth and landed on the sheet in front of him. Joey thought he should be able to do better. For the second try, after filling his lungs with air, he put the marble between his lips and his front teeth and forced air into his mouth until his cheeks bulged out. Then he quickly pushed the palms of his hands against his puffed out cheeks. Pow! The marble shot out about five feet and rolled under his pillow. Major progress! Joey tried seven marbles in all, but with little more success. The marbles were just too heavy. But now, Joey was ready to spit cherry pits if Zak challenged him.

"Joey! What *are* you doing? Please come down for some breakfast."

"Okay Mom. Just a minute."

Joey scooped up his marbles, put them back in the bag, and returned the bag to the bookcase. He hurried down to the kitchen in his bare feet. Joey had been so absorbed in his experiment he hadn't heard his mom get up.

"What were you doing, Joey?"

"I was doing an experiment to find the best way to spit a marble."

His mother shook her head. "Sometimes I wonder about you. Maybe you'll be a famous scientist someday—win the Nobel Prize, or maybe you'll be an inventor," she smiled.

It was quiet in the kitchen for a few seconds as Marion looked at her son. "We're going to church today, the whole family. After church we'll go to Grandma's and have Sunday dinner. She baked some pies."

"With whipped cream?" Joey inquired. He didn't care whether it was apple or cherry pie as long as there was whipped cream on top.

"I suppose so. Please eat your cereal and drink your juice. I've cooked some bacon and scrambled some eggs, too. After breakfast you need to shine your good shoes."

Joey's dad came into the kitchen and sat down at the table. Marion poured big Joe a mug full of coffee. Joey watched as his dad added some cream, a teaspoonful of sugar and stirred the mixture with a spoon. Joey had tried coffee once but didn't like it.

"Good morning, Joey. Did you know we're going to church today?"

"Good morning. Yeah. That's what Mom said. I have to shine my shoes."

Joey went to his room, picked up his black dress shoes, and took them into the garage. In ten minutes, he had his shoes gleaming and ready for church. He put away the stain and brushes and took his shoes up to his room. After washing his hands and changing his underwear, he put on his good clothes, black socks, and shoes. He went in the bathroom and used a hairbrush after rubbing a little dab of Brylcreem in his hair.

It was only ten o'clock and Joey was ready to go. He had to wait for Mom and Dad to get ready and then they would get Grandma and Grandpa. While Joey waited, he decided to look at the Atlas. He started looking at the map of Antarctica and was imagining traveling by a sailing ship, with at least three masts, into the cold ocean water lapping against large glaciers. Joey wasn't seasick anymore, he had gotten used to the ship's movements. He imagined seeing icebergs, penguins, seals, and maybe a walrus. Joey wasn't sure any walruses lived that far south, but he assumed they did 'cause he knew they lived near the North Pole, but that would be a long way to swim. He could see many icebergs floating near his ship. He heard his captain giving orders to avoid the ice.

"Okay, Joey. Let's pick up your grandparents."

In a few minutes Grandma and Grandpa were in the back seat and Joey was sandwiched in the middle. Grandma had on her hairpiece and a pink dress. Grandpa had on a brown suit and his hair was combed. They both looked real nice and had the tiniest scent of Ben-Gay. Joey figured it was on Grandpa. Grandma usually wore a little perfume.

Joey didn't like sermons, but he sat quietly as Reverend Carter talked about a story from the Bible. Joey tried to read the Bible once but gave up. The words were funny and he couldn't figure out what they meant. He memorized a Psalm once but didn't know what it meant either. It was a short one. He couldn't remember things that had no meaning.

Joe Sr. had given Joey a quarter for the offering. As Dr. Carter talked, Joey pulled the coin from his pocket and looked at the date. The date was 1948 S. It was really shiny. Joey turned the coin over in his hands moving the quarter from heads in his right hand to tails in his left. Suddenly the quarter was on the floor. It rolled and rolled and dropped into a metal grating under the pew in front of his mom. Everyone in the church could hear it now; it just kept rolling. Then it spun around faster and faster and then everything was quiet in the church.

Reverend Carter looked out into the congregation and said, "Heads or tails?" Everyone broke out laughing. After the laughter subsided, Dr. Carter said, "This is a good time for some music. We will sing Hymn 92: *In Praise of God for all Things*. Please stand and sing with the choir."

As usual, following the service, Reverend Carter stood outside the main entrance to the church thanking people for coming to church and for their support. As Joey walked out into the sunlight he turned to Dr. Carter and said, "That was my quarter that made all the noise. I'm sorry I dropped it. It rolled into those holes underneath the seats in front of us. It was my offering."

"Thank you for telling me son. If God needs that quarter, he'll show us a way to get it out of the ventilation shaft."

The preacher shook hands with Joey's grandparents and commented to his mom and dad about their son being a nice young man. Joey had always thought Reverend Carter was someone he wouldn't like, but it was just the opposite.

After arriving at Grandma's house they all went in and relaxed. Grandpa made some coffee and Grandma got a bottle of Coca-Cola from the refrigerator. She put some ice in a glass and poured Coke in it for Joey. Everyone else had coffee and slices of pie dough that had been baked in the oven. Grandma had put cinnamon and sugar on the slices of pie dough and arranged them on a plate. Joey counted them. There was enough so everyone could have two pieces.

Joey sat down at the card table and continued working on the puzzle he and Grandpa had started the previous day. Grandpa came over to the puzzle and said, "I only found a few pieces since yesterday, Joey. Looks like you already found several more today. You're pretty good at puzzles." Joey continued to work on the puzzle while the adults went out to the garden in the back yard. They seemed to be talking about vegetables so Joey didn't go out to the garden. After about ten minutes, the adults came back into the dining room and the kitchen.

Marion stepped out from the kitchen and said, "Joey, please wash your hands. We're going to have dinner now."

Joey went to the bathroom and saw grandpa washing his hands. Grandpa turned to Joey and said, "Come on in here, Joey. We can wash at the same time."

When they were all seated at the table, Grandpa said grace. Joey wasn't sure what bounty was but he figured it must be the food they were going to eat. They had pork chops, mashed potatoes, corn on the cob and salad.

Joey occasionally looked at Grandpa as they ate. Then it happened. Grandpa took out his pocketknife and started removing the corn from the ear he had on his plate. Joey watched intently as Grandpa cut off the corn. It didn't take long before the cob was bare. Grandpa added a small slab of butter and a dash of salt to the corn and went after the yellow pieces with his fork.

Joey's mom said, "Dad, I wish you wouldn't talk about the war with Joey. He gets all kinds of strange ideas. Last night he was asking me about pumpkins that grew on trees. He said the pumpkins got their spots from a little girl that got the pox. Please don't tell him any more of your stories."

Joey was confused. Grandpa didn't quite know what to say to his daughter. He didn't want a fight at the dinner table so he kept his mouth shut. But Joey didn't think what his mom had said was fair.

"Mom?"

"Yes Joey."

"I like Grandpa's stories. They make me think about things. I don't know how much is true, but they are fun to listen to. I found out where Cuba and the Philippine Islands are by looking in the atlas. If Grandpa hadn't told me that story I wouldn't have looked them up. And besides, you listen to the stories on the radio, and they aren't true."

Big Joe smiled and said to Marion, "I think he's got you, dear. Joey's becoming a pretty smart cookie."

The subject of conversation changed to politics and something about Korea. Before long it was time for dessert. Grandpa and Joey both asked for cherry pie with ice cream instead of whipped cream. Grandpa had suggested ice cream. Joey thought that was a great idea.

After dinner, Joey and Grandpa were working on the puzzle again. Grandpa said, "Thank you for sticking up for me at dinner, Joey. You're a good grandson. I talked to your mother about teaching you how to shoot an air rifle. She said it would be all right as long as we just shoot at targets. Would you like to learn?"

Joey's eyes lit up. "Really, Grandpa?"

"That's the God's truth, Joey, but I'm all out of BB's. I'll get some from the hardware store next week, and we can start shooting on Saturday. I'll get a package of targets, too."

"Oh boy! I can hardly wait! What time should I come over?"

"It'll be in the afternoon. Your mom and grandma are going to do something. Marion will bring you over. Say, did I ever tell you the story about flying with the Wright brothers?"